Greta and the GLASS KINGDOM

OTHER BOOKS BY CHLOE JACOBS

Greta and the Goblin King
Greta and the Goblin King
Greta and the Lost Army

Greta and the GLASS KINGDOM

chloe jacobs

Entangled Publishing, LLC
2614 South Timberline Road
Suite 109
Fort Collins, CO 80525
Visit our website at www.entangledpublishing.com.

Entangled Teen is an imprint of Entangled Publishing, LLC.

Edited by Stephen Morgan
Cover design by Kelley York
Cover art by Shutterstock

Manufactured in the United States of America

First Edition February 2015

To the Goblin Gang, the most awesome street team, in—or out of—Mylena!
I realize that this book has been a long time coming, and I also want to thank every single reader who emailed me and messaged me to tell me how eagerly they were waiting for it. Your excitement humbles me, and I dedicate this book to all of you.

CHAPTER ONE

Darkness. Fear. A circle of madness and death. Stone children trailing red from the corners of their eyes, collapsing bonelessly to the dirt.

Greta's in the middle of it all, the eye of the storm, and the power whips around her ferociously. Through her. In her. Sending her spinning. Spinning. Spinning out of control.

Someone grabbed her by the shoulders and shook her.

Fire burning. The world shakes. Someone screams.

Screams. Those were *her* screams.

The world wasn't shaking—*she* was being shaken. And the fire wasn't a nightmare, it was real. The smoke tasted like death and burned her lungs.

She fought against the hands holding her. Unbidden, the darkness that had become all too familiar since the battle with Agramon shoved outward, like a bully on the schoolyard eager for a fight.

"Greta, please!" Hands on her shoulders. That voice. It was Siona. "I am trying to contain this, but I need you to wake up and focus."

She snapped her eyes open, told herself to relax and stop struggling before she lost control of the thing within her again and hurt Siona.

In the darkness of the room, she couldn't see her friend or anything else. Siona must have wisely closed the door behind her when she'd rushed in to stop Greta from burning the castle down.

You are stronger than this. It does not own you.

She didn't know if that was her own voice talking…or Isaac's, who'd been unshakable in his belief that she would overcome whatever this was that had been happening to her. Hard to believe, especially since the nightmares were coming more often, and each time it became harder to contain the dark magick trapped inside her.

The magick she'd never asked for and never wanted. Kind of like how she'd never wanted to be here to begin with. Getting stuck in the icy wasteland of Mylena wasn't exactly the thing every teenage girl dreamed of. Especially when a deranged, power-hungry demon kidnapped little kids—including Greta's brother, Drew—and used a spell to split open the universe so that he could terrorize every world, including the human world she'd tried getting back to for years.

Don't let it win. At first it was like talking to a stone wall, but after a long, quiet moment, her body finally started to listen. The snarly beast inside retracted its claws and closed its eyes. The heat dissipated. She took shaky, ragged deep breaths. And then fought to keep the tears from falling.

How could she have thought she was badass enough to take on a demon the likes of Agramon? He'd chewed her up and…well, the portal he'd pulled her into would have swallowed her down if Isaac hadn't reached in and dragged her back out.

"It's all right now, danem." Siona had stopped shaking

her and now patted her shoulder. It was awkward enough that Greta almost chuckled. She groaned instead. Despite all they'd been through together, Siona still refused to drop the Mylean formal address—dolem for men and danem for women.

"How do you always know?" She blinked up into the shadows about where Siona's face should be. Somehow her friend was always there before things got too bad.

Siona stepped back, and Greta thought she could see the outline of her slim shape. "It's my responsibility to watch over you while the goblin king is away," she whispered. "I heard your cries of distress and came to see if I could help."

Greta flushed with embarrassment at the thought that she might have awakened the whole castle with her screams. "Did I burn the bedsheets this time?" She glanced down, but it was too dark—

The door flew open and crashed into the opposite wall so hard she felt the shudder of it like a mini-earthquake. The sconces hanging on the walls out in the corridor let in enough light for her to see that the hulking figure filling the entrance to her room was very Isaac shaped.

He charged in, eyes glowing in the dark.

"I'm okay," she said, worried that he would see the scorch marks in her bed and lose it.

Her breathing hitched as he crossed the room in three long strides. Siona stepped back as he put his knee on the massive mattress—bigger than any she'd slept in before—and pulled her into his arms. His weight crunched the straw that had been packed beneath the layers of wool and linen making up the bed.

He pulled her into his embrace, and her cheek squished against his chest.

"I'm fine. It was nothing," she insisted in a muffled voice.

She felt him shift and knew he was looking back at Siona

for confirmation.

She pinched him on the arm. "It was just a dream," she said. She didn't want him worrying about her. She'd caused him enough problems lately.

"Yes," he finally agreed in a low voice. He ducked his chin and rested it on top of her head. "Just a dream."

But they both knew there was more to it than that.

Neither of them would come right out and say it, though, because in this moment, it was more important that his touch stifle the cold carrying the dream's memory. He wasn't letting her go, and she didn't really want him to. She melted against him and let his strength be the wall between her and the fear she'd carried inside for weeks. It was a weakness she would berate herself for later, but right now, she was just scared enough not to care.

Siona cleared her throat, and Greta automatically pulled back, but Isaac's arms only tightened, and he didn't let her go far. "Do you require anything further?" Siona asked.

"She is fine. You may leave now." He tossed the order over his shoulder. Greta jabbed him in the stomach, and he grunted. "But I…thank you for your assistance."

"Yes, my king." Greta thought she saw Siona's lips twitch before she turned to go.

"Siona," Greta called after her. "Could you leave the door open a little bit, please?"

"I hope you enjoy better dreams the rest of this night, danem," she murmured, and, with a shadowy nod, the goblin hunter left Greta and Isaac alone.

With the small crack of light coming into the room, Greta could see the look on Isaac's face as he peered down at her. "Don't frown at me like that," she said, then reached up to smooth the lines in his forehead away with her fingers. They hadn't talked much about the events of the eclipse. Not about Wyatt and the other human boys, or about the battle in

Agramon's fortress. And especially not about the dark power that had hitched a ride inside her when she'd come out of that portal. But the worry in his eyes said they needed to.

He snagged her hand and kissed her fingers while drawing swirly patterns across her back with his other hand. His chest rose and fell with each of his deep breaths, so close to her she was moved along with them.

She was mesmerized. His touch was still so new, her body demanded she give it her full and complete attention. There was a kind of sloppy reverence in it. His hands were too big to treat anything delicately, and yet he seemed to want to try with her. She should remind him that she could handle his big strong self, that she was no fragile flower who needed to be protected. But that could come later.

She glanced around him to the doorway. It was the middle of the night, and he was in her room on the bed with her, and anyone could walk by and see them alone together. Everyone here already hated her, both for being a human and for bewitching their king. It was one thing for them to be faced with her presence in the goblin castle and not be able to do anything about it because she was a guest, but if they knew just how close she and their king had become, there'd probably be a riot.

"You shouldn't have come in here. Someone might see us."

He didn't remove himself, instead raised an eyebrow and glared at her like maybe she'd just offended him. "Your nightmare screams could raise the dead, but I should just leave you to them?"

The exasperation in his tone almost made her forget the blood, smoke, and screams of her nightmare. She smiled and ducked her head like a blushing schoolgirl. Weird that dating a goblin king in an alternate world would make her feel more like a regular human being than anything else.

A vexed rumble barreled up from his throat. It was still surprising just how quickly and easily she got under his skin. It was even more surprising that he let her see it. Greta had never meant enough to anyone to get under their skin, on their nerves, or anything else before.

She'd always kept her head down and avoided attachments. As a human in Mylena, that had been the only way to stay alive. Well…that, and she'd become right handy with a sword.

And before Mylena? Who could even remember anymore. Maybe there were people besides her family who'd missed her when she disappeared, but she'd only had a few friends and no boyfriends. Greta was never the most popular kid, or the smartest, or the funniest. She'd just been another face in a crowded school hallway.

Isaac put a finger under her chin and tipped her face up. "You are all right?"

She clenched her eyes shut against the tenderness in those four words. "The dreams are coming more often," she admitted. She bit her tongue against telling him how hard it was getting to control that dark thing inside her. "Sometimes I see Drew's face in the circle, and sometimes I don't. Sometimes Wyatt is there shouting at me, but I don't understand what he's saying." She shuddered as the images all flooded back.

Agramon.

His grip tight, digging into her forearm. So deep she's sure the tip of each claw goes through her skin and bone. The pain crawls up and up like rivers of ice in her veins, heads straight for her chest, and she wonders if that's what a heart attack feels like.

He pulls her deeper into the devouring darkness, promises they'll have an eternity there together, but another presence adds his voice to the chaos, calling for her—

"You are worried for your friends," Isaac said. He smoothed her hair back behind her ear. She nodded, but it wasn't worry fueling these dreams, and they both knew it. "There has been no sign of them yet," he said. "But I will send Siona out to search the forest again."

She swallowed. It should be *her* out there, and she'd been able to slip away a few times to join the search, but Isaac worried when she went out alone, and she knew that if he came along, Wyatt would never let her find him.

"You're always in the dream," she said with a smile. "Urgent, cross, and demanding that I return to you."

"None would dare disobey the goblin king." He chuckled. "What else? I don't want you to be afraid."

She pressed her lips together and remembered the black place filled with the silence of smothered screams. The portal had not been a dream, and when she returned there every night, it was impossible not to think that this time she'd be stuck there for good.

The dreams varied. Sometimes she reached for Isaac and he slipped from her fingers, but sometimes she couldn't grab on at all. And on really bad nights she…*killed* him instead.

In the end, she was alone. Always alone.

At first she'd blamed the nightmares on the fact that she wasn't sleeping well, and she'd blamed not sleeping well on the nightmares. What was the Mylean equivalent of the chicken and the egg?

"No, there's nothing else," she said. "It's not a big deal. It just…it seems to trigger…"

They both knew what got triggered when Greta lost control. Since Isaac had pulled her back out of Agramon's portal, she hadn't been quite the same. At first it only happened while she was sleeping, and thankfully, Siona had somehow been able to sense it and always came running to snap her out of it.

But it was getting stronger, slipping away from her easier—sometimes while she was awake now, too.

"What if we went back to my cottage, just the two of us?"

he said.

The first time he'd brought her there, she hadn't understood why Isaac would prefer to hang out by himself in a tiny little stone house that had once been a hunting lodge for his father, not when there was a whole castle at his disposal with servants and everything. But she got it now. There weren't any disapproving looks, judgments, or expectations there.

But he was wrong if he thought their problems would cease to exist if they ran away.

"Your people need you to be here." She knew he couldn't stay there anymore, now that he was trying to accept his responsibilities as the goblin king and do the job the way his father would have wanted.

"We'll find a way to stop the nightmares," he said. If only she were facing an enemy with her sword instead of some unfathomable dark magick, she might have shared his confidence. He smiled. "I'll keep you safe, if I have to come and spend every night in this bed with you."

"Oh, no. Do you think it could be that serious?" She pretended alarm but couldn't keep from grinning.

His eyes glittered in the shadows. "A king must take all necessary precautions."

She hoped he was right about there being a way to stop it. He was so positive, he had to be right, didn't he?

She rested a hand on his shoulder and lifted onto her knees on the mattress, then lightly touched her lips to his. He didn't hesitate, instead tilted his head and captured her lips completely. He kissed her with a molten desperation that made her belly tighten and her heart pound.

His hand spread across the small of her back, and he pulled her hard against him. His other hand dove into her bed-head hair. She shivered at the scrape of his long incisors on her upper lip. His mouth opened on hers. She answered in kind, and his tongue slipped in to taste her.

She groaned, and her fingers curled. She was aware of everything. The slope of his hard bicep, the wrinkles in the fabric covering it under her fingers. She was even aware of the tiny little pockets of space that remained between them.

She still couldn't get used to this touching thing. The kissing thing. It was amazing and intoxicating and left her whole world reeling every time, but it was also treacherous. Trust wasn't her best skill, and neither was diplomacy. She'd spent three weeks in the goblin castle under Isaac's care and protection — going stir-crazy with inactivity — and none of his people seemed any closer to accepting her.

A flicker in the light from the corridor drew her attention. Reluctantly, she pulled back and shimmied her arms between them. The shadows in the hallway seemed to shift. Was someone out there?

"Don't worry," he said. "No one will say anything even if they know we are here together."

"They won't say it to your face, but they'll still talk."

He paused. "Has someone defamed you?"

"Defame? What kind of archaic word is that?" She tugged her shirt back into place. To Isaac's amusement, she still stubbornly wore her hunting clothes, whether she was awake or asleep, even though there was a closet full of feminine dresses and stuff just waiting for someone to show interest in them. "Don't worry, I can handle myself." She also kept her dagger under the pillow.

For the first time, she remembered another reason why he shouldn't be in her room. "When did you get back?" she asked. "I thought you would be gone at least another moon rising." He was dressed in travel gear and smelled of sweat and those ugly Mylean horses that weren't really horses. He must have come straight to her.

"If you had let me into your dreams last night, I would have told you of the change in my plans."

"You don't have to be snarky about it," she said.

She would never be able to keep him out of her head for good, but she was intent on regaining control over her subconscious mind. Not only for privacy's sake, but because it might be the only way to keep the darkness inside her from spilling out all over the place.

She remembered Luke, who'd found her in the snow after she got stranded in Mylena and had taught her how to fight, how to survive. He used to go to his sacred circle in the woods every evening to connect with the Great Mother, and recently, she'd decided to try meditating herself to see if that worked for her. It seemed to help where Isaac's ability was concerned, although it hadn't made any difference with the nightmares yet. So far nothing could keep them away.

Not that having Isaac enter her mind was still the violation she'd once considered it to be. The truth was, she could relax with him then in a way she'd never been able to relax anywhere else in Mylena. In dreams, she remembered just how young he really was. The mantle of his responsibilities as king fell away, and he let her share in all his hopes, dreams, and ideas for the future.

"So what happened out there? What did you find out?" she asked, mindful of the open door and keeping her voice low.

"Just a misunderstanding that I was able to take care of with a minimum of fuss."

"If it was so minor, why did it require the king's personal attendance?"

"I have been remiss in my duties since assuming my father's throne. The people deserve to know their new king. They deserve my personal reassurances that everything is well in hand."

She bit her lip. "But the outbursts are increasing."

"Small skirmishes here and there are expected to arise in any kingdom, but I should have taken the time to address my people long before now. I am rectifying this so that all will be well for the both of us. You will see." He trailed a finger down the bridge of her nose.

She opened her mouth to argue, but the sound of a door creaking open somewhere down the hall filtered into the bedroom. She grabbed his wrist and dropped her voice to a barely audible whisper. "You would tell me if all these problems were because of me? If your people were rising up in protest because their king is openly courting a human?"

Her worry made the dark thing inside her twitch and writhe. She held her breath and focused on battling it back down.

"No one would dare oppose my choice of mate." His voice was rough and broken. "Any member of *any* kingdom who tries will—"

Her worry shifted. His eyes had started glowing, and his entire body threw off seething waves of fury that seemed to come from thin air. "Isaac, calm down," she murmured.

It wasn't the first time something like this had happened. Since the eclipse, he seemed to have more trouble controlling his moon phase. He'd shrugged aside her concerns, but she couldn't let them go. She was worried all the time. Worried that his problems within the provinces were her fault, worried that the thing inside her might somehow be provoking the thing inside him. Worried that this little bubble of happiness they'd found since the eclipse was short-lived and soon to burst.

His raspy breathing eased as she whispered in his ear and let her hands roam over his shoulders and arms and back. She hoped it was soothing, but she'd settle for distracting.

He bent over her and kissed her again, so…distraction for the win.

She had no idea how much time passed before another sound outside her room made him look up this time. She touched her fingers to her swollen lips and swallowed hard.

His eyes flared as he watched.

"You should probably go," she said regretfully. "Someone might see."

Undaunted, Isaac kissed her once more. A simple, quick kiss on the mouth that tempted her more than it should and made her lean after him when he pulled away and got up from the bed.

"I will have Siona attend you in the morning, to make sure you don't bolt before the banquet. You'll stand with me, won't you?"

"What do you need me there for?"

"Visiting the provinces has made me realize it's far past time I make it clear to one and all that my heart is claimed and my commitment to you is true."

She sputtered. "Wait, what? What does that mean?"

"I want no one to doubt what you mean to me, and the sooner I make it public, the sooner everyone will have no choice but to accept you."

Did that mean she was right and he *was* having trouble because of her? She curled her fingers into the tangled blankets.

"Um, are you sure that such an announcement will accomplish what you think it's going to accomplish?" She winced, picturing a castle full of Myleans rising up against the both of them with pitchforks and torches. No wonder he thought she might bolt.

"Don't worry," he reassured her with all the arrogance of a true king. "It will all work out."

Famous last words.

CHAPTER TWO

The long, heavy skirt swished against Greta's legs, and its hem brushed her stocking-covered ankles as she turned away from the pockmarked mirror that had probably been hung on the drafty castle wall about a million moons ago.

She looked down at the yards of rich purple-dyed wool billowing around her from the waist down with a gut-wrenching cringe, feeling like a complete fake. She pulled the skirts wide. "Why the hell did I let him talk me into this, again?"

Siona, who was also wearing a dress instead of her typical hunter's garb, cocked her head and looked Greta up and down with a smile. "You look very…"

Greta threw up her hands. "I look like a complete idiot, that's what."

"You look gentle."

"You mean *genteel*?"

Siona laughed. "Ah, no, my friend, not quite. But that hard, bounty-hunter edge of yours is a bit softer in this color, don't you think?"

Greta huffed and spun away to look back into the mirror. She might have to get used to wearing these dresses. It wasn't so bad, was it?

No, it wasn't bad, not until she stood beside Siona and couldn't help but compare the two of them.

Greta was no slouch in the height department, but Siona still towered over her. And Greta was tiresomely blond and pale, where Siona had those startling amethyst eyes and jet-black hair, just like her cousin the goblin king. It didn't help that Greta was also too thin and had dark circles under her eyes from disturbed sleep. The oddly styled dress only made her feel even more like an imposter in Mylena, whereas Siona looked regal and elegant and perfect.

Siona came up from behind and met her gaze in the hazy glass.

"And why exactly is gentleness such a good thing?" Greta asked. She was becoming less convinced by the second that this was going to work. Dressing her up and parading her around in front of the masses—even if you promised them food and protection from the elements for an evening—was not going to make them forget who, or *what*, she was.

"It will be easier for the people of Mylena to come to accept you if you appear less defensive. You don't make it easy for anyone to approach, you know."

She smoothed the skirts over her hips. This was the first time she'd really noticed that she did, in fact, *have* hips. Her regular clothes were always strategically loose, for more than one reason...none of which had anything to do with female vanity and everything to do with survival. Before coming to the castle with Isaac, she'd spent every day worried someone would discover she was human. Survival had meant always keeping her guard up. Isaac and Siona wanted her to believe that she was safe now, secure, but how could she abandon the habit that had kept her alive for so long?

She snorted. "You don't honestly believe that a dress is going to magically change everything, do you? Everyone's going to take one look at me in this costume and know that it doesn't fit."

"I was here when the seamstress took your measurements. It's a traditional style and fits you perfectly." Siona put a hand on Greta's arm to test the fabric. It was finer than Greta's regular clothes, but it would still have been considered coarse if compared to the silks and satins she remembered from once upon a time. Mylena might have varying levels of wealth, but the best quality available here was still leagues apart from the human world she'd come from.

"That's not what I'm talking about, and you know it." She turned away from the mirror, and Siona took a step back.

Greta mourned the loss of her other disguise. She'd been a better fake sprite than she'd ever be a goblin king's…what? Girlfriend? She'd bet a lot of Myleans would use another word.

Thankfully, no one had used it to her face. She didn't care what they thought about her, but she also didn't want to be responsible for Isaac being hurt, and if he heard someone insult her, he would take it as a personal affront.

"I do understand how you feel," Siona whispered, fingering a pleat in the skirt of her own dress.

Greta shook her head. "I seriously doubt that." She waved to encompass the gorgeous goblin's innate perfection. "Look at you. You're beautiful, strong, and best of all, born of a species that happens to *belong* in Mylena." Then she pointed at herself. "I can never look like you or be like you, and everyone knows it. They hate me, and they're never going to let me forget it."

"There are some who would say that I don't belong here. Not here, and not anywhere."

Greta gasped in surprise. "What? Why?"

Siona's gaze clouded over. Greta stepped closer, shocked

by the sadness and pain contorting her face.

Today was the first time Siona had ever shared something personal. She didn't want to pry, but if Siona needed to talk, Greta wanted to be there for her. That's what friends did… she assumed. She hadn't actually had many.

"Do you think…I mean, if you want to tell me about it, then I would—" She heaved out a frustrated breath and shrugged. "It's no big deal if you don't want to talk about it, but if you need to…"

Siona looked equally as uncomfortable, but she said, "The king doesn't speak of my mother out of respect for my wishes, but…"

Greta knew that Siona's mother had died when she was young, but that was all. Was that because there was some secret scandal behind the circumstances surrounding her death?

"But what?" Greta placed her hand on top of Siona's.

After a moment she said, "My father was brother to the last goblin king, but my mother was faerie."

Greta's breath caught in her throat, but she didn't say anything, just squeezed her friend's hand and urged her to go on.

"Apparently, the king had hoped that the union of my parents would mean an alliance between the goblin and faerie races, but his other brother couldn't understand that, and eventually he amassed a following who agreed with him."

Greta glanced at the high cheekbones and delicate features that, now that she knew, betrayed the goblin's faerie ancestry. She'd already suspected that Siona wasn't all goblin. But half faerie? It was hard to believe a faerie and a goblin had ever found enough common ground between one another to, well… you know.

"You're talking about Isaac's father and uncles?" It was no secret that one of Isaac's uncles had been a douche bag who'd killed his own brother, but there must have been another sibling that she hadn't heard about.

Siona nodded. "After they wed, my parents lived in the goblin court, but whenever anything went wrong, my mother was somehow to blame. A failed crop, a missing child, a bad storm. Everyone turned and pointed their fingers at the one who didn't belong, the one whose magick was strong and foreign to the goblin people."

"That's horrible." Being reviled for something you had no control over was something Greta could relate to.

Siona gave her a weak smile. "When my father's murdered body was found in the woods, my mother was immediately accused of that, too—even though the small amount of evidence pointed to the king's brother."

Greta sneered. "Wow. From what I've heard, that guy was as bad as they come."

"In the end, there wasn't enough proof that he was responsible, and it was much easier for everyone to blame my mother. Only the goblin king believed her when she said she was innocent. He knew she was carrying a child. In the end, he resisted the clamor of the goblin people and allowed her to return to the faeries instead of letting them execute her."

"I guess that must have been before the queen decided to shut the gates of the Glass Kingdom." Greta had never cared to go beyond the Luna Pass, where the faeries were said to reside, but even if she'd wanted to, the Glass Kingdom had been off-limits for at least as long as she'd been in Mylena.

Siona's lips pressed together tightly, and she nodded.

If these people were so quick to condemn an innocent woman just because she was different, what makes Isaac think they'll ever accept me?

"This all happened before you were born?"

Siona nodded.

"If you were born in the faerie kingdom, why did you

leave? Why come here where your mother was treated so horribly?"

"The faeries mistrusted my goblin blood as much as the goblins mistrusted my mother's faerie blood. I was quite young when... they banished me. I tried to return, but..."

"Banished? Your mother just stood by and let that happen?"

"My mother"—she glanced away—"had already died by that time."

To be thrown out like so much garbage. It wasn't hard to imagine just how big a chink that would leave in a person's self-esteem. "That's awful."

Siona shrugged. "The goblin king took me in and forbade anyone to harm me. At first it was...horrible," she admitted with a grimace. "But after a while, it was less so. Thankfully, given the passage of enough time, many seemed to forget that I was part faerie."

Greta doubted that, but now she understood a little better why this beautiful girl had become a hunter—for the same reasons as Greta; so no one would notice her. There was an independence in such a line of work that many other vocations available to Mylean women lacked. Too bad everyone knew she was human now. The independence she'd enjoyed was quickly disappearing the longer she stayed in the castle with Isaac. It should be chafing more than it actually had, but exploring their relationship had taken up a lot of her attention of late.

"The only person besides the king who truly accepted me was my cousin."

"Isaac."

Siona nodded. "He never questioned my heritage. Never made me ashamed of it. And when he became king, he promised me nothing would ever change. That I would always be family, always welcome in his kingdom."

Greta held her breath. "Neither of you had many other

friends growing up, did you?"

"We had each other."

She smiled. "I'm glad for that."

Siona's posture stiffened as if she didn't want to talk about it anymore, so Greta turned and walked across the large room to the wardrobe.

"What are you wearing on your feet, danem?"

She hated that Siona still called her that...and the goblin knew it. Greta stopped and looked down at her boots, crossing her arms. "I don't care what it looks like. If you think I'm going to put those flimsy little slippers on, you can forget it." She pointed to the pair that had been left for her along with the dress. "How am I supposed to hunt in those? Five minutes in the goblin forest and they'd be toast. I'd end up with frostbite."

Siona sighed. "You're not supposed to hunt in them. In fact, you're not supposed to be hunting *at all* anymore."

She ground her teeth. "Who's going to do the job if not me? This place'll be overrun by the Lost in no time."

"That's not your duty anymore, danem. There are other hunters in Mylena besides you," Siona answered, hands on her hips.

"No offense to your abilities, Siona, but you can't do it alone, and too many of the other hunters are nothing but cutthroat mercenaries. They'll kill anything, good or bad, for the right price. Not to mention," she continued, "how else am I going to make a living? Hunting is the only thing I know how to do in this world." In any world, really.

"You know you don't have to worry about that anymore."

Greta swung her arm out. The room was bigger than Luke's entire cottage had been. In fact, her old bed would have looked like a ratty rug tossed on the floor of her pater's little cottage. "This? This is only temporary. It isn't where I belong, and I can't stay here forever, but Isaac refuses to get it into his thick skull that he won't get his way in all things."

"You don't expect him to tromp through the forest with you and forget that he has duties and responsibilities here, do you?"

"Of course not." But how could she give up her independence entirely when she didn't know from one minute to the next if this crazy thing between them was even going to work out? When she didn't even know what this crazy thing between them was?

He's planning to announce to the whole kingdom that you're important to him.

He'd said the word last night. *Commitment.* But what did that even mean? He might like kissing her, but kissing didn't automatically mean they were going to spend the rest of their lives together. A king couldn't just make decisions like that without thinking about the needs of his kingdom, and she was definitely not what Mylena needed. This announcement was probably just a way for him to ensure she would be protected.

She rubbed her forehead. "There has to be some compromise, doesn't there?"

Greta had lost everything when she fell through the portal and ended up in this icy place. But in the last few weeks, even the small comforts she'd found in Mylena had been taken from her. Her human friends were gone, her disguise was destroyed, and now she felt like a darkness was eating her up from the inside out.

Last night wasn't the first time she'd scorched her own bedding, and she was afraid of what would happen if Siona wasn't there to wake her up the next time. She clenched her hands into fists in the folds of her skirts.

Big fluffy snowflakes drifted down outside the window. Some stuck to the glass and turned to water droplets, tracking down the thick green-tinted glass, while the rest kept right on going.

"I should be out there," she said. "I've wasted the whole day away when today I might have tracked down the boys."

"It has been a complete moon cycle, danem. What if—"

"No. They're out there," she said. "And they're fine. Probably fine." She was trying to reassure herself now. "But I have to be certain." Greta knocked her forehead against the thick, cool glass and closed her eyes with a shattered sigh. "I owe them that, at the very least."

Wyatt and the other boys had been missing since the eclipse. Greta had left them in the cubby beneath Luke's cottage before she and Ray went to Agramon's lair, but by the time she'd recovered from her injuries enough to return, four days had passed. She hadn't really expected them to sit tight and wait for her, because she'd thought she could track them.

But every time she'd managed to duck out of the castle to search, she'd come up empty. She hadn't been overly worried at first. Wyatt was a master of survival. He'd kept those boys alive and hidden out in the goblin forest for months, and she'd never had any clue they existed. In fact, she might still never know other humans existed in Mylena if he hadn't decided to make himself known to *her* when he'd found her passed out in the woods.

There was a knock at the door. Greta glanced over her shoulder as Siona opened it. One of Isaac's guards whispered to Siona.

"What is it?" she called out.

Siona nodded at the guard, who spared Greta a cold look and a stiff bow before he left. Siona turned back to Greta with a frown. "Nothing you need to worry about. You should relax and ready yourself for the evening's festivities," she said.

Greta put her hands on her hips and glared at her friend. If she'd had her dagger, she might even have been tempted to pull it out and show the goblin hunter how she used it to relax. "Don't do that. Don't pat me on the head and send me off for a nap like a child. What's going on?"

Her lips pressed together. "The guards have found evidence of an intruder in the castle. I must go to inform the goblin king."

"Didn't you say that the gates were being opened for the banquet this evening? Why would anyone bother to break in when they could walk right through the front door in just a few more hours?"

She shrugged. "We'll find out."

"All right. Let me change and I can come help."

She shook her head. "Everything is under control. Your skill would be wasted with such a minor thing," she insisted. "The banquet is soon to begin, and—"

Greta held her skirts wide. "Siona, it's a dress. How long could it take to put back on later?" She turned around and looked over her shoulder. "Undo me, and then I'll meet you in the courtyard."

"Will you always be so stubborn?"

She grinned. "Consider it a gift from me to you."

Her friend grunted, but she came over and undid what felt like a hundred buttons all the way down Greta's back. After she left the room, Greta still held the purple fabric to her chest while it gaped to her waist in the back. She heard the door open and then close again.

Her first thought was that Isaac had come to see her. She grinned expectantly before realizing it was more likely that Siona had changed her mind about meeting her downstairs, so she laughed and said, "Seriously. I don't need any more help with this thing. Go on and I'll catch up in a few minutes."

Her chuckle died out, though, as she turned to shoo Siona away—the figure filling the doorway wasn't Siona. It wasn't even Isaac.

"I thought you'd be happy to see me," he said.

She blinked, but the figment didn't dissolve into thin air.

"*Wyatt?*" Her feet were frozen to the floor.

He hadn't moved a muscle since slipping into the room and closing the door behind him. Just stood there staring at her like she was staring at him, as if he didn't believe it was her, either.

"Oh, thank God you're okay." The words burst out, and she finally took a step forward. So did he, and then he crossed the room and pulled her into his arms and was hugging her so tightly that breathing was iffy. "I've been so worried," she gasped.

She felt his heart beating strong and fast and her knees went weak with relief. Thank God he was real and not part of her nightmares.

His arms tightened, and he bent his head to the curve of her shoulder. She was still so surprised he was there that she was at a loss for words.

"You're alive," he murmured, his voice hoarse.

She felt his hands on her back where the dress gaped. She'd forgotten all about her state of undress. Her breath caught, and she reached between them to clutch the fabric to her chest. She took a step back, clearing her throat. "Of course I'm alive, and I've been looking for you everywhere. What happened to you? Where did you go?"

She peered into his face. It was all hard angles and deep lines, and he'd lost weight. So different from the last time she'd seen him, which hadn't really been that long ago.

She remembered the worry in his eyes the moment before she left him. The eclipse had been imminent, every creature of Mylena caught in its vicious thrall. And she and Ray—impulsive, impatient Ray—were going to Agramon's fortress to free the rest of the human boys held captive there. He'd hated the idea of staying behind, but Jacob, Sloane and the others needed him. And Wyatt was ever, heartbreakingly, reliable.

"When you and Ray didn't return after the eclipse, we all thought you were dead."

Alarmed, she clenched his arm. "Ray didn't come back?" He'd pushed her into Agramon's portal, somehow thinking that he was doing her a favor by sending her back to the human world. But as the darkness descended, she remembered seeing him run. She'd just assumed that he escaped the fortress alive.

A devastating sadness settled into Wyatt's expressive blue eyes as if she'd just dashed his last hope. "Don't assume the worst. He could still be out there," she insisted for the benefit of the both of them.

"Yeah, of course. He's a resourceful kid, so he's probably just lying low." He didn't sound confident, but they both had to let it go.

After a moment he blinked and looked over her shoulder. She felt him stiffen. "When I heard you were here, I knew I had to try to get in and find you." He paused, gaze falling on the bed. "It looks comfortable."

Her cheeks burned. Even though she didn't owe him any explanations, she remembered their kiss, the questions and promises that had been locked up in it, and felt compelled to try. "I was hurt during the battle with Agramon. The goblin king saved me."

Wyatt's jaw visibly clenched, but he nodded. "I understand. I guess I knew something was up when I kissed you, but—"

"That was probably a mistake." She knew she started blushing as soon as he said the word "kiss," because she could feel it in her cheeks.

"Have you kissed *him*? Was *that* a mistake?" he asked in a tight voice. "At least I would never lie to you, manipulate you, or hurt you. Can you say the same about him? How many times has he done it already?"

Greta put her hands on her hips , but her bodice started

to fall and she remembered the dress was still undone. She readjusted her grip on it. "Whatever is between me and Isaac is none of your business."

"You're right. I don't want to know." He grimaced.

"He's a good guy," she said anyway. "And because of him, it's safe for us to be in Mylena. Humans no longer have to worry about persecution just because we exist."

He looked incredulous. "You're so sure about that?"

She stepped back. "Yes," she said firmly. "After Agramon was banished, Isaac went before some kind of council and argued on our behalf. If it wasn't true, do you think I would be standing here getting ready for a party instead of locked up in the dungeon down below?"

"If everything's so perfect, then why have there been hunters out scouring the woods ever since the eclipse, and why did I have to break into this place like a criminal?"

"Did you even *try* knocking on the front door instead?" She crossed her arms. "The gates are closed because there's been some unrest in Isaac's kingdom recently," she admitted hesitantly, feeling a little guilty for sharing Isaac's business. "But they're being opened tonight because Isaac is throwing a big event to…ah…introduce me to his people."

Wyatt stepped forward and took her arm. Anger simmered in his gaze. "I haven't had a nice cushy bed to sleep in at night or a fire to warm myself with the last few weeks. I've been out *there*"—he pointed out the window—"where you used to be, too. And let me tell you that no matter how much your goblin king boyfriend wants it to be true, his subjects and the rest of Mylena aren't even close to giving up hundreds of years of hatred for humans. If you go in front of the entire kingdom tonight, what makes you think they won't revolt against you both?"

"That isn't going to happen." She jerked back. Her grip tightened so hard on the collar of her dress that her knuckles ached.

"You've got a lot of confidence in someone who would have killed you with his bare hands just a few weeks ago."

She swallowed, shook her head, and glanced over his shoulder at the door. Could she say for sure that if Isaac came in right now, he would welcome Wyatt with open arms? Or would he be angry? "Things change," she said determinedly.

"Not that much. Don't fool yourself." He matched her step back with another step forward and lifted something in front of her face. It took a split second to focus on the gold chain dangling from his fist. Her locket. He undid the clasp and placed it around her neck, his fingers soft on her skin.

She opened it slowly and let out a long breath at the sight of her parents' photo. Wyatt gently took her hand and pressed something else into her palm. She closed her fingers over the hard, round object and swallowed hard. "He's never going to understand who you really are. He'll never be able to understand why you kept this walnut in your pocket all these years. And he won't understand why you asked *me* to take care of the only two things in this world that you cherished."

No fair. "You underestimate him," she said.

"Mylena is never going to be where we belong." He held out his hand. "Come with me, Greta. Let's get out of here before something awful happens to prove it to you."

She swallowed, ignoring his outstretched hand. "I can't." Her throat burned and her chest ached. "I can't just leave. I care about him, Wyatt. I'm sorry, but I have to try and make this work."

"What if I told you that I found the portal out of this world?"

Her breath caught. "What? You did? Where?"

"I'll tell you, but you have to come."

She hesitated and felt guilty. If she went with him, Isaac would be devastated. Everything he'd done for her...

But if she didn't go, that would be admitting once and for all that she was never, *ever* going home.

He dropped his arm and backed away. "I suppose I have your answer." His voice cracked as if tears clogged his throat, and he looked so disappointed that she bit her lip.

He turned to leave without another word.

"Wyatt, wait," she pleaded, blinking back tears of her own. "You don't have to go right away. Stay and meet Isaac, and you'll see that — "

"I can't stay, Greta. You shouldn't, either, but I don't have the time to convince you. I have to get back out there."

He sounded more than just disappointed. He sounded worried. "What's going on?" A sliver of suspicion and fear pierced her sadness. "Wyatt, is something wrong? Where are the boys?"

A knock at the door startled them both. Wyatt spun around, and suddenly there was a dagger in his hand. "Wyatt, no!" She reached for his wrist and held him back. He tugged against her.

Something rose up from her core, like a cloud of ash barreling to the surface. She sputtered and coughed, her vision blurry and her fingers tingling with heat.

Wyatt gasped and jerked away just as Siona entered the room.

She took in the situation in the span of a heartbeat. She very slowly closed the door behind her and put her back up against it. "Do you require assistance, danem?" she said calmly, searching Greta's face.

It was hard to concentrate. She itched and burned, like fire ants crawled beneath her skin. Greta glanced at Wyatt, horrified that he might see what she'd been trying to hide from everyone. He gripped his wrist with a confused look on his face. *Oh, God.* Was his skin slightly red there, like a burn?

Greta sucked up Siona's serene confidence in great gulps

and, finally, control seemed to return, pushing the dangerous energy back down. Thankfully, Wyatt seemed more concerned about their visitor and had failed to notice her discomposure.

She swallowed. "What are you going to do, Siona? Kill the dangerous human for me?" She made it a joke, but Wyatt didn't look like he found it funny.

Siona crossed her arms. "I was thinking more that you may need help with that dress after all," she answered with a smile.

Greta squeezed Wyatt's arm. "This is Siona."

"What is she? Goblin or faerie?" he asked, looking the hunter up and down quizzically.

"She's a *friend*," Greta said sternly with a sharp look. "A friend who saved my life and who's been helping me try to find you all this time."

Wyatt had the grace to blush and immediately apologized, those Boy Scout manners of his kicking right in. "Nice to, uh, meet you, danem."

"It is good to see that you are finally found, Dolem Wyatt," Siona replied in her most unexpressive hunter's voice, but her eyes sparkled as she looked him over with an equal measure of interest. "What can we do for you this moon rising?"

He ignored the question and turned his back to their curious audience. "Whatever's going on with you"—he looked down at her hand as if it might shoot balls of fire, so he obviously hadn't been as oblivious as she'd hoped—"we can deal with it together."

She shook her head. "It's not…nothing's going on." She tried to sound reassuring. "I just need to give this a chance."

His expression hardened, and his voice dropped so only she could hear. "I won't waste more time begging you to come with me. But please don't trust them, Greta," he pleaded. "Don't trust anyone."

"Wyatt, nobody here is going to do any—"

"Just be careful," he said urgently. "I'll wait two nights before I take the boys to the portal." His finger trailed up the line of her bare shoulder and the column of her neck until he cupped her cheek, his strong, callused hand flat on her flushed skin. Her eyelids fluttered, and she bit her lip. "If you change your mind or if you need me, I'll come, okay?"

She let out a long breath and nodded. Was this it? If he'd found a way home and she remained here…did that mean she was never going to see him again?

"Wyatt?" she whispered, voice cracking with emotion. *Don't go. Don't leave.*

She couldn't say it. He had to leave. He was right about one thing—he would never belong in Mylena. There was nothing for him here.

Is he right about me, too?

Was she deluding herself that things could change, that this world could accept her and she and Isaac could be happy together?

His hand slipped to the back of her neck. He was going to kiss her.

Not fair.

Greta sucked in a hard breath and drew back. She owed Isaac better than that. She owed *Wyatt* better than that.

She pushed against his chest hard enough to let him know kissing her wasn't an option.

"Are you going to deny that you feel something between us?" he said.

He needed to go, and it was already too hard to let him walk away.

"Of course not," she said. "But the time for us is…"

"Over?"

Impulsively, she threw her free arm around his neck. "Be careful," she whispered.

He squeezed her tight. "Once I knew you weren't dead…I

had to at least try, right?" he murmured. When he stepped back, he threw her a crooked grin. "Who knows, I might not be going anywhere if I can't make it back out of this castle."

She looked down at herself. Had she really been standing here all this time with this stupid dress undone? "Give me a minute and I'll take you to the gates."

Siona interrupted. "The goblin king requires your presence in the hall, danem." She tilted her head and smiled at Wyatt. "But I will personally ensure that Dolem Wyatt makes it to the front gates without incident."

"Thanks, Siona." She turned back to Wyatt. "Not everyone here is out to get us. There are people in Mylena who *can* be trusted."

He squared his shoulders and dropped his arms. "I hope you're right."

A coldness settled over him as he turned and walked through the door, chin held high as if he expected Siona to take him directly to the dungeons, no matter what she'd promised.

He didn't look back.

CHAPTER THREE

Greta was alone again, and she felt it in more ways than one. Turning back to the window, she peered out and down, but she was on the wrong side of the building to see the gates.

"This is quite a sight."

She spun around at the sound of Isaac's deep voice. Her gut clenched, and her heart pounded. No matter what doubts she had, or how often they clashed, or how aggravating he got, his voice was enough to remind her why she continued to believe that working through it all might just be worth it.

He leaned a shoulder against the frame of the open doorway, looking her up and down with that intense focus she still hadn't gotten used to. A glint of satisfaction lit his eyes, and a smile pulled at his lips as he took in the stupid dress.

"Oh, no. Don't you get used to this," she warned, bracing a free hand on her hip even as warmth spread through her like a rushing tide. "I don't know what you're up to, but you better not start thinking you can tell me what to wear on a regular basis."

He chuckled and came forward. That couldn't be good.

Teasing, charismatic Isaac was always harder to get a bead on than brooding, snarly Isaac.

He stopped a few feet in front of her. She took in the crisp white linen shirt under his richly embroidered black cloak, a drastic change from last night's dirty traveling clothes.

His hair was slightly damp, but he still smelled of pine and wood smoke. It was the sort of thing that couldn't be washed away. It made up who he was. It was the same scent that followed her to bed every night.

"Damn, you look good." Her mouth went dry and she couldn't look away. "Every inch a king."

A goofy grin spread across his face, and her chest virtually exploded. It was like an unexpected ray of sunshine and… well…she loved that *she* was the one who'd just made it happen. There was no doubt that this particular boy had never lacked in confidence or arrogance, but *she* was the one who put the playful gleam in his eyes. She actually made him…happy.

"How much trouble have you gotten into today?" he asked with a smile.

"Don't even." She snorted. "I've been sitting around here going stir-crazy for hours while your people poked and prodded at me."

"You need to start thinking of them as your people, too." As a reminder of what he was planning to do at the banquet tonight, it worked.

She chewed her lip, which was starting to feel pretty ragged. Any more anxiety and she might worry it off altogether. "Are you sure this is such a good idea? Telling everyone about us, I mean? Couldn't we just let them figure it out on their own? You know, like we were normal kids or something? I doubt that even in Mylena there any other couples who feel the need to make a proclamation of their relationship."

He reached for her hand and tugged her forward. Her stomach fluttered, and she went with a smile. It was still hard to trust someone to get close without her sword between them for protection, but with Isaac she could do it. With him, it almost felt natural, kind of freeing. And as much as he drove her crazy a lot of the time, she couldn't resist the chance to touch him.

"Who ever said that we were like any other couple…" He leaned in and lowered his voice. "…from any other world?"

She tilted her face up and welcomed the press of his lips. He claimed her with a deep, hard kiss that took her breath away again and again. In seconds she was lost in him. She even forgot about the stupid dress until she realized the only thing holding it on anymore was the force of their bodies pressed together.

"If you want to keep me compliant, you'll tell me the real reason you think this banquet is necessary," she murmured, hiking the fabric up to her shoulders when he pulled back. "Why do we have to do this now?"

He smiled and traced her collarbone, much like Wyatt had done only minutes ago. Guilt warmed her cheeks.

"This is the best way to get as many of my people together so that I can address the kingdom." He nudged her to turn around, then began to refasten all the buttons of her dress. She started to throw a grateful smile over her shoulder, but the brush of his fingers gave her goose bumps.

Silly, it's not like that was a hugely intimate part of her body, but this touching thing was still so new to her.

Holding her breath, she focused intently on his progress, dreading when he would reach the very last button. But he took his time, and that was almost worse, because every caress was both torture and heaven. Finally, he pushed the thick braids over each of her shoulders and leaned down to place a kiss just below the tender spot right beneath each of her earlobes.

She knew her face was red when she turned back around and presumed her whole body appeared the same, because she felt the deep flush go all the way to her toes.

She cleared her throat and tried to remember what they'd been talking about.

"You're so certain getting everyone together in a confined space and springing the news that their king is dating a human is a good thing?" Her hands were clammy just thinking about it, and she clenched them in the folds of her skirts. At least all those pleats were good for one thing. "What if I wait on the sidelines with my sword ready? You know, just in case it all backfires?"

He shook his head. "You'd like it if the room turned blood-thirsty, wouldn't you? At least then you would know how to deal with it."

She groaned. Maybe he was right. Maybe she'd only imagined the tension in his shoulders whenever he returned from handling these little skirmishes across goblin lands. Maybe her uneasiness about this whole thing came from her own insecurity and doubt.

"I want you at my side." He pulled at the tail of one of her braids. "And don't bring your sword. Tonight I want my people to see you as you are."

"The sword is a part of who I am, Isaac. Don't think that just because I've been hanging out here for a few weeks, any of that's changed," she warned.

"I want them to see beyond the formidable hunter to the vulnerability I've witnessed."

"Well, then, you'd be the only one." She crossed her arms. "But it's your party, you can die if you want to."

He let go of her hair with one last tug. "This trust we've spoken of before…you do know what it means, right?"

"Okay, okay. Just tell me when to show up and I'll be there."

"I don't think so. I'm not letting you out of my sight again before the banquet. You'll accompany me downstairs now."

She grinned. The autocratic goblin king had returned.

"Now who's lacking the trust?"

CHAPTER FOUR

One of Isaac's attendants, Soren, stood waiting for them at the top of the stairs when they came out of Greta's room. His bulbous nose was usually stuck up in the air, but when he noticed her, those cavernous nostrils flared in a disdainful sneer as he contemplated ways to make her disappear. At least, she could only assume that's what he was thinking, since he hadn't ever condescended to actually speak to her.

Today his expression was carefully blank as he greeted Isaac with a deep bow. "Everything is in order," he confirmed.

Isaac nodded and turned to Greta. "You are ready." It wasn't a question.

She didn't object. She wouldn't embarrass him by admitting to the fear that almost froze her feet in place.

He held out his hand. She would have preferred to walk into this thing without anyone thinking she had to lean on him for support, but that was the old Greta talking. The new Greta took his hand because they were in this together and a show of solidarity and commitment was going to be crucial to pulling it off.

Downstairs, the hallways and common areas were packed with people. Suddenly, something came sailing through the air toward her face. She caught it an inch from her nose.

Her skin sizzled. Her head throbbed. She bent over and clutched at her chest as the magick inside crawled up her throat like bile, burning and bitter. It was obvious now that the surge of power was a reflex that arose when she was threatened, or when her body *thought* she was being threatened—which was probably why it had reared up most often during her nightmares.

Not now. This cannot *happen now.*

"Greta!" Isaac's voice was low and raspy, strained along with every muscle in his body.

She blinked. He was struggling with his demons almost as deeply as she was with hers. She heard the sharp concern in his voice and saw the claws that had automatically protruded from his fingertips at the first sign of her distress.

No, no, no.

She doubled her efforts to control the magick flooding her, threatening to unleash itself. She couldn't let her weakness put Isaac in danger of going Lost.

Holding back the magick *hurt*, like a dagger twisting in her belly, or a deadly disease systematically destroying all her healthy organs and leaving black sludge in its wake.

She gripped Isaac's wrist. "It didn't touch me," she said quickly. "I'm fine." She swallowed hard and tried to focus on something solid. The object in her hand…which was nothing but a hunk of crusty bread.

A goblin child no taller than her ribs stood shaking like a leaf a few feet away, with Soren's hands on both his shoulders to keep him from bolting. Just a child. Thankfully, Isaac noticed the child at about the same time, and she felt the waves of fury visibly reduce.

"Are you hurt?" He wasn't asking about the bread.

"It's under control." For now. If, like she suspected, the

magick responded when she felt stressed or threatened, and Isaac's moon phase went into overdrive when he sensed it rising, the combination was a bomb whose fuse would only keep getting shorter and shorter. It wasn't as if either of them could avoid every aggravating situation that might come along.

What she really needed was to get rid of this dark power once and for all. As soon as possible.

Isaac motioned to Soren without letting go of her. "Bring the child here," he ordered. His voice sounded harsh over the silence that had fallen in the corridor, but within the folds of her skirt he squeezed her hand.

The boy came forward with his head drooping low enough for his chin to touch his chest. Isaac stood over him, looking huge and intimidating. He took the piece of bread from her and held it out. He waited patiently for the boy to look up at him. "It seems this slipped from your grasp. Lucky that my friend caught it for you."

The boy looked at her and nodded with big round eyes full of fear. Her chest constricted and she smiled as brightly as she could. She would never blame a child for imitating what he'd seen the adults do—not that she was about to admit to Isaac that this wasn't the first incident where foodstuffs had been thrown at her head.

"Why don't you head into the hall and find something better than stale bread to eat?"

The boy's shoulders fell, and somewhere in the gathering crowd, a woman sobbed in obvious relief.

The child took off in the opposite direction as fast as his stubby little legs could carry him.

Thankfully, Soren started to usher people into the banquet hall, and the sounds of mumbled conversation and movement started back up again as the hallway cleared.

"Stuff like this is only going to keep happening," Greta

finally whispered when they were almost alone and she could breathe again. He had to know it.

"Not after I make it clear what you mean to me," he insisted with a determined edge to his voice. Yes. He knew.

Wyatt's words came back to haunt her. The certainty that it had been a mistake to agree to this made her sweat. Isaac wanted to keep her safe, but if he made a decision as a man that jeopardized his position as a *king*, didn't it fall to her to keep *him* safe?

Survival might be her specialty, but what the heck did she know about ruling the goblin kingdom? Trust. She had to trust that *he* knew. And so if he thought this was a good idea, then…

She looked up and smiled. "Okay, let's do this thing."

Pride and relief shone from his eyes as they made their way into the hall. She found herself searching the crowd for Wyatt…but he wasn't there. And she should be glad, because he *shouldn't* be there. Hopefully, he was already far away, taking those boys back home.

She pushed aside the wave of regret because there was no place for it here, now. She didn't regret staying, only regretted that making such a choice had cost her a friend—of which she had too few to begin with.

The main hall of the goblin castle was usually divided into functional smaller chambers. There were areas where goblin children sat for lessons, others where goblins could request supplies, get food, and even spend the night if it would be too far to travel home before dark or if the weather was very bad—not an unusual occurrence. All this had been business as usual before Isaac became the big cheese, but he had continued the practice.

Tonight the dividers that usually separated the main hall had been removed, and every one of the sconces on the walls had been lit.

She saw the king's treasurer across the room. He was a harried and overworked little guy, and they'd seen a lot of each other whenever she'd come in to claim payment on a bounty. They'd even sort of been friends. Or rather, they'd been the kind of strangers who exchanged pleasantries and the odd ribald joke. That had ended when she was outed as a human, but at least he hadn't publicly ostracized her, and the brief nod he sent her way now gave her hope for the evening.

Isaac's hand fell on the crook of her arm. He bent his head. "Are you ready?"

Greta had never seen so many people in one spot before and felt decidedly vulnerable. Many of the goblins, sprites, and ogres had to have come from hours away, maybe lured by the promise of the free food. After all, Mylena's farmlands were all but barren after centuries of winter. Many of these people—Greta included—had never seen so much food in one place before, and to lay hands on even a portion of what the goblin king was giving away free tonight would have cost the average person the equivalent of a firstborn child.

There were three kingdoms of Mylena: the goblin kingdom, the gnome kingdom, and the mysterious faerie kingdom. The sprites and ogres and other unrepresented species had no choice but to seek sanctuary within one of these or take their chances in the free territories—which were even less habitable than the rest of this frozen world.

The goblin kingdom was by far the most popular for these refugees.

Nobody ever opted for the Glass Kingdom, home of the faerie race, for a whole crapload of reasons, not the least of which was because they'd closed their doors to everyone. In fact, the doors hadn't opened even once in more years than anyone could remember. It was also said to be cursed, that every year the gates remained closed, the Glass Kingdom blended deeper into the mountains until one day nobody would ever find it again.

Isaac's face was so close she could see the flecks of deep purple in his eyes. "You should have let me bring my sword," she murmured, the corner of her lip turning up.

His laughter turned heads throughout the packed hall, but his gaze was locked on her to the exclusion of all else, making her blush so hard her cheeks might go up in flames.

She cleared her throat and focused on the crowd, ignoring when his laughter turned to a knowing chuckle.

Greta had never seen so many people gathered in one place and found herself getting nervous again. As she shifted to ask about the security arrangements, the doors at the end of the hall blew open, letting in a rush of cold air and whirling snow that was just as showy as the entourage that poured inside after it.

Her breath caught.

Gnomes.

Everyone said gnomes were vicious schemers and liars. They'd thrown their lot in with Agramon and tortured dozens of humans in the depths of the demon's dungeons, so maybe that was true, but all she really knew for sure was that they were hands down the butt ugliest creatures Greta had ever come across.

The gnome king, Leander, was certainly no exception. She picked him out right away, even though she'd never seen him before this moment. He sauntered into the room like he owned it, a dozen or so of what she assumed to be his personal guard forming a scruffy-looking half circle behind him.

He was gaudy and coarse at the same time. Jewels hung from his neck and sparkled on his fingers, and he wore a deep red cloak, reminding her of a glittering Santa Claus without the fat belly or the jolly. He even had a beard, but it was gray and scraggly, separated down the middle, each end twisted into a point that touched his barrel chest. The available real estate of his bulbous nose looked as if it had exploded with warts, making it red and swollen looking.

As ridiculous as he appeared, she didn't dare laugh. He wore jewels because that was the only thing of value his land produced, and no one could be faulted for succumbing to gout when ale was a cheaper way to heat the body than wood for fire, which grew slowly, if at all.

Goblin lands weren't exactly fertile, but they had prairies, a thick wood, and minerals from the Brimstone Caves, and so had fared the never-ending winter better than most.

As the gnome king stopped in front of the high table, his dark eyes glittered with hatred for the both of them. But only weeks ago he and Isaac had been allied in their hatred of humans, so she couldn't exactly fault him for that, either.

Greta's job as a bounty hunter had taken her to the beautiful but deadly acid mists of Eyna's Falls in the north. It had led her to an ancient, deserted, overgrown faerie palace crawling with creepy centipede-like things the size of ponies with pincers that could easily crush bone. She'd also hunted in the scorching heart of the Brimstone Caves, home to fire ants the size of cockroaches, huge bats that could drain the blood from a pasture full of cattle and still go back for more, and whatever else happened to wander inside and lay claim to a dark and smoky section of cavern.

And although she'd ventured as far as the southern counties of the gnome kingdom as well, she'd never gone to Rhazua, where Leander himself resided, preferring not to tempt fate in the lawless city.

The gnome king sneered at Isaac. "You put this creature here at your side? As your equal? I wouldn't have believed it without seeing for myself, but the rumors are apparently true. The young goblin king has been bewitched."

Not so long ago, Greta had lumped Isaac and the gnome king together as being cut from the same cloth, but now she knew better. She stiffened at the disgust and loathing in Leander's voice, but refrained from defending herself…or Isaac. When it came to hunting, he'd always let her handle her own business without interference; she supposed she could return the favor now.

"Leander." Isaac rose slowly. He didn't seem as surprised to see the gnome king out in public. Then again, he was notoriously good at hiding his emotions. She'd been on the receiving end of that deadpan look enough times to know.

"I hope you and your retinue enjoy goblin hospitality. I've saved a special place here at my table so you'll have no difficulty hearing my announcement when the time comes." Isaac pointed to his left with a nod and three goblins rushed toward the empty seats to fill goblets and bring bread.

The gnome king harrumphed and made a loud production of seating himself, yelling for the good wine and complaining about the speed of service.

Isaac slipped her a subtle grin that she understood perfectly. "Keep your friends close and your enemies closer" was apparently a universal concept.

Just when she thought the hall couldn't hold as much as another dwarf, a group of big ogres entered.

The building should have been freezing considering how often those doors had been thrown open, but the body heat from so many people had kept the temperature warm enough for the fires to have been left to smolder, coats to have been tossed aside, and the ripe scent of underwashed bodies to permeate the air.

Another of Isaac's guards bent close to whisper in his ear. His expression tightened and he nodded.

"What's going on?" she whispered to Isaac.

He shook his head. "Don't worry about it."

She ground her teeth. "You know I hate when you say that. If something is wrong, I want to know. I can help," she insisted. "I'm not just a pretty face, you know."

"Are you saying that I can't handle my kingdom without you?" He did that imperious eyebrow thing that made her want to scream.

"I wouldn't say you *can't*," she teased. "But you know you wouldn't want to."

"Which brings us back to the reason for being here tonight." He patted her hand. "You will trust me."

She shrugged and lifted the only utensil on the table in front of her. "All right, but when the fighting breaks out and I save your life with this wooden spoon, you're going to admit that you should have let me bring my sword."

Their gazes held until someone else came to whisper in his ear. Greta faced forward and caught a small group edging through the crowd. There were four, each draped in long gray cloaks with hoods pulled up over their heads. At first glance they might have been mistaken for sprites, but Greta's internal alarm system was going haywire.

Faerie.

It was virtually unheard of for faerie kind to mingle with other Myleans. Of course there'd been that one…and he'd been intent on murdering her. As much as she wanted to give everyone in Mylena a chance, the faeries didn't leave her with much to hope for.

Where did they come from, if not the barricaded Glass Kingdom? When had they arrived? What did they want?

"Where's Siona?" She just realized there was no sign of her.

"I do not know," he admitted with a frown.

Cold, sharp fear sliced through her chest. "Isaac."

"I see them." Well, at least she knew he hadn't invited the faeries without telling her.

His whole body had stiffened beside her, humming like a bowstring being snapped. When he curled his hand into a fist on top of the banquet table, she saw that the claws were out, and her heartbeat kicked up a notch.

He rose and called in a booming voice, "You there. Attend me."

The faeries glanced up, showing no surprise at being summoned by the goblin king. They turned toward the head table, stopping opposite Isaac just as Leander had done. Speak of the devil, the gnome king took the opportunity to slip back into the crowd, a tankard still clutched in his hand.

Three goblin guards closed in. The scrape of steel being drawn from leather sheaths made her nervous. If worst came to worst, she'd have to use the small dagger strapped to her ankle.

Isaac got to his feet, so Greta quickly did the same. He lifted his hand, and after only a slight hesitation, the guards behind them resheathed their weapons. She opened her mouth to protest. Who knew what kind of magick these faeries had up their sleeves? The last one of their kind she'd tackled had caged her inside a spinning tornado of flesh-burning smoke.

But when two of them lowered the hoods of their thick woolen cloaks, revealing their faces and the decorative embroidery of their outfits, Greta gasped. They were so young, no older than herself.

"Your Highness," said the girl, sinking into a formal curtsy.

She had the face of an angel. Her pale skin glowed and her bright blue eyes were disconcertingly sharp. She had long, super-pale blond hair that fell to her waist and seemed to blow back in a bit of a breeze, even though the main doors had shut once more.

The same went for her companion, who must be related. A brother, if Greta had to guess. He had the same coloring and the same eyes, and he looked about the same age. They might even be twins.

It would be easy to come to the conclusion that these two were harmless, but the moment she let herself believe that would probably be the moment they attacked.

Isaac crossed his arms and nodded at the two young faeries. "Your Highnesses. What calls the faerie prince and princess away from the Glass Kingdom after all these years?"

Highnesses? These two were faerie *royalty*? How did Isaac know?

Looking more closely, it was actually pretty obvious. The two faeries were so embarrassingly round eyed. They wore impractical clothing and were flanked by two warrior faeries almost as young as the prince and princess. They still looked formidable, but nothing like the ancient, fearsome Lazarus, whose icy power had preceded him before he even entered a room.

Isaac was being polite, but tension and suspicion surrounded him like a heavy cloak. She was pretty sure nobody but her could see it, though. *He* might still have doubts about how well he was going to fill his father's shoes, but *she* didn't doubt for a second that Isaac had been born to be a king. He hid his true feelings well and handled the games and intrigue of this world like a pro.

The faerie guards stepped back a few steps as the boy bent into a stiff bow before Isaac. One of the warriors glanced up. He had crystal-blue eyes and blond hair. Not perfectly blond like the prince and princess, but like he'd tossed around in a bit of soot before getting dressed that morning. She decided that this one was a little tougher than the others. In fact, he was pale and wiry like Lazarus had been, with similar features. Just younger.

And hopefully less psychotic.

Greta followed his gaze.

Siona.

Greta released a relieved sigh. *Where the heck were you?* she mouthed with a frown.

Distracted, Siona shook her head. Her gaze was drawn to the faerie guests. She managed to convey her signature brand of calm, cool disdain as she looked over the newcomers…

except for a deep flush of color staining her cheeks.

Greta started to relax. It certainly didn't seem as if an icy showdown was about to erupt here in the goblin court.

Everyone had pretty much ignored her so far until the young princess said, "We have heard tales about you, Danem Greta. Word of your strength and skill as a bounty hunter has found its way to our borders."

The young girl ducked her head and dipped into another perfect curtsy, but she didn't stand back up. After a long moment Greta realized she was going to stay like that until Greta returned the sentiment, so she gave it a shot. Her curtsy was wobbly and pathetic.

The girl straightened, folding her hands in front of her and turning back to Isaac. "We come as emissaries of Queen Minetta. My name is Leila, and this is my brother, Byron."

"Your Majesties," she said tightly, managing another pathetic curtsy for the prince's benefit. "I've made the acquaintance of your kind before, although I can't say that the circumstances were ideal."

Leila's brow raised. "You met one of us?"

"A bounty hunter named Lazarus." Her tone made it clear that he hadn't made a stellar impression.

"Ah. Please don't consider him to be representative of the entire faerie race. You understand, of course, that one does not speak for all."

Considering that's exactly what she'd always hoped the rest of Mylena would come to accept about humans, Greta knew she had to give the prince and princess the benefit of the doubt. Convincing Isaac, who was already bristling with suspicion, might be more difficult, but he'd accepted *her*, hadn't he? Was it possible that even the elusive faeries could become allies? What if Mylena could get to the point where it was no longer divided by race at all?

"Unfortunately," Leila said, "Lazarus was banished from

our kingdom long ago. However, I recently heard that he…" She trailed off. It was obvious she knew exactly what had happened to Lazarus.

Isaac cleared his throat. "You are welcome to stay to hear my announcement and partake of refreshment before returning home," he said tightly, making it clear that hospitality did not equal trust.

Both the prince and princess graciously bent their heads. Leila's smile was warm as she looked up at Greta again. "Perhaps we'll have an opportunity to speak again later."

"That would be nice," she said, and it was true, even though Isaac tensed beside her. It could only benefit them to have some insight into the mysterious faerie race while there were representatives of the faerie queen herself right here.

The faeries melted back into the crowd. Even though Greta was watching them, one second they were weaving around goblin folk, and the next she couldn't find them at all. She envied that neat trick. She'd once had the ability to blend in almost as well…before the secret of her true nature had been revealed to all of Mylena, and before she'd become the goblin king's…um, what, exactly?

If Greta was really going to stay in Mylena with Isaac, then maybe formalizing their relationship wasn't such a horrible idea. It would give her some credibility, right? Maybe she could even help Isaac bring Mylena out of the dark ages. This might be the start of some real positive change for this world, and when the history books were written they could say she was the one who put an end to prejudice and hatred across all the species.

She glanced over at Isaac. *Keep dreaming.* His eyes had gone black and the hair on his arms stood on end. He was obviously reacting to the mounting tensions that the arrival of the faeries had brought to the crowded room. Was he having second thoughts?

Nervous, she curled her fingers around his and squeezed. "Maybe we could get out of here for a few minutes," she suggested lightly. "You know, catch our breath." His gaze cleared as he focused on her, and she grinned. "Come on, you know you want to get some alone time with me."

"I know how fond you are of ravishing me in closets," he whispered with a grin.

She shook her head. "One time…and you're never going to let me forget it, are you?"

"But when I do get you alone again, I don't want to be rushed."

The Great Mother save her, that sounded *hot*. Maybe hotter than she was technically ready for, but heck, never let it be said that Greta wasn't all for bringing their relationship to the next level.

Her imagination was deep into overdrive when Isaac raised an eyebrow and shook his head. "It is time," he said.

She swallowed hard, forcing her head back into the game— so to speak.

Isaac stood again, his chair skittering back across the floor with a loud screech that made her wince. When that only succeeded in getting half of the massive room's undivided attention immediately, he grabbed his tankard and thumped it on the table in three booming knocks. Thankfully, it was empty.

Three goblins each raised a horn to their lips, but these were nothing like the musical instruments Greta had known in the human world. They emitted a single sharp blast of sound that captured the attention of the entire room and made Greta's ears ring in the process.

The noise level went from raucous to hushed before the echo of the horns had dispersed into the rafters of the ceiling. All eyes were on Isaac…and her, as if everyone already knew that this was somehow going to be about her.

She wanted to duck and hide, but forced herself to square her shoulders and look straight ahead. Isaac deserved someone strong and confident at his side, and even if she wasn't that person…she'd gotten good at pretending to be lots of things.

Although she tried to keep her gaze steady and calm, as soon as Isaac spoke, she looked. At him. She saw only him. There were so many different sides to this boy, but he always mesmerized her, especially when he played this role. The *goblin king*.

Power and conviction rolled off his shoulders and bled from his pores. He was absolutely invulnerable but still approachable, the *people's* king. Because underneath it all, the fact that he cared about Mylena was unmistakable.

She was in awe, and if she didn't know he'd lord it over her forever, she might even tell him that one of these days.

His voice sailed over the crowd like a crack of thunder. "It is no secret that for many hundreds of years, our lands have been under a curse. The Great Mother deemed Mylena unworthy of her gifts and abandoned us to the endless winter."

Greta winced. Did he really have to go there?

"And for many hundreds of years we have blamed humans for this curse, but we were wrong to do so." He paused for effect. "*I* was wrong to do so. Humans are *not* the scourge we have been warned against for so long. In fact, it was a human. This human"—he took her hand—"who finally released Mylena from Agramon's evil and reawakened the Great Mother from her cold slumber." He seemed to spear each and every person in the crowd with his hard gaze, daring to be contradicted.

The grumbling and gasps built on top of each other until the entire hall was buzzing again.

King Leander stepped forward, pointing at Isaac. "How do you come to the conclusion that the Great Mother has returned to Mylena when the lands remain encrusted in ice as always, and the endless snow continues to fall, even at this very moment? This human has bewitched you!" He swung around in a flamboyant circle, twisting the ends of his ugly beard with a twinkle in his eyes that promised trouble. "She released a demon that had been safely confined for hundreds of years, and now she has bewitched the goblin king in order to spread her evil to all of us!" he yelled.

Isaac lifted his hand for silence. The rumblings lessened, but did not quiet completely.

"The Great Mother *is* returned to us."

A door opened at the back of the hall. Suddenly, goblin maids started filing into the room one after another with their arms full of...something. Greta blinked as she tried to figure out what they were carrying.

Flowers!

They started handing flowers to everyone, and in a perfectly choreographed move, one of the maids passed off a large bouquet to Isaac. He held it up to her with a vulnerability in his gaze that shook her to the core.

No. She had no regrets about staying.

She took the flowers gently, surprise washing over her. "Thank you," she whispered. She dared not squeeze the stalk of the bouquet. The stems felt so thin and delicate in her hands, the most delicate thing she'd touched in years.

He leaned in and pressed a kiss to her lips right there in front of everyone—not that many people noticed with all the excitement.

The blooms were small and underdeveloped, but they were real. She brought them up to her nose. They smelled real, too. You don't realize how much you've missed something until it's thrust in your face. The heavy aroma tickling the inside of her nose as she breathed in the perfume of flowers brought on an ache that threatened to bowl her over with homesickness.

Greta had *never* seen a flower in Mylena. Not one. Nothing

so fragile and beautiful could survive the harsh, cursed climate. "Where did these come from?" she whispered, wondering if there was a secret royal greenhouse hidden away somewhere.

"Here, the snow may still be falling, but farther south the change is already noticeable. The ice is melting, the air is growing warmer." Had he actually seen the fresh green shoots poking out of the ground? "I wouldn't have believed it, either, but it seems that spring is on its way."

Spring. Could it really be true? She grinned. "Do you know what this means?"

He nodded. "The curse is broken. It means that Mylena can change, and its people can change. They have no reason not to accept you any longer."

She hated to point out the obvious and put a damper on his expectations, but even if the suns blazed down upon Mylena until it was hot enough to splash around in the newly thawed lakes wearing nothing but a string bikini, there would be those who would say that the heat was just another curse to be blamed on the humans. There would always be something, some reason for people to hate.

But what if he was right? What if the two of them could beat the hate, be a force for change, and have a real life, a normal life, together?

Isaac's voice boomed as he straightened and claimed everyone's attention once again. "In the time of our ancestors, the kings and queens of Mylena would have gone before the Great Mother and sought her approval of their choice of life mate. But the breaking of our curse is a sign that the Great Mother has already approved of my queen, and so I will ask no one's permission to take her as mine."

He turned to her, looking deep into her eyes. "I ask for none but yours."

Her breath caught. Her vision blurred. *Queen?* That wasn't the commitment speech she'd been expecting. Suddenly there was a heck of a lot more pressure and responsibility bearing down on her, and she couldn't breathe.

The entire hall stilled and waited for her response. Isaac's expression tightened as he waited, too. He saw her uncertainty, but she couldn't make this one easier for him, not if she wanted to stay true to herself.

"Isaac, this is…" She didn't even know…

She tugged on the hem of his jacket until he bent down. She hissed under her breath. "Just how soon is this wedding, or coronation, or whatever you've got planned supposed to happen?"

A flicker of humor broke the severity that had marked his expression since making his announcement. "Do you honestly believe that anyone could force the indomitable Greta the bounty hunter to do anything before she was ready? Even me?"

She bit her lip to keep from smiling. She wouldn't want anyone watching to think she wasn't taking this completely seriously. "Not that you wouldn't give it a good old Mylean try, right?"

"When you're ready," he assured her. "Together."

"Okay." She nodded.

She hadn't even realized how still he'd gotten until she watched him let out a carefully controlled breath. "We'll stand together for the goblin kingdom and the good of all Mylena?"

She would stand by his side with a sword in hand any day of the week, but this? Could she really do *this*? Become a queen? *His* queen?

"For the good of Mylena and any other world we happen to come across along the way," she agreed with a shaky grin.

He held out his hand, and the look in his eyes said *don't panic* as he turned and thrust their clasped fists into the air.

CHAPTER FIVE

The distracting parade of flowers was a good try, but Greta wasn't surprised when the castle rattled on its foundations with thunderous disapproval.

She was still reeling from the announcement herself and doing her best not to let anyone see it. She didn't want to add to the turmoil in the room.

At least she wasn't being slaughtered by an angry mob… yet, and she soon realized that the loud cries of "Foul" weren't coming from everyone. Leander seemed to have riled up his group of gnomes to the point where they drowned out any and all reaction from anyone else. In fact, as she watched, a couple of burly, dirty gnomes started a fight with a trio of goblins down on the floor just a few feet away from the head table.

She started forward to jump in and put a stop to it, but she was slowed by the yards of heavy dress fabric hanging off her, and then she remembered that she also had no weapon besides the small dagger under her skirts.

One of the gnomes pulled a knife. She lunged halfway

over the table anyway without any thought for the dress as the bastard stuck it in one of the goblin guests near him, a rail-thin young guy who looked like he'd only come for the free meal.

Isaac shot out for her arm with an iron grip that made it clear he wasn't letting her go anywhere. He shouted at his guards, but suddenly two faeries who must have come with the young prince and princess stepped from the throng of people into the fight and did exactly what Greta wanted to be doing—started kicking ass.

Before anyone could breathe, the snarling gnomes were grabbed by the scruff of their necks and tossed to the floor, faces pounded into the grit-coated floors.

There must have been many more faerie soldiers present than had come forward to be introduced to the goblin king, because they were in the thick of at least four other fights, putting a stop to them before any more weapons could be used.

Two of Isaac's men stepped in. They called for some room, lifted the injured goblin carefully, and started to carry him away. One guard shot Isaac a discouraging look and gave a short shake of his head. There was no mistaking that message.

Isaac's jaw tightened, his gaze stormy and dark. He called for order.

Leander had moved to stand behind a wall of his gnomes—those who weren't in the process of being locked in irons. He backed up nervously as a couple of the faeries closed in, but he still paused to sneer up at Isaac and Greta.

"You have engineered your own end, young goblin king," he called in a high voice. "Mark my words, the people won't stand for this abomination. The human will never be a queen of Mylena!"

With that, the gnomes pushed their way to the doors and threw them open. Greta's heart sank as the blowing snow and whistling wind blasted through the hall. It seemed a fitting end to such a violent outburst, and only more proof that the bitter winter might be here to stay.

Leander and his goons were finally gone, but the moment of optimism she'd let into her heart had already faded, marked by the mass exodus of everyone else from the hall.

She and Isaac were ushered out and into a private room down a short corridor.

"Everything will be fine now. The hard part is done," he murmured when they were alone. He touched her chin and smiled, but there was strain in his face.

"Were we even in the same room? Have you sniffed too many of those fresh flowers?" She shook her head. "The gnome king almost—"

He crossed his arms. "I can handle the gnome king."

Jeez, he was stubborn. "We'll handle him *together*. But he's not our only problem. There wasn't a single person in that hall that was happy about your announcement."

"You mistake a few rowdy antagonists for the whole of Mylena when that is not the case."

She rubbed a hand over her face, feeling suddenly weary.

"Have you changed your mind, then?" he asked. "Do you wish to be released from our bond?"

She looked up, surprised by the offer even though the look in his eyes said there was no way he was letting her go. "Of course not. I was caught off guard, and I'm still trying to figure out what just happened."

"Let me sum it up for you, then," he said, taking her hand and bringing it to his mouth.

Her hands were her livelihood. They were dry and cracked from the cold climate. Far from feminine. But she was proud of the calluses. They proved she'd survived. Against all the odds, she'd survived. Still, the spot in the center of her palm was soft, and when he opened her fingers and pressed his lips right there, it felt just as intimate as a kiss on the mouth.

He said, "Tonight I made it clear to every territory of Mylena that Greta the bounty hunter, Greta the brave, Greta the human…will one day become Greta the goblin queen."

"Did you ever stop to think that despite what we might feel for each other, maybe this is not what your kingdom needs? Your people need someone they can relate to, someone who knows what they've been through and what they struggle with every day."

He smirked. "Do you not know just as much about the harsh realities of living in Mylena as any goblin, gnome, sprite, or ogre?"

He had a point. "That's not the *point*. You know what I mean."

"I know that the goblin kingdom needs unity with all the other races of Mylena. I know that I want to be the one to bring it to them. And who better to help me unite the provinces under a common rule than one who has no fealty to any particular province, one whose motivation is for the good of all?"

Her heart sank. "So this is about politics?"

There was a sharp knock on the door. "Enter," Isaac called in a terse voice.

Siona came in, accompanied by three goblin guards. She'd already changed out of her formal dress and back into her hunter's garb. Greta desperately wanted to do the same thing.

One of the guards had a nasty scratch bisecting his left eye. Greta winced. If she hadn't been in the hall tonight…

Siona stopped a foot in front of her and got down on one knee. "My queen," she murmured.

The other guards were slower to follow suit, but with nervous glances sent Isaac's way, soon all of them knelt in a semicircle before her.

Pretty much the most uncomfortable she'd ever been in her entire life, Greta sent Isaac a panicked look, but he didn't seem the least inclined to do anything about it.

"By the Great Mother, get off the floor, all of you. I'm not anybody's queen, at least not yet." She reached out, grabbed Siona's hand, and yanked her to her feet. "If you do that again I might have to punch you," she growled into her ear.

The guards stood and stepped back, only to cross their arms behind their backs and turn to Isaac, as if waiting for instructions.

Siona gave her an evil grin. "You're going to have to get used to it eventually, you know."

Greta ignored that. "So, what's going on?" she asked. "Has anyone checked on the injured goblin?"

"I will go," Isaac said. He turned to Siona. "Stay with her."

They were far from finished with their discussion. "Isaac," she said.

Both of the guards glanced back at her sharply, obvious fear clouding their eyes. Their king hadn't been around much, so not many people besides the few maids who attended her had seen the two of them together. She'd almost forgotten that no one but her dared use his given name, and their reasons were good ones that had little to do with having a healthy respect for their monarch. There were consequences for saying the goblin king's name out loud where he could hear you.

It reminded her that maybe she should address him differently when they weren't alone, not because she cared about those kinds of consequences—it was way too late for her to avoid them—but maybe in an effort to maintain appearances, since winning over the people was already going to be tough enough for the both of them.

"Later," he said. The gentleness in his voice sounded almost like a private apology. She crossed her arms and nodded.

When everyone was gone, she turned to Siona and grumbled, "What am I getting myself into?"

"It must be difficult."

"What?"

"Relationships. They can be problematic at the best of times, but when you've been alone for as long as we—*you*—have…I suppose it might seem virtually impossible to navigate all that emotion. Someone always ends up suffering for it."

"Is that personal experience talking?" She regretted the words immediately when Siona's expression blanched. Yesterday, Greta never would have believed that Siona considered herself just as alone as Greta did—or just as damaged—but the more you learn about people, the more you relate to them.

"It's not always this hard, though, right?" It felt strange to be talking to someone about this stuff. Luke would never have tolerated it. To show uncertainty or admit she was scared was a sign of weakness. Luke wouldn't have denied her right to *have* feelings, just to show them. Like, ever.

"I'm not always going to ruin every friendship I try to have, am I?"

Siona dropped her gaze. "I don't know," she admitted, fiddling with the hilt of the dagger at her waist. "I've never really…" She trailed off and shrugged.

Jeez, what a pair they made.

Ah, what the hell. Greta stepped forward and reached out hesitantly, fingers trembling as they closed around the other girl's cold hand and squeezed lightly. It was weird how quickly their positions had flipped. Now Siona was the one exposing a bruised and vulnerable side and Greta was clumsily trying to soothe. Apparently neither of them was any good at it, but maybe that was okay, too.

With a cough and an uncomfortable dropping of gazes, they both turned away.

At a knock on the door, Siona looked up, her face quickly turning white.

Greta rolled her eyes and stalked to the door. "Oh, come

on. You act as if there's an assassin out there."

Siona leaped forward. "At least let me answer the—"

Impatient, she put up her hand. "Just stop right there. Do you really think someone looking to kill me is going to knock politely and stand out in the corridor waiting?"

When she pulled open the door and saw the faerie prince and princess with a pair of faerie guards standing stiffly on either side of them, she groaned. "Damn it. I *really* hate it that she's always right."

Greta automatically reached for her sword before remembering that it wasn't strapped to her hip. They'd planned this perfectly. She probably would have done the same. Pretend to come in peace, then hang out until the time was right...

Siona was at her side in an instant, pulling Greta back into the room.

At least it didn't look as if the prince and princess were carrying weapons. Only the pair of guards at their sides. One of them had a bow slung across his back and a pair of daggers, just like Siona's, at his waist. The other had a sword.

"Your Majesties," she said in what she thought was a perfectly deferential and calm tone of voice. "The goblin king isn't here right now."

The faerie guard who'd been eyeing Siona in the hall earlier slid his cool gaze over her. Siona shifted, but he'd already moved on, as if she was just a perfunctory part of his examination of the room in general. And yet, there was an awareness in his posture. His body stayed slightly angled toward the goblin hunter, and Siona was blushing again.

The faerie prince's lip curled as he looked Greta up and down. On the other hand, the smile the princess gave her was warm, maybe even friendly. "We wish you no harm," she said. "In fact, it is you that we wished to see. We had hoped this might be an appropriate opportunity to talk."

Siona was tense but not screaming at her to run for her

life, so Greta shrugged. "All right, come on in." She lifted her head toward the two bookends flanking the prince and princess. "Although I would prefer if your pals remained out there."

She stepped aside to let the faeries through. Neither the prince nor the princess gave their bodyguards a second look as they closed the door. Siona silently moved to stand sentry, putting herself in front of the barrier.

The princess spoke first. "We want to let you know that the faeries understand the goblin king's desire for a unified Mylena."

They did? And how did they know about it when she'd only figured it out half an hour ago? She shifted her gaze to Siona, lifting her eyebrows in question. The goblin hunter leaned back against the door and made a face that matched Greta's feelings perfectly.

"It won't be an easy task, but we've come to offer our support," Leila continued.

Greta wasn't sure what to say to that, either. What would Isaac want her to say?

"Don't get me wrong, I'm sure that's very…appreciated. It's true, the announcement was a bit of a surprise to everyone"— understatement of the year—"but I don't think we'll need any help. Isaa—er, the goblin king has everything well in hand."

Did that sound queenly? Like she knew what she was talking about?

"You obviously have no concept of what has been happening beyond these walls," the prince said.

"What do you mean? Nothing's happening."

He lifted a thin, sculpted eyebrow. It reminded her of the arrogant look Isaac always gave her. She needed to perfect that look. "After tonight, you doubt it? Hostility among the races has increased all across Mylena."

"I'm aware that things are…unsettled. But it's a big leap to go from a few disturbances within goblin territory to the kind of unrest that has a chance of affecting any of *your* people."

"The gnomes came into the goblin king's territory tonight, into his very *home*, and caused violence against his subjects." The prince looked as if he actually took pleasure in having been there to see it all.

Leila interrupted gently. "Danem Greta—if I may call you Greta." She paused until Greta nodded. "Tensions are high well beyond the border of goblin lands. Do you really not know how deep it goes?"

Greta shot a glance over their heads at Siona. Her friend's tight nod made her stomach clench with fear.

Leila gave her a pitying look. "We're sorry to be the ones to relay this difficult information." Somehow, looking at Byron, Greta doubted very much that *he* was sorry for anything.

She started for the door. "Listen, I'll pass along your offer of friendship and all, but I don't think there's really anything that you can do to—"

"We have felt your suffering, Greta. We can take away that pain for you."

She stopped in her tracks with a sharp hiss. "How do you know about that?"

"My apologies, but the demon's magick coats your spirit like thick black tar."

She shuddered. "It does? You can actually *see* it?" Just the mention was enough to stir it up like a cloud of dry dust, and she clamped her teeth together.

"I can. It must be painful for you." Leila gave her a sympathetic look. "And it could be very dangerous to others as well."

"How would you help me?"

"Our queen Minetta has the ability to free you of the magick. If you'll come with us back to the Glass Kingdom—"

She frowned. "Sorry, I guess I meant *why* would you help

me?"

Leila's brows drew together in confusion, as if she hadn't expected to be questioned.

"Why the sudden effort to make friends?" Greta clarified. "I mean, your kind has never paid much attention to what goes on in Mylena anyway, right? So I don't get why you suddenly want to play nice with one little human. What would I owe you in return for this grand gesture?"

The girl frowned.

At her side, Siona piped up in a dry voice, "I've found that the human manner of speech takes some getting used to. Once you realize that sarcasm features prominently, it becomes easier to understand."

Leila nodded. "The faeries are known for feuding among themselves, but when Queen Minetta assumed the throne, she brought the majority of our people together under the roof of the Glass Kingdom for the first time in hundreds of years. However, she also became so fearful of outside threats shattering the fragile truce that she shut the gates."

The princess looked at Siona. "None have been able to leave since then, and those who remained on the other side when the gates came down were not able to return." She made it sound as if Siona would have been welcomed home eventually, if not for those locked doors. Was that what the goblin hunter had been hoping for all these years?

"Now that Agramon has been banished, my brother and I petitioned Queen Minetta to reopen the gates so that faerie kind can rejoin the rest of Mylena and mend relationships with the other races."

What kind of queen locked all of her subjects away from the whole world for so long? What kind of queen even had the *power* to do something like that?

It didn't sound like an unreasonable thing to wish for—freedom. Being trapped inside for just a few days gave Greta the shakes. She had never considered the predicament from the faerie point of view. To her, they'd been reclusive and antisocial because that's what they *wanted*.

"I don't quite understand why you need us to travel with you to meet your queen. If the faeries want to make nice and they're willing to help me out, why doesn't she come here?"

"Such would not be possible. Queen Minetta does not leave the Glass Kingdom."

It wasn't hard to tell that there was more to it than that, but before Greta could ask, a crash outside the room interrupted them.

Attack! Her blood sizzled and a surge of power sparked from her fingertips before common sense kicked in and she realized that *she* wasn't the one in danger.

The door rattled on its hinges with a massive thud. "Oh, no." She immediately lunged forward, but it was too late, the magick had awakened, responding to the possibility of threat with the eagerness of a coming storm.

Desperation mingled with the fear, the pain…and an uninvited thirst for more. She stammered Siona's name, but her friend was already at the door. She had it open before Greta could get there.

One of the faerie guards waiting out in the corridor was on the floor, shaking his head and trying to get to his knees. The other was in the process of having his nose bashed into the stone wall.

"Isaac!" Greta called.

"Dryden!" Siona called, before slapping a hand over her mouth. She looked like she wanted to jump in and help the faerie boy.

Isaac looked at her, and Greta gasped at the feral light in his eyes. His form had even started to fill out, taking on the wilder, huskier shape of his moon phase. Close. He was so close to the edge, so close to going Lost.

She tasted smoke, felt the heat of it shoving at her insides, burning her lungs as the magick fought to get out. And it *hurt*.

As if he could see it, the dangerous light in Isaac's eyes flared and he growled low in his throat. She'd never seen him this bad except when the eclipse had taken hold.

Something in the Mylean air made every goblin, ogre, gnome, and other creature vulnerable to a kind of moon madness that threatened whenever they lost control of their emotions. She had believed it was just another facet of the curse that had blanketed the world in unending winter, but the curse had apparently been broken and Isaac was obviously still susceptible, so she'd have to reevaluate.

Byron pushed himself in front of his sister, brandishing a short sword. Where the heck had that come from?

"He's not Lost!" she cried just as Isaac noticed that Byron was standing between him and what he'd come for—*her*. "But everyone needs to stand back, now!"

His gaze swung madly left and right. She stepped forward and reached for his hand. She held on tight, fighting to push the magick down and focus only on him. She whispered calming words under her breath. They weren't just for him, but her, too.

As she clawed back more and more control, he watched her, seething. But finally, he seemed to calm, and the moment her pain felt completely banked, he let out a deep breath and his eyes returned to normal.

She suddenly realized the most disturbing and distressing thing about Isaac, the goblin king, the boy she'd linked her future to and hopelessly fallen for…

She was poisoning him.

He had just been *this close* to going Lost, and it was her fault. She didn't think she was imagining it. The trouble he'd been having with his moon phase was because of her. Somehow, she was tormenting him with her darkness through the link they shared, *her* demons inciting *his*.

Oh, God, this couldn't happen again. "Isaac, it's fine," she lied.

"Greta," he rumbled.

"I'm fine," she repeated.

He turned to Siona with a hard glare. "What are they doing here?"

Leila stepped forward. "We understand your reluctance to trust our intentions. The faerie race has long retreated from the affairs of Mylena," she said. "But your announcement this moon rising has already set events in motion that will affect us all. My brother and I are here to make alliances, not enemies. We have relayed our proposal to your plighted queen"—Greta looked to see whom they were talking about before she remembered and stopped herself—"and we will wait in our camp outside the castle gates for your decision. If we don't hear from your emissary by the next moon rising, we will assume that you do not wish to have our assistance in the war that is sure to come your way."

Isaac stubbornly crossed his arms, unfazed by the faerie warnings. "You can leave my lands now. I won't be calling upon you."

"Why don't we all just—"

Isaac clamped his hand on her arm before she could smooth his harsh words. She bit her lip and shut up.

With that, Leila dipped her head with a sigh. She and Byron turned to leave. Siona's tight expression didn't change as she moved out of the way and let them through the door. "I will show our guests to the castle gates," she said.

When they were alone, Isaac rounded on her. "You could have been—"

"Don't say it," she snapped, hands on her hips.

"They tried to have you murdered once before. Just because they come now in fancy clothes with simpering smiles on their faces doesn't mean their purpose is any different."

"*One* faerie tried to kill me, and he's gone. If these ones wanted me dead, they had ample opportunity to make that happen before you got here, but they didn't hurt me. In fact, they could be the only people in Mylena who *like* me."

"The faeries can't be trusted. You *know* that."

"What kind of people would we be if we believed that of everyone?"

"Wise and cautious ones," he said stubbornly but then sighed and rubbed a hand over his face, looking weary.

"Isaac, what if…" She wrapped her arms across her mid-section. "What if they could help us…me? I mean, me."

He stopped and pulled her against him. "We need no one but each other."

"The princess said that Queen Minetta can do something about the nasty gift Agramon left me with." Frustration and fear choked her. "If we went to the Glass Kingdom—"

"I won't take that kind of chance with your safety," he said gruffly.

"It's not your chance to take. It's mine."

"We don't need them," he insisted.

"We need *someone*. When were you going to tell me how bad the uprisings have gotten? You said everything was under control, that you were just dealing with normal, everyday grievances, but that was a lie, wasn't it? The people are revolting against you, and it's because of me!"

"Not because of you," he insisted. "This is *my* doing. Since my father died I've been a king in title only, but today I wanted to promise that I will be there not just for my people but for all of Mylena."

As an attempt to make her feel better, it fell way short. "You were absent because you were busy helping me free a bunch of humans from a demon. A demon, I might add, that would have enslaved all of Mylena and countless other worlds if we hadn't stopped him."

"All of that is true…and none of it matters," he admitted. "The goblin people want a leader who understands their daily challenges, not one who strays afar to fight fantastical battles."

He wanted to honor his responsibilities to his kingdom *and* his commitment to her. She wanted the same, but she was much less confident about making it work. When it all fell apart and she and Mylena ended up on opposite ends of a double-edged sword, what would he ultimately choose? How could she even ask him to choose?

Her determination to do whatever it took to make Mylena accept her doubled, but she couldn't do it as a burning fuse atop a powder keg of dangerous dark magick. The faeries were right. She had to get rid of it, and she had to do it fast, or the next time she lost control, she could not only destroy all of his efforts to make her worthy of Mylena, but Isaac himself might end up *Lost.*

"You can downplay this all you want, but Mylena isn't accepting me just because you say so, and especially not when their king could go Lost just by being in the same room with me," she warned.

"Does it look as if I am Lost?" He pulled her into his arms, determined to prove a point. He bent down and kissed her. Softly. Gently. Until her body all but melted into him.

"But—"

"I can control it," he assured her in a whisper that caressed the corner of her mouth. "I have no choice but to control it or risk losing you. Losing everything."

She couldn't let him assume all the risk. He deserved a queen who was as strong and capable and worthy as he was, not one who was a hated, damaged liability, who was more likely to lose him the kingdom he already had than help him secure a unified Mylena.

CHAPTER SIX

There had been word of another attack near the border. After the gnome king's loud and public threats in the hall the night before, Isaac decided he should personally go check it out, with a retinue of guards backing him up.

Greta had wanted to bring up the faeries' proposal again after they'd both had a chance to sleep on it and calm down, but he was gone before she awoke—probably to avoid what he knew was going to be an argument.

She'd strapped on her swords and daggers and slipped out of the castle alone. It might be better this way. She doubted any amount of sleep would change his mind about the idea of putting her body and maybe even her soul at the mercy of the faerie queen, who was, by all accounts, more dangerous and powerful than any that had lived before.

At the subtle sound of crunching snow behind her a few hours later, she quickly ducked behind a thick tree and peered around it, but she already knew who it was before the figure came into view.

The hunter stopped and tilted her head like she was

listening intently. She was too good at her job to give in and go away. Greta swore under her breath and stepped into view. "What are you doing here, Siona?"

"I knew it was you. There's no mistaking your ripe human scent," Siona answered with a teasing grin. "Not to mention, you've been getting sloppy about covering your tracks."

"I have not." She bristled. "Why did you follow me?"

"Do you really have to ask?"

She sighed. "Does he know?"

"Of course he knows, but he also knows how important finding your friends is to you, and he trusts your ability to take care of yourself." She raised a slim brow. "He does *not* know, however, that this excursion isn't about finding your friends."

Of course Siona had figured out what she planned to do. She understood better than anyone what this magick was doing to Greta. "Why didn't you tell him?"

She paused. "I agree with you. I think you must do what you can to rid yourself of the black magick, and I only want the best for Mylena's future queen."

Greta groaned. "Don't say that word."

"Do you doubt that it will become reality?"

"I'm trying not to think about it, so do me the courtesy of playing along, will you?"

Her voice was softer when she said, "I'll stay by your side and we'll enter the Glass Kingdom together."

There was a lump in her throat as Greta swallowed and nodded. "Thank you."

They spent the afternoon slogging their way through wet, slushy snow instead of the ice-crusted snow she was familiar with, the kind that sounded dead when you stepped in it. The air was cold as usual, but not brutal. Maybe Isaac had been right and the curse was broken.

"Is this what springtime really looks like?" Siona asked.

Greta didn't quite know how to explain because it had

been such a long time. "It's like getting the same meal every day. Tea and toast, tea and toast, tea and toast, until the tea and the toast don't even taste like anything anymore. But then suddenly one morning there's milk for your tea, and the morning after that, some jam for your toast, and then the next day maybe a piece of fruit on your plate. Springtime is like waking up every morning to…more. More color, more sounds, more scents, more *life*. First the snow melts and it gets all muddy, but at least that's a little bit of color. And then the trees start to bud and the birds start to sing."

"Singing birds?" Siona sounded skeptical.

"Of course!" She grinned. "And when the birds come back and start singing, then you know the warm weather is really on its way."

"I've never seen a bird that wasn't for eating before, and even those are wretched-looking creatures." She turned wide eyes on Greta. "I think singing birds would be a miraculous thing to behold."

Greta didn't want to actually promise anything. She wasn't even sure that spring was really coming. Would Mylena's more delicate birds somehow find a way to return if the ice thawed? It seemed doubtful. It wasn't like they were just hibernating, or had flown south to wait out the curse in warmer climes. Some Mylean species had adapted to the weather, but there must have been hundreds, or even thousands, of species that had simply gone extinct.

"Trust me, when it's five in the morning on a weekend and you left your window open overnight, you won't think birdsong is so miraculous." She chuckled, then realized Siona had no idea what she was talking about.

She cocked her head, suddenly tense. "Something's up ahead."

"It could be nothing," Siona whispered.

Greta's sword was already in her hand. "I'm going to

check it out."

"Danem," called a voice from the other side of a thicket of trees. "I am unarmed."

The faerie princess, Leila.

As much as she'd been on her way to find the faeries, Greta's instinct to protect herself was still strong, and the magick started thrumming in her veins. She glanced at Siona. Her friend was already putting away her daggers and gave Greta a focused look of encouragement. She felt the darkness fading immediately.

She took a deep breath and sheathed her sword. She'd tried to talk Isaac into relaxing his suspicious nature. Maybe she should take her own advice. Siona was right. Coming in with weapons raised was sure to give the faeries second thoughts about helping her.

They pushed through the trees and found Leila waiting, arms folded delicately in front of her. She wore a flowing white dress beneath a heavy winter cloak ruffled in pure white fur. How the heck had that girl survived even one Mylean snowstorm dressed like that?

Greta peered around her. "What are you doing here alone? Where are your guards? Do you require assistance?"

"No need to worry about me, although I appreciate the sentiment. The rest of our group is camped not far from here, but I wanted to meet you personally."

"How did you know we were coming?"

She smiled. "We aren't in the habit of allowing others to sneak up on us."

Greta nodded. That was something she could appreciate.

"Can I presume from your presence that you've decided to let Queen Minetta help you with your problem?"

That's exactly why she'd come, but now that the moment was here, she was hesitant to commit, Isaac's warnings echoing in her ears. "I have some questions first."

"Of course." Leila looked at the darkening sky. "But since the moons are soon upon us, please come back to camp and stay the night. I would like to be able to reassure you that faerie hospitality does not need to be something to fear."

Greta turned to Siona and lowered her voice. "I've seen the way you look at them, especially that boy who was at the banquet, the guard. You know them, don't you? From when you were living in the Glass Kingdom?"

Siona paused before nodding slowly.

"And what do you think?"

"About what?"

"About their proposal. Can they really be trusted?" Siona drew back, looking startled by the question.

"Well?"

"You should never trust anyone," Siona whispered finally, biting her lip. She took a deep breath, and the lines in her forehead smoothed out. "But I agree that it seems doubtful they intend to slit our throats."

"All right then. I guess we're really doing this."

"Greta, what about the goblin king? When he finds out—"

"If he really wants me to be his queen, he's got to learn that I won't just sit back and let him be the one to take all the risks. As much as he wants to protect me, I need to protect him and the goblin kingdom, and I can't do that if I'm the thing that puts him in danger." She winced. "Not to mention, it would be nice to help him make allies instead of being the reason he has more enemies."

Siona gave her a weird look. "That says a lot, danem."

"About what?"

"About how far you've come. Not too long ago, you wouldn't have given a second thought to matters of Mylena, not unless it affected your own survival or benefited you personally in some way."

A flush of embarrassment crept up her neck. Siona made

her sound so self-centered. She wanted to object, but had to face it—the assessment was spot-on. But in her defense, until now all she'd had to worry about was her own life and death, not anyone else's.

Sometimes she wasn't sure she was actually better off for having grown a conscience and a sense of social morality, but if it helped Mylena accept her, then it would be worth it.

Siona's gaze remained intense for a long moment. "You continue to surprise me, danem," she said.

"In a good way, right?" Greta chuckled and punched her lightly in the arm. "Come on, no more of this danem crap. Don't think I didn't notice that you called me Greta just a minute ago."

They followed the princess back along the narrow trail, now shrouded by darkness as the suns had lowered. After a few minutes, she stopped in her tracks and folded her arms, turning slightly. "You might as well come out and join the group," she called.

Siona spun around in surprise and drew her daggers, but there was no sound, no movement in the woods.

The princess chuckled. "Come, Dryden," she said lightly.

A deep flush rose in Siona's cheeks, either because she was embarrassed about not having picked up on the fact that they were being tailed…or because the faerie suddenly walking out of the woods right in front of her was the same guard whose name had burst from her lips when Isaac attacked him back at the castle.

Dryden was tall, taller than Greta or Siona, and probably even taller than Isaac. But he was thin and wiry like most faeries, and moved like a timber cat.

When he stopped and looked down at Siona, her face only got redder, but she squared her shoulders and didn't move a muscle. It was obvious there was more happening between the two of them than could be seen or heard.

Finally, the faerie guard kept walking, but his shoulder

brushed Siona's very lightly as he passed. She turned and followed him with her gaze until she noticed Greta watching, then cleared her throat and ducked her head. She seemed to notice only then that she still had her blades in each hand and flipped them over with a snap of her wrists before shoving them back in the sheaths.

The faerie dude went to Leila's side and took the lead as they continued through the woods. Not five minutes later, the glow of a campfire became visible. "You weren't kidding about being close by," she said.

Suddenly they were surrounded. Her palms itched and her stomach tightened in readiness. It was a survival instinct Greta had cultivated since arriving in Mylena, but she bit her tongue and forced her hand to open.

Looking at the tents, Greta was reminded of the dugout, the shelter that the boys had built for themselves deep in the heart of the goblin forest. Those tents had been built to be stripped down and packed up quickly if needed, whereas these were larger and more elaborate, the kind of accommodations one would expect of traveling dignitaries who had little to no experience with actual traveling.

A female faerie met the princess in front of one of the camp's biggest tents with a steaming mug of something in her hands. There were a few lines fanning out from the corners of her eyes that suggested she was older than the others, but she still only looked about forty or fifty. From what Greta knew of the faerie race, the woman could be 250.

Leila took the mug with a grateful smile before turning back to Greta. "Please make yourselves comfortable. We have another guest whom I'm certain you'll wish to meet. Danem Jessa will show you to him, and we can talk more later."

A guest? The older faerie woman nodded to Greta but completely ignored Siona, who lagged a step behind. Maybe this was one of the faeries who'd rejected Siona because of her mixed blood.

"Excuse me, danem," Greta called after the faerie. "But exactly who is this other guest of yours, and when did he get here?" Didn't they realize that when you were dealing with a hunter, surprises were *not* appreciated?

Jessa kept going past the crackling bonfire and a group of faerie guards, all of whom seemed very interested in checking Greta out as she passed.

The faerie woman finally stopped and pulled open the flap of a much smaller tent at the outer edge of the camp. "This will be yours for the evening," she said in a tone as brisk as her steps had been, with a tiny bow of her head. "Please don't hesitate to let me know if you need anything. Someone will fetch you for the evening meal."

When the woman left and no one else stepped in to stand guard, Greta took note. Was this their way of proving they meant no harm and wanted her to trust them?

Before Greta could duck through the tent flap, a hand reached out and pulled her in.

"What the—" She stumbled forward and whacked her forehead off the crossbeam holding the canvas over their heads. "Ow, damn it."

"Greta."

She blinked back the stars in her vision. "*Wyatt?*"

Behind her, the canvas folded shut over the opening, and it was dark inside the tent.

"I can't see you," she said, reaching up. "Did they hurt you? Are you okay?" Her fingers found his scratchy chin.

"No, I'm fine."

Siona shifted away from the opening, brushing against the canvas and allowing a slim crack of light to come through. Thank the Great Mother. He looked intact. "What are you doing here?"

He glanced at Siona. She shrugged. Greta looked between

the two of them, confused. "What's going on?"

Siona removed her long coat and dagger belt. "I escorted Dolem Wyatt out of the goblin castle, as promised."

"Actually, she followed me all the way back to the Brimstone Caves." He looked at Siona with a grin. "Almost as if she expected me to get lost."

"You did make more than a few wrong turns."

"You only think so. Those turns were cunningly calculated to throw enemies off the scent."

A small smile played at the corners of Siona's mouth. "In that case, you could use a little more practice."

"Are you saying that you're an enemy?"

Greta raised a brow at the back-and-forth between them and wondered just how much time they'd spent together.

Greta turned to Siona. "Is that why you were late to the banquet last night?"

She nodded. "I knew it would be important to you that Dolem Wyatt reach his destination safely."

"That still doesn't explain how you ended up here."

Wyatt's expression dimmed. "The boys were gone when I arrived."

"Gone?"

"There were signs of a struggle."

She gripped the hilt of her sword and frowned. "Not the faeries?"

Wyatt shook his head. "No, but Siona and I came across them when we attempted to track the prints leaving the scene, and they offered to help me. She left me with them last night, and we started our search today. Unfortunately, there's not much to go on. The snow has been melting, and any prints that were left in it are gone."

She turned to Siona. "What do you think is really going on with these guys?" she asked.

Siona waited a long time before answering. "It is quite

possible that everything the prince and princess have said is true. If that's the case, then it would make sense that they would offer assistance to your friend."

"Because they think that by helping me with my problem and helping Wyatt find the others, they're going to get on my good side and I'll put in a good word with Isaac."

She nodded.

"I'm going out there to talk to Leila. I'll try to see what she knows about the boys."

Wyatt stood with her. "I'm going with you."

She stopped and shook her head. "I don't think that's a good idea."

"I don't recall asking you if it was. Those kids are *my* responsibility, not yours."

"Fine, have it your way." She strapped on her sword, realizing that nobody had attempted to take it from her yet. "Stay behind me," she said flatly. "If something goes wrong, I'll—"

He cut her off and picked up a wicked-looking dagger from the furs. He strapped it to his belt. The veins in his hands popped, snaking up his thick forearm and under his rolled-up shirtsleeves. "Don't bother. I've been taking care of myself for a long time now."

Her cheeks flushed and she nodded. "Okay, let's go."

They weren't mobbed as soon as they left their tent, but their movements were definitely noted. Two guards by the fire pit stood at attention. Greta made eye contact with the faerie closest to her, who happened to be the same one Siona hadn't been able to keep her eyes off of. "We'd like an audience with the prince and princess, if you don't mind."

Without showing an iota of emotion, he led them back to Leila's large tent. He pulled open the covering and stood aside. "Enter."

Siona slid him a shy glance as she slipped by. Greta noticed the way his head dipped very slightly, as if he was smelling her hair when she walked past.

Inside this particular tent, there was lots of light. Tiny tin holders cradling small, flat candles had been strung in rows from loops stitched into the canvas ceiling, reminding her of the little paper lanterns that used to hang from the covered deck in her backyard when she was a kid. They'd been all different colors, and her mother had loved to turn them on at sunset and set the patio table for dinner outside. Dad would complain that they attracted the bugs, and when her brother, Drew, was really young, he would laugh and try to swat the flies landing on his plate, sending mashed potatoes everywhere...which had only made him laugh harder.

She swallowed the unexpected melancholy and tried to decide whether she should bow before the faerie royalty or not. If Byron had been in the tent she definitely would *not* have. But it was only Leila, so she gave it a clumsy go.

Leila came forward with a smile and took her hand, pulling her up straight. With a nod toward Wyatt, she said, "Didn't I promise that we could help you find your friends?"

Wyatt crossed his arms. "Danem Greta was never lost, Princess, but it's a good try." His tone of voice was respectful, but reserved.

"Do you know where the others are?" Greta asked. She winced. "I mean, thank you for your hospitality, Your Highness, but I was wondering—"

Leila shook her head. "Unfortunately, we do not yet know where the young ones are. But that is exactly why you must come with us to the Glass Kingdom. Queen Minetta will know. Your visit will be beneficial on more than one level."

"How do you know your queen will be able to tell me where a small group of relatively sneaky human children are hiding, when they could be anywhere in Mylena?"

"That is one of our queen's gifts."

"It appears that she has a lot of gifts. How exactly does this one work?"

Siona spoke up, her gaze never leaving the faerie princess. "Every faerie mind is connected to Queen Minetta's mind, and through her all faeries are connected to one another." Siona paused and crossed her arms. "Unless that connection is forcibly severed."

If they'd been alone, Greta would have reacted to the slight thread of pain in her friend's voice, but she knew Siona wouldn't appreciate any show of support in front of the faeries and Wyatt, so she said nothing.

"Theoretically, the connection she shares with her people means that she can access the power of any of her people as well," Siona said.

"Wow, that *is* a neat trick," Greta said. She didn't know whether to be impressed or completely creeped out. What else would Queen Minetta be able to do with that kind of connection? How easily could it be misused? She'd been fighting with just one source of magick for only a few weeks and it was ready to break her.

Greta met Siona's gaze, searching for any hint of warning from her, but the look on her face was stoic and calm. "All right, I'll go with you." She had no choice.

Byron spoke from the doorway. "Be ready to leave with the rising of the suns."

She turned around. Wow. Did the expression on that guy's face ever change, or was he permanently constipated?

Greta nodded. At least this way, only she could be held responsible if things went bad. Isaac need never be involved.

They got up to return to their tent a little while later.

"Could I keep Siona with me for a few moments?" the princess asked, hands folded neatly in front of her. "I would like to…get reacquainted."

Siona stiffened, and Greta was about to object on her

behalf, but then she nodded and smiled. "Of course, Your Highness. That would be lovely." She turned to Greta. "I will join you shortly." Her smile looked pasted on, but her eyes asked Greta to leave it alone.

Greta shrugged, but tried to let Siona know that she would be close by if needed. "Sure. See you later."

She and Wyatt returned to the little tent alone. Full dark had fallen, but Leila had sent along some of her little candles, and it only took a minute to get them hung from the canvas ceiling.

Greta took off her sword belt and collapsed onto the furs. "I suppose we better get some rest."

"You're not serious about all this, right?" Wyatt crouched down on one knee in front of her. "We've got to get out of here."

"You want to leave? But I thought—"

"You're here now," he said. "You and I can track the boys down together. We don't need anyone else."

She shook her head. "No, I can't. This is our best chance."

"For what?" he said, pulling back. "Finding the boys, or for you and your boyfriend to suck up to some faeries?"

She gasped. "It's our best chance for a lot of things, Wyatt. You don't understand everything that's at stake right now."

"Oh, really? Then why don't you explain it to me."

She put her hands in the fur and curled her fingers. She wasn't ready to talk to him about her own issues. "What do you want me to say? That this could be a mistake?" she asked. "Yes, it might be a mistake. But you don't realize what's been going on here. This whole place is on the verge of war. If there's even a chance I can stop that—"

"Why would you risk yourself for a world that neither understands you nor cares if you live or die? This isn't your fight, and nobody's going to magically change their mind about you just because you make it your fight," he insisted, making her blush. Was it really so obvious that she craved

Mylena's acceptance?

He leaned forward and took her hand. "Leave the Myleans to their own problems."

"And how long will it take for two people to search all of Mylena alone? Another week? A month? Longer? Could you live with yourself if even one of those kids died because we were too stubborn to accept the help that has been graciously offered?" She extricated herself from his grasp. "And then what? Assuming they're even still alive after that long. How do you think we're going to rescue anyone when we don't know who or how many we'd be up against?"

"We'll figure it out." His voice shook.

"Don't you see, this is the way we figure it out," she said gently.

He shook his head. "How can you trust any of them?"

"I don't. Not entirely. But not everyone is out to get us. There are people in Mylena who *can* be trusted."

He crossed his arms. "If you're wrong about this—"

"I've been wrong about a lot of things, and if I'm wrong about this, too, then we'll find another way."

The tent flap fluttered, and Wyatt didn't say anything. Siona was back. She entered and then stopped. "Do you require some privacy?" she asked delicately.

He shook his head. "No, we're done."

Greta sighed. "Why don't you both get some sleep and I'll stand watch." She glanced up. "Siona, will you relieve me in a few hours?"

"No, let me take the first watch," Siona said. "With the banquet and everything else that's happened, I have a feeling you need more rest than I do."

"Thanks." Greta didn't bother to argue. It was true. She was so tired her eyelids started drooping the minute she spread her coat down over the cushy blankets and collapsed on top of them.

CHAPTER SEVEN

When she closed her eyes and let out a deep breath, the dream was there almost before she was even fully asleep. It rolled into her head like a movie reel starting to spin.

She hadn't even opened her eyes, but she knew Isaac had taken her back to the secluded glade in the forest where they'd had their first kiss. That kiss had been part of another dream, but was still so real she remembered every moment of it. In fact, she remembered all of the dreams where he visited, because in a way they *were* real. Real enough to be experienced by both of them, at least.

Her heart hammered with anticipation. She desperately wanted to see him, but that might not be such a good idea now that Wyatt had shown up.

The link between them clicked into place as the dream coalesced. She was sitting, her back propped up against something wide and firm that took deep breaths and smelled rich and earthy, like the forest itself.

Strong hands turned her around to face him. She set her teeth and ducked her head, resisting looking up, resisting the moment when they would argue.

"Not yet," she whispered, grabbing fistfuls of his soft shirt in her hands and ducking her forehead against the warm wall of his chest. "Let me pretend I can't feel you bristling for a fight. Just for a minute. Okay?"

"Greta." She could hear the frown in his voice, but he dragged his hands up her arms. "Why—"

"Shh." She shook her head and breathed deep, amazed that there could be so much reality packaged up in a dream. "Please, Isaac. I just want…"

"What wishes do you make of me now?" His voice was a low murmur that teased the wispy strands at her temple until she felt the hesitant press of his lips. "I'll grant every one."

She lifted her head finally and looked into his face. The forbidding goblin king who'd once contemplated her death because she was a hated human was long gone. In his place was the boy she couldn't resist.

She knew his duties as the goblin king would ultimately change him. It had already started. But if she was to be the goblin queen, too, how would it change her? Could they weather those changes together, and come out stronger for them?

"No more wishes," she said, curling her hand around his neck to play with the short ends of his hair, pulling her bottom lip between her teeth as she contemplated how to get him to kiss her without having to ask.

His gaze fell to her mouth and stayed there. With the softest touch he could turn her to mush. She held her breath. Give her a sword and she knew what to do with it, show her a track in the snow and she could hunt down whatever had left it. But this emotion crap always threw her for a loop.

When Isaac's mouth covered hers, she gasped. Each time between them was different, hitting her from another direction.

Her lips felt tingly and swollen when she finally turned her head to catch her breath, but then she looked back at him and was breathless all over again. Silky black hair curled at the nape of his neck, but she didn't reach out and touch it. His amethyst eyes were mesmerizing pools deep enough to drown in, but she didn't let herself.

His expression darkened.

"I guess playtime is over," she said with a groan.

His bicep was hard under her hand. The corners of his eyes tightened. "Did you slip away the very moment I left, or did you wait until I'd rounded the corner? Have you *no* regard for your own safety?"

"I'm used to taking care of myself," she said. "And you said the faeries exaggerated the attacks, that things weren't as bad as they made it out to be so I should be perfectly safe. Or was that a lie?"

His mouth compressed in a tight line. "The threat to your safety is great if you insist on traipsing about unprotected, no matter the situation. You must have regard for your position—"

Here it comes. She'd been wondering when he would use that angle to try and rein her in. "I *know* what the dangers are, and that's why I had no choice." Her voice broke. "We can't ignore the fact that I'm getting worse, and the faerie queen can help."

"You still should not have gone alone," he murmured, touching their foreheads together. "This is something we should manage together."

"You know I want you with me, but I have to stand on my own two feet." She took a deep breath. "If we're going to be together, your people need to be convinced that I would never do anything to wittingly put them in danger, and the way I am now...I'm putting people in danger." She closed her eyes. "I'm putting *you* in danger."

"I'll worry, but I understand."

She opened her eyes, surprised. "Siona is here, so I'll be fine." She had a weird compulsion to keep explaining. "And you have a hundred other things to deal with. I can't keep taking you away from your responsibilities." This was going well. She'd expected a much bigger argument, truth be known, but he was very calm about her decision.

"You will make the finest queen Mylena has ever known."

Her heart tripped. His trust made her feel empowered and more nervous at the same time. She hoped he was right, but there were so many things still to overcome.

She frowned. "Listen, I need to talk to you about Wyatt. He's here, too. The other boys are missing. Someone took them, and the faeries have offered to help us find them."

So much for calm. His gaze darkened and he gripped her shoulders. "Where *exactly* are you right now?"

"Uh, we're still camped in the goblin forest," she said. "Why? What's wrong?" This wasn't about Wyatt. It was something else.

"The forest?" He shook her so hard her teeth rattled. "You must awaken. The gnome king has sent his army into the forest." His voice seemed to be fading. She was waking up. "Awaken and protect yourself."

"*An army?* Isaac, what's happening?"

"He thinks to take my kingdom. Get Siona and leave the forest as quickly as you can," he warned. "Protect yourself. Stay alive."

Now she understood why he hadn't freaked about her going with the faeries—because he'd already figured out what she was up to and decided it was the lesser of two dangers. If she was with them, she wouldn't be out in the goblin forest searching for her human friends…except that she *was* in the goblin forest.

Urgency twisted his features. She could sense him trying

to shake her again but couldn't feel his touch anymore. The dream was slipping away like fast running water through her fingers, as if he was too upset to keep it together, or she was pushing him out.

"Isaac—"

"I'm coming, Greta. Wake up. Wake up now!"

CHAPTER EIGHT

She jerked awake, already reaching for her sword.

"Siona? Siona, where are you?"

It was still dark, but not completely. She could see her hand in front of her face…and she could see that she was alone in the tiny little tent.

Pushing to her knees, she listened through the canvas for sounds that didn't belong before dragging on her coat. Her dagger and its sleeve were missing.

She crawled out into the open as Isaac's words echoed in her head. A shiver went up her spine. *Protect yourself. Stay alive.*

The air felt as if the Great Mother was set on refuting the very suggestion that spring could be on its way, and she squinted into the early-morning shadows. The ground that had started to get soft and muddy in the milder weather had turned back into hard, icy ruts at some point during the night. A spooky mist clung to the ground. Prickles ran up and down her arms as she spied Siona and Wyatt standing very still only a few feet in front of the tent.

"Hey, what are you doing out here?"

The goblin hunter raised her fist sharply into the air without turning around. Greta took the hint, falling silent as they all strained to listen to the sounds of the forest. But there *were* no sounds. Not here, and not beyond the tree line surrounding the camp. That couldn't be a good thing. What had spooked the forest?

Siona cried out as two figures rushed her from the misty darkness. *Gnomes.*

They came from the other side of the campfire. It was now just a dark circle of soot, but one of them leaped over the little crater anyway instead of running through it.

The gnomes were closing in on the faerie tents. More emerged from the mist to her left. They came right for her and Siona. She counted five in total. Each was dressed in tattered, grimy rags and ran on hairy, bare feet. They were surprisingly swift and quiet.

The first two were short and squat with thick, bushy eyebrows over scrunched-up faces. One had sharp, jagged teeth protruding out of an overbite from hell, and the other bore a dark shadow across the left side of his face that didn't seem to be caused by the slanting angle of the meager light.

It was the last three that might prove to be a problem. They looked like they'd been burped out of a swamp bubble. All of them were tall. Wide. Noses the size of golf balls and hands that could close around her head with room to spare. One of them sneered at her and curled his fingers into a meaty fist that would probably knock her right into the next universe with one solid swing.

She drew her sword as Wyatt let out a harsh gasp. A gnome had his arm twisted up behind his back. Anger surged, overcoming her initial fear.

"I'm certain you gentle gnomes would much rather continue on your way than disturb this faerie camp and a couple of bounty hunters on the king's business." Siona's voice rang out, with emphasis on the part about the faeries. Everyone knew how powerful the faeries were even if they didn't think much of a couple of girl bounty hunters.

The triplets moved forward together. These guys hadn't clued in yet that they might be in more trouble than their prey.

"The ugly one's a human," one snarled at Wyatt. Greta quickly switched places with him and gave the gnome a dirty look, shuddering at the sight of those long, yellow nails clutching a pointed staff. No way was he putting one finger on her.

"Human? You don't say," she replied. "Then you do realize that you're threatening the soon-to-be goblin queen, right? You might want to think twice about—"

"Yeah, she's the one we been lookin' fer!" He grinned at his cohorts before turning to her, showing off yellowed teeth surprisingly the same color as his fingernails. "Thanks fer settin' us straight."

Greta swore.

She glanced down at the dagger in Wyatt's hand—her dagger—with a frown. That wasn't going to do him much good. "Don't be a hero," she told him sternly. "Find a proper weapon and stay safe."

He gave her a nod. Wyatt was excellent at self-defense. Thankfully, he was also *not* a macho idiot, and he knew when to stand back and let her do her job.

"Get behind me," Siona ordered, stepping closer to the both of them.

"Sure thing, right after I take care of these three big ugly dudes." Greta stepped forward and swung her sword in a showy arc.

"Why should I let you take the big ones?" Siona continued, matching her. She had a grin on her face, getting into the spirit.

"Don't think I can handle them, do you?"

Siona glanced sideways, sizing Greta up with a haughty air of you-can't-possibly-compare-with-my-sheer-goblin-awesomeness. "I think when I'm done with these two I'll be finishing those ones off for you after you collapse in failure."

"Oh, it's on, babe." She tossed her braid over her shoulder with a big smile. "Try to keep up, will you?"

Greta gave her full attention to the triplets. "What do you say, boys? Wanna dance?"

Somewhere close by, the sound of clashing steel rang out. It sounded just like a bell signaling the start of a boxing match, the kind she remembered her dad watching on TV.

Two of her three opponents pulled knives. One as he was circling around, the other waving it right up in her face. The third just took a swing at her midsection with his oversized club of a hand.

As cocky as she'd pretended to be, uncertainty choked her as she ducked the gnome's fist and came back up to block the second's jab with his long-bladed knife. She'd never felt so slow, so sluggish, and her reflexes were shot. At the clang of steel on steel, her wrist throbbed, sending pain up her arm to her elbow. She bit back a groan, hiding it behind a sharp breath.

She heard movement in the woods to her left, and her heart pounded. Her body wasn't responding like it should. The harder she tried, the weaker she felt. All except for the rising pressure in the pit of her stomach, as if all the strength she needed to fuel her body was being funneled into the black hole of the chomping, snarling, smoky evil thing inside her. Her breathing became more labored, and she swore.

Siona swung a narrowed look in her direction. "You seem to be having some difficulty," she called. "Do you require assistance?"

This *should* have been a piece of cake, but the hits kept coming. She managed to deflect for the most part, but it wasn't pretty, especially when she realized it would have been much worse if Wyatt had not been holding off the dude at her back with his dagger.

"Over my dead body," she muttered, fighting to keep her breathing regulated.

"That might be the case if you cannot hold up your end, danem."

"You're starting to sound irritatingly like my pater, Siona," she snapped. "Cut it out."

One gnome remained weaponless. He was actually more dangerous than the rest. He knew how to use his fists, striking hard while she was busy dodging knives. She was going to have a black eye and maybe even a few bruised ribs.

It made her angry. Creatures more dangerous than these had ganged up on her before. She'd hunted quarry through the tightly packed, half-dead trees of the goblin forest, and in pitch-black caves where slimy things crawled. Hell, she'd taken on ogres, ghouls...and even a fully turned faerie in the middle of a magick-induced spinning tornado of corrosive smoke.

"You will be my first human." He was looking her up and down. He even licked his lips, but that wasn't nearly as disturbing as the erection pushing out the front of his dirty trousers, cut off at the knees.

"Don't count on it." A chill ran down her spine. "I'd rather slit my own throat..." She adjusted her grip on the weapon, wishing her palms weren't so sweaty. "Although I'll settle for slitting yours instead."

She made her move, stepping forward and swinging her arm in a wide arc. Instead of being fluid and sure, it started out wobbly and slow, but she pulled herself together in time and angled the tip of her blade in line with his throat.

Luckily, he was slower than she was. Not by much, but she got the job done, leaving a thin slice in his neck that immediately started to spread apart.

She refused to flinch as blood sprayed, splattering her hands like green paint coming off a brush. The gnome's mouth worked, spittle flying. His eyes bulged and his hands flailed as if he might take flight.

Greta didn't wait for him to fall, letting the momentum of her swing carry on into a slashing thrust of her blade across the sternum of the other gnome moving in behind her.

That one screamed and careened backward a few steps, dropping his knife. His palms flattened over his chest. Blood seeped between his fingers before he collapsed to his knees. She was already shifting again, turning to face the last one.

But he wasn't the last.

Her heartbeat pounded in her ears as she glanced up to find dozens more gnomes pressing in on her and Siona, and a dozen more again surrounding the faeries. The princess herself wielded a sword, but while the consensus in Mylena was that the faeries were a deadly bunch, that reputation apparently didn't come from direct battle skills. She was slow and clumsy with a weapon, making Greta wonder why she hadn't pulled some freaky magick trick out of her hat to protect herself.

Byron fared better with a blade. He was only a short distance away, but surrounded by gnomes and too far to help his sister. Where the hell was Dryden? In fact, a number of the faerie warriors seemed conspicuously absent from the fight.

The princess cried out as a gnome caught her with a thin slice across the arm. Wyatt noticed and started for her side.

"Wyatt, wait!" Greta called. He kept going, making a beeline for the princess like a knight in shining armor. The dagger was his only weapon, at least until he punched a gnome in the face, elbowed him in the gut, and jerked the sword out of his grasp.

He might be capable against one gnome, maybe two, but he wasn't a warrior. He was going to be massacred. Damn it.

She swallowed the sizzling magick thick in her throat,

blurring her vision, crushing her chest. She rushed after him, but the way was quickly blocked against her and he was devoured by the mob.

Siona pressed her shoulders to Greta's and they slowly moved in a circle. "This is a distressing turn of events," she threw over in a tight voice.

Gritting her teeth, Greta nodded even though Siona couldn't see. "We might be slightly outnumbered now."

"Just slightly."

She struggled to break through the pain choking her and find that Zen place where training took over and erased all thought, all doubt, all room for error.

She lifted her sword once again, but a sudden blur crossing the edge of her vision made her jerk back. Maybe it was just a trick of the changing light as the suns rose. But then there was another blur. And another.

The blurs reminded her of flitting hummingbirds, moving too fast for the eye to process. As another moved into the camp, she saw enough to know that they were man sized and armed to the teeth. The only other time she'd come across anything as fast was…

Finally! The missing faerie warriors. Thank God. With their arrival, Greta was able to fight her way to Wyatt's side.

"Siona, stay with me!" She couldn't afford to lose another friend in the fray.

At a subtle whistle behind her, she turned and blocked the swing of another blade and shoved it back, then shifted to meet more steel coming at her from the right.

The faerie warriors were closing in on the other side of the horde. Maybe that had been their plan all along. By surrounding the gnomes who were themselves surrounding their prey, the enemy was suddenly left with nowhere to go.

Greta might have agreed the plan was a good one…if not for the fact that they were still ridiculously outnumbered.

The attacking gnomes were all faceless to her now, as much a blur as the faeries. She couldn't even see Wyatt or the princess. Byron stood shoulder to shoulder with Dryden, but they were obviously tiring. Ahead of her, Siona blocked and countered again and again, but even she couldn't hold out much longer. Even as Greta thought it, the goblin hunter was a half second too slow and four gnomes were on her.

"Siona!" Greta tried to go to her, but she was boxed in just as tightly.

She fought her way through. Bloody bodies started piling up around her, but they kept coming. There were so many.

An army.

One of the gnomes cut her.

She cried out, immediately losing her tenuous grip on the magick. In a split second it went from pacing her insides like a caged animal to throwing itself against the bars with a vicious snarl.

Her whole body burned, the hilt of her sword getting so hot in her hand she feared it would fuse right to her palm.

Suddenly, an enraged roar echoed from the shadows of the early morning, chilling and deadly. If that sound had a shape it would be twenty feet tall and just as wide, thick as a mountain and darker than midnight.

Greta laughed.

She'd know that particular roar anywhere. The burning pain from the cut in her arm and the darkness in her soul actually faded a little, and when Isaac burst onto the scene, she'd never been so happy to see anyone in her life, even if he looked fierce and wild, on the very thin edge of control.

Blood trickled from a cut in his forehead and his eyes were wide and manic. What had he gone through to get here so quickly?

She edged closer only to get shoved back, and the harder she tried to reach him, the more gnomes got in her way. But they were no longer attacking her. Their focus had shifted to the more dangerous threat.

Isaac took hit after hit from every direction. What if they'd been after him all along? What if they'd known that attacking her would be the best way to draw him out?

Suddenly he grunted and growled, twisting around. Greta gasped at the arrow shaft protruding from the thick muscle of his left shoulder. Another arrow hit him, sinking deep into his abdomen.

They were going to kill him.

Two more arrows hit Isaac. One in the arm, another in the chest, barely missing his heart. He didn't even notice. His attention was on her.

She screamed at him to protect himself, but his focus didn't even flicker. She fought the wall of bodies standing between them, but for every gnome that she put on the ground, another two took his place. With arrows protruding from his body, he threw gnomes over his shoulder and bashed heads together.

The monster rattled its cage again. A rush against her senses, almost like drowning, like having water flood into her mouth and cascade down her throat at the same time it pushed out her ears and nose and leaked from her eyes.

She didn't want to give in, but she couldn't help it this time, and once she did everything changed. Power filled her, gave her strength and certainty the likes of which she'd only ever felt once before…in Agramon's circle, when the portal magick had coursed through her.

She opened her eyes, not even sure when she'd closed them. Everything looked different, one-dimensional. The world had taken on a yellowish-brown tone, like the tiny sepia photograph of her parents in her locket.

"Isaac," she murmured, hearing the hollow quality of her voice.

Magick. Power. Letting it free would be easy. So easy. It

was there. Right there.

But the more she used it, the more it would own her. The more it would consume everything she was and replace her with darkness. She had no doubt about it, because it didn't belong to her. It was unnatural, and there'd be consequences for using it.

Isaac roared. He was dangerously close to turning. Next to most of the gnomes he was a monster. Huge arms. Huge legs. Huge fists. Full of rage. He looked like a bear swatting at a swarm of bees seething around him.

A blade slipped into her side, right between her ribs. Damn, it burned. She stumbled and bit off a scream, not wanting Isaac to hear it, but he did anyway.

Wyatt must have noticed, too. He called out her name, and she saw him suddenly, fighting to reach her.

Isaac's bellow of fury shook her to the core. He tried to charge but stumbled. She couldn't tell which blow had finally been strong enough to take him down, but he clutched at his head.

"Isaac!" Her voice begged him to stay with her. He had to hold on.

She pressed a hand to her side, grimacing as blood flowed warm and thick between her fingers. Her head swam. She swallowed blood from a cut in her lip and straightened to her full height. The gnomes knocked her back down. One of them held a dagger to her throat.

The air was heavy and hot like an electrical storm getting ready to unleash its fury, and the magick crashed through every barrier she had, real and imagined.

Her sword fell from her hands. The power exploded outward like pulling back a bowstring, physically shoving the gnomes back a few feet, too. Yes, so easy. Except that it tore her apart on the way out, and it hurt so much. So... *good*, the way pain could sometimes be so intense it became indistinguishable from pleasure.

Greta gasped and fell to her knees, watching the black cloud that threatened to encompass everything, destroy *everything*.

Oh, God, no. It's going to kill everyone. Gnome and faerie. Isaac. Siona and Wyatt.

Everything seemed to be moving in slow motion. She screamed. Isaac roared.

She blinked through the haze of pain. He'd seen her go down. He would lose it. He would go *Lost*. She sobbed. Was it already too late?

Siona was suddenly at her side, keeping the gnomes back. She clasped Greta's wrists tightly.

Greta didn't care. She craned her neck to find Isaac. Soldiers kept closing in, but he'd stopped fighting them to get to her. When the first sword stabbed him, she screamed and struggled against the hands holding her back like a woman possessed.

"Isaac!" She welcomed the sizzle of heat this time. *Don't fight the power.* But something was blocking her access to it. Siona? *No!*

Isaac suddenly stopped and called her name. Still almost thirty feet away, he gazed into her eyes with an intensity and focus that chilled her to the bone, like a spike being driven into her heart.

He called out for her to stay strong.

She tried to tell him not to worry. She could save him now. The power to do it was right at her fingertips. It might kill her, but it would save him.

His mouth moved, but she couldn't hear what he was saying. Only when the light in his eyes went out and he looked away did she realize…

This was his good-bye.

"No." Her whispered denial turned into a scream. He couldn't sacrifice himself! Not when she'd already decided to be the one. "No, no, no! Isaac, don't you dare! Don't give in."

She shoved Siona aside and pushed herself to her feet.

Too late. Too late.

He dug his fingers into the earth as the change washed over him. His body contorted and flexed and grew. His growl deepened, his jaw elongated. His eyes were the last to turn. From that beautiful, expressive amethyst to a blood red.

Too late!

He leaped through bodies and landed right in front of her.

She flinched. *He won't hurt me. Won't hurt me. Not me.* But she wasn't so sure anymore.

She jerked back instinctively with a breathless sob to avoid his razor-sharp nails. He tossed her out of the way and launched himself at a gnome that had been coming up behind her and tore his throat out.

She whispered his name, praying for recognition to flare. Blood dripped from his muzzle. Muzzle, *not* chin. It smeared across his face.

Another arrow screamed through the air and lodged itself into his back, and another.

He reared up and swung in a wide circle, roaring as the gnomes converged again.

"Leave him alone!"

Siona wrapped both arms around Greta's waist and kept her from lunging after him.

Isaac was wild, filled with a rage so terrible it seemed impossible that anyone could overcome that. *He will. This is just a slip. It's just—*

Throwing his head back, the thing that had been Isaac let out a furious roar. The whole of Mylena must have heard it. It shredded her heart.

Her stomach clenched at the thought of the havoc he would cause and the bounty that would be issued as soon as word got out…

That the goblin king was Lost.

CHAPTER NINE

The gnome army was completely focused on Isaac now, but Siona held Greta back and the faeries refused to step in. "Help him!" she cried.

"He's too dangerous." Siona tightened her grip on Greta.

She was so furious her chest rattled with it, her vision glossed over with hot tears, her hands shook. "Nobody hurts him!"

"Danem, we must go, or it won't be the goblin king who is hurt." Siona tugged her away insistently. A goblin turned Lost was one of the most fearsome creatures in this world. Strong and deadly, like a wolf and a bear and a devil all rolled into one horrifying killing machine without conscience or mercy.

She shook her head. "I can't leave him."

Before she could grab her sword or draw on her magick, Dryden stalked forward…and then everything went black.

She woke up with a jerk and a gasp that hurt her jaw and sent pain shooting down her side. Someone put an arm around her shoulder. Wyatt, *not* Isaac. She leaned into him and tried to take stock. She couldn't decide what hurt more, her face or her side.

The magick was so close, blurring her vision, singing in her veins. She felt less resistance to using it than last time. Her conscious mind knew how to access it now, *wanted* to access it, even as she felt it coating her spirit with suffocating black oil…

Siona knelt down beside her. The surge of unpredictable darkness receded, but the pain in her side wasn't getting any better.

She opened her eyes and struggled to sit up. She looked for Dryden. He stood behind Siona with his arms crossed. She burned through him with her gaze.

"Jerk! You sucker punched me."

Siona patted her shoulder. "Dryden's methods were… harsh." She frowned up at him. "But we had to get you out of there."

She shook Siona's hand away. "Where is he?"

Everyone looked away from her, and nobody answered.

"What did you do to him?" Her voice cracked with worry, bringing the magick rushing back to the forefront. She gritted her teeth against it, but apparently having given in to it so completely, even just one time, had put a serious crack in her control.

"We didn't do anything," Wyatt answered. Siona was back to soothing her with a hand on her arm. "If he survived the gnomes, then he's still out there."

If he survived the gnomes.

"Where are we?"

"Not far. You're pretty heavy, you know that?"

She grunted and looked down at herself. She was covered in blood and immediately pressed her hand into the wound at her side. "I'm bleeding."

"The wound isn't serious. You took a blade in the side, but it didn't go deep. The bleeding should stop soon."

She nodded and pushed herself to her feet, using Wyatt as a crutch. He handed her sword back, and she nodded thanks. Where would Isaac go? What would he do now that he was…

She couldn't even think the word.

This is my fault. The heartbreaking guilt choked her. He never would have given in to the beast if he hadn't felt like he had to save her.

Well, if she'd wanted the goblin kingdom to accept her, she was off to a pretty hellacious start.

She turned to Siona with a shiver, sick to her stomach. "I have to go after him."

Siona's eyes widened. "Danem, you can't. It's already too late. You saw him, you know it's true. It isn't safe for you to be anywhere near him now…or ever again."

Greta shoved her sword into the sheath at her waist and gritted her teeth. "I'm going."

Wyatt crossed his arms and frowned. "Don't be ridiculous. I don't think Mylena has ever known a more dangerous creature than a goblin king gone Lost."

"And what do you know about Mylena? All you do is hide from it," she snapped.

Wyatt recoiled, lips pressing into a thin line. She immediately groaned. "I'm sorry, I didn't mean that. I just…" She shook her head and turned away. "I need to go."

Siona pulled her away from Wyatt and the others. "What can you possibly do for him now? I hate it as much as you do, but unless you wish to be the one to stick the blade through his chest and end his misery, you must let him go."

"And what if he hurts someone? What then?" She swallowed the hard lump in her throat. She knew the exact moment he'd given up on coming out of that fight intact. That moment when he'd felt her giving in to the magick and decided he should be the one to let go instead. Her weakness had failed him.

"If it comes to that—but it won't—but if it does, then yes,

I have to be the one to take him down. Nobody else."

The pity in the hunter's eyes made Greta want to hurl. "You will only be hurt if you do this," Siona said, "and I can't let you be lost to Mylena, too."

"Siona, don't be melodramatic. I'm the only one in Mylena who *can't* be Lost."

"I'm not talking about running with the moons, danem. This is about the goblin kingdom and what is best for Mylena." She paused. "This is about the darkness growing inside you. It threatens to consume you just as completely as the moons rule Mylena. There is *no* getting him back. Now there is only ensuring that the dream he had for a peaceful, united Mylena is continued by the successor he has already named."

"But we could find him and help—"

Siona gave her a sympathetic look. "Would you really risk going after him now when it's because of you he went over the edge?" Greta winced, but Siona had a point.

She swallowed hard. "I'll control it."

"You can't." She said it so matter-of-factly, and all doubt about whether or not Siona had somehow been bolstering Greta's control over the magick was gone.

Siona's voice softened. "He chose you to be the one to continue in his place if anything happened to him. You need to think about what's best for his people. Your people, now."

That probably wasn't technically true. Proclaiming Greta his *future* queen did not make her the current queen just because he was gone now…whether that's what he would have wanted or not. She didn't know who'd been slated to take the throne before last night's banquet, but she was pretty sure no one would just *let* her have it. Not without a fight.

"That's what I'm doing." She didn't want to hear about moving forward without Isaac. This was a problem, but she'd figure something out. In the meantime… "I can't leave the goblins unprotected while the gnomes ransack the kingdom.

They need Isaac."

"You can't go back to him or the goblin people like… this."

Wyatt stepped in. She wondered how much he'd heard.

"Whatever you're planning, you can't go anywhere without getting that wound looked at first." He wouldn't look her in the eye. He sounded pissed. And worried.

They were both right. Maybe not for the reasons they thought, but the scent of her blood on Isaac's trail might be worse than waiting a few days to make sure her problems were taken care of and she could track him down safely.

"All right." With a final glance into the shadows of the woods, she nodded.

"Really?" Siona looked startled and a little guilty.

"I guess. Going to the Glass Kingdom will kill a bunch of birds with one stone. I need the faerie queen's help, she wants the goblin king's allegiance, and Wyatt needs to know where to find the other boys."

"Then let's get you patched up," Siona said.

Greta looked around. "Um, did you leave all our stuff behind?"

Siona put her hands on her hips. "Should I have fought through the horde of gnomes to rescue your tattered old pack?"

The flowers Isaac had given her were in that pack. "No, of course not." She swallowed her tears.

Dryden approached, having apparently anticipated that they would need a few things, because he carried a bag and handed it over when he stopped in front of them.

"Everything that we managed to salvage has been divided up. This is yours for the three-day journey," he said in a gruff voice, his gaze lighting on Siona and pausing there for a long moment. Was it just Greta, or did his icy faerie crust melt just an iota when he looked at her? "There are bandages and some dried rations inside. Be ready to leave in an hour's time."

So efficient, but where had he been when the fighting started? Who'd fallen asleep at their post, or gone off to take a piss at exactly the wrong time? Why hadn't the faerie warriors been patrolling the area surrounding the camp and noticed those gnomes coming long before they were right on top of everybody?

The three of them found some privacy but Greta refused to take her shirt off until Wyatt turned his back, so he stood guard a few feet away while Greta's injury was cleaned and dressed.

Siona frowned as she looked Greta over. "I'm fine," she reiterated.

"I don't have another tunic for you to wear," Siona said.

"That's okay. Just because I spent a few weeks in the goblin castle doesn't mean I don't remember what it's like to live day-to-day." With a shrug, she reached for the bloody, torn shirt she'd put on clean and fresh only yesterday morning. "So, if we're heading in the direction I think we're heading, we should make Eyna's Falls before noontime, and I'll try to clean up a bit as we walk along the river's edge."

"We aren't following the river. We must cross it."

"And just where do you expect to cross it?" There was only one way—

"At Solem's Bridge."

Her mouth dropped open. "But that means passing the *bjer*. Are you abso-freakin'-lutely nuts?"

Siona's forehead creased, but she didn't laugh and say, "Got you good!" and her stoic expression wasn't exactly reassuring.

"Whose idea was this? Wait, let me guess. The faeries. Don't they realize it's a suicide mission?"

"The faerie queen has already heard of the battle with the gnomes. She has ordered her people to return to the Glass Kingdom before the moons are full in three days' time or be banished, and the gates shut again…this time forever."

"How has she given these orders?"

"Her mental connection to the faeries allows her to stay in touch."

She remembered mention of that neat trick. "Great, but they've got to know it's impossible reach the Luna Pass from here in three days' time."

"Unless you cross Solem's Bridge," Siona said.

Greta groaned and pulled her coat back on. They rejoined the rest of the group, which, from the look on Dryden's face, was waiting on them to leave. She stalked up to him. "If you think I'm going to try to cross Solem's Bridge without a plan for defeating the *bjer*, you've got another think coming," she said.

He raised a pompous brow. "I have it on good authority that we have two bounty hunters in our midst. I believe it's in your job description to manage such threats, and I assumed you would wish to carry your weight on the journey."

With that, he made his way to the front of the mini procession that had already formed. She felt like calling after him that going to the Glass Kingdom had never been her idea in the first place, so she wasn't going to pull *any* damn weight, but that seemed counterproductive, so she bit her tongue.

This was the first time she'd traveled the wilds of Mylena without constantly looking over her shoulder. Having this many pairs of eyes watching the woods was a novel experience. It reminded her, though, that somehow these same faeries had missed a large group of bloodthirsty gnomes raiding their camp, so she wasn't about to let her guard down.

There weren't quite as many faeries left as there'd been before the attack. The fighting had taken its toll, and only four faeries—including Dryden—remained to protect the prince and princess on the journey back to the Glass Kingdom.

Greta had already calculated that they'd reach Solem's

Bridge well before nightfall. That didn't leave her with a lot of time to remember what she'd heard about the *bjer* guarding it.

"Have you formulated a plan for gaining access to the bridge?" Dryden's voice startled her. She hadn't expected him to willingly draw her into conversation, but when she noticed Siona watching, she had a pretty good idea why he'd used this excuse to approach them.

"I'm thinking," she answered tightly. "Have you ever seen a *bjer*, or known anyone who has seen one?"

Whenever Greta started out on a job, the first thing she did was gather as much information as she could about what she'd be hunting. She'd learned to hang back in the shadows of taverns and public houses, listening to the locals tell stories. It was a good place to start even if the tales had a tendency toward exaggeration. If a goblin was standing in the middle of Maidra's with a crowd of rapt faces glued to his every word, raving about a twelve-foot-tall beady-eyed monster with talons the size of rapier blades, she knew she was likely going after a pretty average ghoul.

"In your pursuit of the Lost," he said, "you never hunted the *bjer*?"

"You're kidding, right? Why would I actively seek to cross paths with something like that?"

He raised an eyebrow.

She crossed her arms. "I don't go *looking* for trouble," she insisted. "If it isn't causing problems, I'm all for live and let live."

"An admirable philosophy," he admitted, surprising her until she thought she might blush. "But it doesn't bother you that anyone who has ventured within the boundaries this creature has arbitrarily claimed does not return?"

She shrugged. "If that's the case, either accept that Solem's Bridge is a dangerous place and post a Use at Own Risk sign, or put a bounty out on the *bjer* so someone takes it down."

"But not you?" He sounded surprised. "You don't want the glory that would be yours for such an impressive catch?"

"I'm not in it for glory," she said with a frown. "And I don't hunt lonely monsters that are just looking for a place to call their own. I hunt the Lost."

He gave her a funny look like she was something he could barely conceive of.

She changed the subject. "One thing I know about this creature is that it's part of the troll family. Bigger than an ogre, smaller than, well, probably nothing. And apparently it doesn't see too well, but it's got a crazy good sense of smell, which is one reason why no one's been able to sneak past it."

He nodded. "The bridge has been unpassable since the creature settled there."

"You know this, and you still want to try?"

He didn't flinch. His expression was like stone, and it made her think maybe there was something else, some other reason for this insane decision, that they weren't telling her.

She shrugged and turned her attention back to the problem of the *bjer*. Solem's Bridge used to be part of a high-traffic trade route between the northern and southern counties, cutting right through the mountain pass. But *bjer* were majorly territorial, and the moment one had decided to call this particular bridge home, that section of road had become the equivalent of a tumbleweed town. The trade route had shifted west. It was a much longer, indirect route between the counties, but safer for the farmers and tradespeople who needed to travel along it.

"Maybe we can wait for the *bjer* to leave. It must hunt for food, right? It can't just sit in front of the bridge forever," Wyatt said from behind her. Greta looked over her shoulder and made room for him to join in the conversation.

"Trolls are nocturnal creatures," Siona said, having closed in as well. "If we get to the bridge before full dark, it might actually be possible to walk right by its den before it wakes."

"Are you sure?" she asked.

"No, but unless you have another option to consider…"

It seemed as good a plan as any given that they had no idea what they were walking into.

Speaking of which, she pulled up short and pointed toward a crude sign a few paces ahead, warning travelers to veer west. They couldn't be far from the bridge. "I think we should stop here and do some recon," she said.

Siona and Dryden both frowned.

Wyatt grinned. "Greta and I can go check things out to make sure the coast is clear," he said.

She threw him a sharp glance. "Actually, I was thinking I should probably go alone."

"You're not going alone," he said. "You're still hurt. What if something happens?"

Siona interrupted. "I will go as well."

Greta shook her head. "Listen, the more people tromping around that bridge, the more attention we're going to draw to ourselves. I think it would be best if—"

"I agree that we should not draw attention to our presence," said Dryden, "but you can't go alone. I will be the one to go with you."

She wasn't impressed with that word, "can't," especially coming from him. And the last thing she wanted was to go anywhere alone with this guy. He reminded her too much of Lazarus. "I don't need you. Anyway, I thought you wanted the hunters to handle the *bjer*."

Byron stepped forward with a look like he was sucking lemons. "You'll take my warrior with you. We wouldn't want you to get hurt. Losing you at this juncture would be… counterproductive to our goal."

She rolled her eyes. "Yeah, it would suck for me, too." She turned to Dryden. "Fine. Let's get out of here. We're burning daylight."

Wyatt came over and pulled her back as they were leaving. "You shouldn't be the one to do this," he said in a low voice. "I don't trust that guy to keep you safe."

He was probably right, but luckily she didn't rely on anyone to keep her safe but herself.

"I'm fine, really." She hoped he wouldn't see through her lie. The wound in her side was still bleeding, making the bandage heavy against her skin, but she was a better choice for this than anyone else, even injured.

"And it's just a recon mission. No fighting." She squeezed his hand. It was obvious that he was still disappointed by her decision to remain in Mylena, but she needed things to be all right between them. She couldn't lose Wyatt, too, not now.

He nodded and squeezed back. "When you return, we need to talk."

She said good-bye and waved to Siona, who didn't look much happier. The two of them stood side by side, watching her go as if she was never coming back. It sent a chill down her spine as she turned and jogged to catch up with Dryden.

They moved quietly through the forest. While the suns were still high, quiet could take precedence over swiftness.

When they neared the clearing leading to the cliff's edge and the bridge, it didn't take long to find the *bjer*'s den; there was no hiding footprints that big, and all of them led to a crudely made shanty stuffed just inside the woods.

It looked as if someone had ripped the trunks of four trees right out of the ground and tried to make a tepee out of them, stacking the branches with all the needles still intact as a thin roof. It was a little too structured to just be a pile of fallen trees, but someone less observant might have overlooked it.

She and Dryden held their breath. They stood not twenty feet away from the ramshackle tepee, staring at a break in the logs—presumably the entrance. From within it came the loudest, longest snore she'd ever heard, followed by a nasally cough, a snort, and the unmistakable sound of something shifting on the ground. In fact, she could almost feel the earth move with it.

When the snoring resumed, she sighed and relaxed her stomach muscles, but her senses were still going haywire. She had that feeling of prickles running up her spine and looked behind her, certain someone was standing right there. "Do you feel that?" she whispered.

"As if we're being watched?" He nodded.

"I can't see anything."

"Stay on guard," he said and turned away. She stuck out her tongue at his back. As if she was ever anything *but* on guard.

She was pretty certain whatever might be out there spying on them *wasn't* the troll-sized guardian of Solem's Bridge, so it would have to wait its turn. They took a few more steps, and a twig snapped loudly beneath her foot.

They both froze, but after a long moment, during which the only sound was Dryden's regulated breathing beside her, she sighed. "We're going to have to walk right by the *bjer* to get to the bridge." She mouthed the words as soundlessly as she could.

He nodded and pointed. She turned around and knew right away that the troll wasn't going to be their only problem. The bridge itself spanned a chasm that had to be at least fifty feet wide…and it looked *exactly* the way one would expect a rope bridge that hadn't been maintained by anyone for years and years to look. Rickety. Dangerous. Suicidal.

Damn it.

She motioned him to go back the way they'd come. When they were far enough into the woods to talk freely, she stopped and ran a hand over the back of her neck. "So that's settled. Even if we can sneak past the *bjer*, there's no way we're crossing that bridge."

"Yes," he said, the look in his eyes so cold ice crystals had formed on his eyelashes. "We are."

CHAPTER TEN

When they got back, the faerie princess was waiting. She rushed forward with a nod for Dryden and a smile for Greta. "So, we're ready to proceed?"

"I know you're in a hurry, but we can't go back that way," Greta rushed to say before Dryden could get a word in. "The *bjer* was sleeping when we got there, but there's no guarantee he'll stay out until dark. Not only that, there's a strong possibility that the bridge won't hold. It's dangerous."

Leila glanced up at Dryden. Neither of them said anything, but a long moment later, she looked back at Greta. "I appreciate your concern, but I think we'll have to take the chance."

She'd already figured the conversation would end up going something like that. She didn't like the idea, but she had to admit that they were right. She needed to get to the Glass Kingdom as soon as possible. She couldn't let Isaac down. He needed her to be whole, so she could protect his people because he couldn't.

"I won't unnecessarily risk my friends' lives for anything, so there are going to be some ground rules."

"What do you propose?" asked Leila.

She angled a glance Dryden's way. "Siona and I have the most experience dealing with potentially hostile situations, so everybody follows our lead."

He nodded.

Greta turned away. "Then let's get moving. The daylight won't last much longer now, and apparently we have a bridge to cross."

They made it back to the clearing near Solem's Bridge about an hour before sunset and it was immediately obvious by the snoring that the *bjer* was still ensconced inside its crude shelter.

Greta had already warned everyone not to make a sound, not until after they were across the bridge. She'd drawn her sword a few hundred feet back, where the glide of steel being pulled from its leather sheath wouldn't be overheard, and now she gripped it tight in her sweaty, shaking fist.

Wyatt held back as the others kept going. He drew her dagger from the sheath he'd strapped to his waist. She remembered a time when he'd refused to take one of her weapons because he didn't believe in violence, but things had changed. He had changed. There was a brittleness to him now that hadn't been there before.

"Are you okay?" she asked, tentatively. "You didn't get hurt in that fight, did you?" She felt guilty for not making sure of it sooner.

"I'm fine," he answered in a terse voice that only made her feel worse.

She bit her lip. "Are you worried about the boys?"

"Yes," he said between clenched teeth. After a few more steps he stopped in his tracks with a heavy, frustrated sigh. She kept going for a second before realizing he wasn't beside her anymore, and turned around to find him glaring after her. "Is it so hard to believe that I'm worried about *you*?"

"What? I'm fine, see?" She held out her arms and bit the

inside of her cheek to keep from wincing.

"You're so full of shit," he said.

Her mouth fell open.

He spun around and started walking again. "Hey," she called, jumping forward to keep up with him. "What the hell?"

He rounded on her and pressed a hand to her side. He was careful, barely made contact, but even such a glancing touch tore a gasp of pain from her lips and blurred her vision.

"You can't keep this up," he said.

She groaned. "Okay, it hurts, but I'm used to working through the pain. I'll be fine."

"Do you even hear yourself?" he said. "You should be doing homework and going to the movies, not *working through the pain*."

"Wyatt, that's—"

"The only reason you had for staying in Mylena is gone now, so why are we still doing this?" he pressed. His deep blue gaze caught hers and wouldn't let go. "Come home with me."

She opened and closed her mouth, trying to find the words. "Wyatt, I can't. Not like this."

Maybe he was right that her reasons for being here no longer applied, but she couldn't even think about whether to go back or stay until she'd dealt with the darkness hitching a ride inside her.

"What is it? What happened when you and Ray went to Agramon's fortress?"

She'd seen him watching her and had known this conversation had to happen at some point. "It's hard to explain."

"Try," he said. "When you didn't come back in a day or two, I hated myself for letting you go, thinking you were both dead. When I finally found you I was relieved to see you whole and healthy, but now I think I should have looked closer." He leaned closer again. "What happened?"

"It was horrible," she admitted, swallowing hard. "I can't

go a night without dreaming about it. He was draining the life out of the children. It was all part of an elaborate spell to open a portal. And I was helpless, Wyatt. So much blood fell before we could stop him, and then…" Her voice cracked.

Wyatt put his hand over hers, letting his thumb smooth across her pulse point. "He hurt you."

She shrugged to hide her reaction to his touch.

The pain was mostly just a memory, but now she had worse things to haunt her. Like the black thing that slithered deeper and deeper into the very heart of her, even as they spoke.

"He did something more than just hurt me. Some of that magick is still trapped inside me, and every time it comes to the fore, I'm less inclined to fight it, or it's more determined to be let out. I can't actually tell the difference anymore."

There was a war going on in there for control. A war she didn't know if she could win.

"How? What happened?"

She grimaced. "I was pulled into the portal with him, and I honestly thought I would be stuck there forever. There was no end to it. No way back and no way forward. There was nothing but darkness and cold for what felt like…always." She shuddered. But that wasn't really true. Even there in the gap between worlds, she'd had one thing to hold onto. "Isaac got me out."

"But?" he prompted.

"But I think something came back with me."

"At the goblin castle…I didn't imagine it, did I?" He looked down at his hand, turning it over. "When I touched you, it burned."

"It's inside me, and I can't control it. It's getting stronger." She swallowed hard, overwhelmed by guilt. "But the faerie queen can help."

"How do you know that? Just because they said so?"

"I know there's a good chance they have some ulterior motive, but I don't have a choice. If they can help, I have to try."

"What if we—"

"There's no time. It's too dangerous. *I'm* too dangerous. I can feel it nibbling away at my soul like I'm some kind of all-you-can-eat buffet. When there's nothing left, then what happens?" She let go of the mask she'd been wearing and let him see all the pain and fear she felt. His eyes widened.

"Then I'll be a monster, Wyatt. Just like one of the Lost. Maybe worse."

"That's not true."

"Yes, it is. And who could stop me? You have no idea the kind of power churning away in here." Even now, it pushed against her chest and spine, but she couldn't take any credit for holding it at bay. She had a feeling that was all Siona.

"Fine," he said. "Then we'll go with them. But when this is over, I want you to seriously think about what you have here—if anything—and what you could have by coming back home…with me."

She bit her lip.

He tipped his chin. "You can't even say it anymore, can you?"

"Say what?"

"*Home.*" The emphasis he put on the word was full of disappointment and sadness. "Greta, even if the goblin king wasn't Lost, you don't belong here." He leaned closer. "You only think you do because you're too scared to face the idea of going back."

"That's not true," she muttered. It was easy for him to talk about going home. He was essentially still the same responsible, honest, compassionate person he'd always been. His family would welcome him back with open arms. But it was different with her. The image of a stone-cold Drew frozen in that magick circle haunted her. The faces of all the Lost she'd hunted haunted her. Luke's face haunted her. *Isaac's* face haunted her.

"I'll think about it."

"Greta—"

She raised her hand. "I said I would think about it, and I meant it," she said. "But later, okay?"

He nodded and they went to catch up with the rest of the group. Siona turned around and held her finger to her lips in warning as they approached. The *bjer*'s snoring continued. The uneasy weight that had rested on her chest since the moment she'd started leading her friends to this place lightened just a little. If the *bjer* was still asleep, there was a chance they could make it across the bridge unscathed.

Everyone took short, careful steps, watching where they put their feet to make sure there were no twigs that could snap beneath boots, no rocks to trip over.

Only ten feet away from the bridge now.

Greta looked up. Two tall posts stuck out of the ground at the cliff's edge, and the thick rope from either side of the bridge had been tied off at both the top and the bottom. Three or four horizontal wooden planks jutted out into nothingness before the weight of the structure pulled the rest of the stepping boards below the edge of the precipice.

Nobody whispered. Nobody sneezed or coughed or stumbled. Nothing crunched or knocked together or fell to the ground.

They should have made it.

CHAPTER ELEVEN

A monstrous roar rang out in the gathering twilight, setting every hair on her body on end. Everyone stopped in their tracks. She jerked her head up, trying to determine where it had originated, because it wasn't coming from inside the ramshackle homemade tepee.

Another soul-skinning roar threatened to rupture her eardrums. She was sure it was coming from somewhere behind them, but there was also something else ahead. She was sure of it.

"Everyone get back from the edge!" she yelled, rushing forward with her sword ready, swinging her other arm to urge them behind her.

Dryden and Siona took up position on either side of her like faerie-shaped bookends, just as a huge hand smashed into the earth at the edge of the cliff, causing everyone to jump. It tore through the layers of snow and ice and imprinted into the frozen ground beneath, sending rock and pebbles cascading in all directions like ants scurrying to get out of the shadow of a boot.

Greta's heart thumped as the massive hand flexed and curled for purchase before it pulled the rest of the monstrous figure up and out of the chasm. With a crash that must have rocked the whole world, it landed on two blackened, bare feet that would have crushed her flat, broken every bone, splatted her head like a melon.

He had to be at least twelve feet tall—and that was not an exaggeration for the tavern tales.

She'd expected the troll to be big, but this guy was twice as tall as Isaac, with dark—almost black—leathery skin. Her gaze kept traveling up and up, past calves and thighs the size of tree trunks. His paunchy belly jiggled when he breathed and hung down over the waist of a pair of filthy half-length trousers cut just below the knee—the same amount of canvas could have made pants for an entire goblin family. The fabric was encrusted in several places with who knew what... probably the remains of all the unwary travelers he'd killed and eaten.

She shuddered. When her gaze got to his chest—as wide as four of her—she knew they were toast. His arms could clothesline all of them off the edge of the cliff like sweeping the contents off a table.

By the time she reached his face, she had to crane her neck and squint to meet his red-rimmed eyes.

"Oh, no," she whispered. If this was the *bjer*—which it had to be—then what else was on its way?

She heard a low growl behind them. With her sword up—as useless as that might be—she half twisted to get a look.

From the dark mouth of the falling-down tepee structure emerged a canine-like creature the size of a Mylean carriage horse. It looked just as mean, too. Its snout scrunched up in a long, rumbling snarl that showed off yellowed, sharp teeth, and it padded forward with slow, stalking movements.

"What is it?" Wyatt asked, a slight tremor running through

his whispered voice.

"It's a *rizos*," Siona replied, obviously assuming he meant the canine creature, although given the way he was looking back and forth between the dog and the *bjer*, he might have been talking about either one.

"Who goes?" The *bjer*'s voice boomed over the tops of their heads like thunder. His breath might actually blow Greta right off her feet if he bent down to her level. The *bjer*'s words echoed out beyond the cliff.

Byron stepped forward, shoulders pushed back. "I am Prince Byron, heir to the Glass Kingdom in the Northern Provinces," he called in a loud voice. She was impressed by the authority and power in his voice, like it came naturally. She could never have pulled off that kind of confidence, no matter how much practice she got.

"Kings or criminals, it makes no matter to me. None shall trespass across the territory I have claimed." The *bjer*'s lip curled much like its pet's, which was still growling at their backs.

"You have no proper claim on this land," Byron started, but at the deep flush of rage filling the *bjer*'s cheeks, he smartly changed tactics. He stretched out his arm to stay the creature. "But my entourage has no intention of contesting your rights. We only wish to—"

"You seek to cross." From the look on his face and the way he licked his lips, this was the part where the *bjer* killed everyone and stripped their bones like he was gorging on BBQ chicken.

The dog beast lunged forward, snapping its jaws and barking madly. Obviously, it was also familiar with what came next and looked forward to getting thrown a few juicy scraps.

Dryden beat off the *rizos* with a slash across the snout. It let out a yowl, but that quickly turned into a growl as it ducked its head and crouched down on its haunches.

Greta could sense everyone starting to freak out. As strong and fierce as Siona was, as smart and capable as Wyatt was...and as wildly unpredictable as the rest of the faerie group was, they couldn't take on this troll and its scary pet. She looked at those crazy massive fists. They would crush her without even trying.

You have the power to save everyone. Her whole body hummed.

She gritted her teeth against the urge to use magick. *Don't do it.* There had to be another way.

She raised her arm to catch the troll's attention. "Would you accept payment?" she called. "What would it cost for you to allow us to cross?"

He looked down his massive nose. She motioned toward Leila and Byron with a wave worthy of any salesman. "These people are faerie royalty. Anything you want, they can get it for you. You just have to name your price and allow us to pass safely."

Beside her, Wyatt stiffened. Yes, it was a risk, but they had to try something, right? If the *bjer* asked for the moons, well... one of them would just have to figure out how to deliver.

He perched those huge hands on his hips and straightened to laugh, belly jiggling in front of her face. As a group, they took an instinctive step backward, but the beast behind them started growling again, and the collective movement halted just as abruptly. They were boxed in.

"Why does your kind always believe that I would want anything from the likes of you?" He sounded surprisingly civilized for a troll. Greta supposed she'd been expecting a raging beast, not an intelligent monster.

"You never know, right? Perhaps we can come to an agreement."

Siona tensed, too. Out of the corner of her eye, Greta saw her glance at Byron and Leila with a frown. They nodded and

Siona leaned close to Greta and whispered, "Just because he can carry on a conversation doesn't mean he won't rip our throats out."

True, but if he was willing to negotiate, their chances of making it through this just got a hell of a lot better.

Another roar echoed from somewhere in the woods behind them. It sounded much closer than before, as if it was following a scent...their scent. They might not have time to negotiate.

"It can't hurt to at least listen to what we have to offer, right?" she said quickly. "And if you decide that you want nothing, my group and I will go back where we came from and leave you alone. No harm, no foul."

Byron started to object. Was he *trying* to get them all killed?

The *rizos* snarled again, and the faerie prince shut his mouth. The *bjer* uttered a sharp command. Greta spared a glance behind her. The beast let out a disappointed whine before sitting back on its haunches. Thick, murky drool escaped each side of its slightly parted jaws and stretched in long lines toward the ground.

"I will afford you the same terms I have given all who trespass and seek to cross the bridge," said the *bjer*.

That word, "trespass," was ominous, and the idea of terms didn't make her feel any better about their odds. "What terms are those?"

There was a scary gleam in his eyes. "Not that it matters. Everyone always chooses the same option...and everyone always loses."

"We have no time for games," Byron said, sharp impatience cutting through his tone. "Tell us your terms and let us be done with you."

He only laughed again. "First I will give you the more than generous opportunity to turn around and leave now if you promise to go back, spread word of the legitimacy of my claim on this territory, and never return."

The troll was very possessive of the little parcel of land he'd claimed. This wasn't about negotiating dinner—except maybe for the *rizos*—it was about protecting what he considered his. That gave her an idea.

"My apologies, dolem," she said, "but we can't just leave, as much as we regret trespassing on your property." Her chest was tight with nervousness. "We need to get across that bridge."

"The offer will not remain open. If you choose to ignore it, all of you will suffer the consequences of that decision."

Byron opened his mouth—no doubt to argue—but she quickly stepped in front of him and resheathed her sword, then held out her hands in a show of good faith. "What is your name, sir?"

The *bjer* blinked and reared back in surprise. "No one has ever asked me that before."

She pasted a smile on her face. "If we are to negotiate together, I think it's only fair that we both know who we're dealing with, don't you?"

The *bjer* nodded eagerly, clearly bewildered. A sliver of sadness wormed its way into her chest. Maybe it was stupid and would come back to bite her in the ass, but she felt bad for him. Here was a creature who'd obviously spent his entire life alone, being hated by everyone he met just because of who he was. By the Great Mother, that was something she could relate to.

Beside her, Byron and Leila seemed to seethe with impatience and dissatisfaction. The magick rose up, clogging her throat, but she was determined not to let it take over.

"My name is Greta, and these are my friends." She took a deep breath and held out her hand, waiting for the *bjer* to reciprocate and hoping he didn't see it as an invitation for him to throw her over the edge of the cliff.

He reached out. His hand engulfed her arm almost to the elbow, pumping it up and down twice. She gasped. One more time and her limb might not be attached anymore.

"I was once called Midas," he said. His gaze hopped from her to Byron and landed on the sharp blade in Dryden's hand, still held at the ready.

She sent him a harsh glare. "Put that away," she snapped under her breath as she forced a smile for Midas. "It's a pleasure to make your acquaintance, Midas."

Dryden wasn't putting his weapon away. In fact, he seemed to want a fight. His very posture was begging for it. Midas's gaze narrowed, his mouth turning down in a suspicious frown. "Do not make the mistake of believing that false courtesy will be enough to gain passage across my land," he warned.

"Of course not," she hurried to say. "I'm sure we can abide by your terms. Please just tell us. What is the other option?"

Midas straightened back to his full height and put his hands on his hips. "I will grant access to the bridge *if* you can make the payment I require."

She let out a sigh of relief, but Midas shook his head. "I will only accept a truly unique treasure. Something I have never been given before."

"But how will we know what you have already received in the past?"

"You won't. You must take that chance." His gaze narrowed as he leaned forward. "And your time runs short."

CHAPTER TWELVE

Greta felt sympathy for the *bjer*, but if they didn't give him what he wanted, he was going to run them down and scoop them up for his stew pot. Of that she had no doubt.

She could practically hear Siona strategizing, feel Wyatt's tension, and see the faeries readying their swords. She wanted to tell them that she'd already played this out in her mind, and responding with aggression just wasn't going to work. They couldn't fight hard enough and couldn't run fast enough, not for everyone to make it to the bridge safely.

"Will you allow a moment of discussion?" she asked politely.

Midas took a half step back, but he waggled an oversized finger. "Don't try to trick me, and don't waste my time," he warned.

She nodded, certain that too many Myleans had under-estimated this guy already. "Please, Midas. It's hard to think with the *rizos* salivating over us. Could you call it off?"

He hesitated but finally snapped another command at the beast. It turned and trudged back to its shelter. Greta shuddered as its red eyes glowed out at them from the dark shadows.

In fact, it was getting dark out here, too. The suns were almost on the horizon and the sky was hazy with clouds, which didn't help visibility. They were burning away too much time.

She turned to the group. Having the *bjer* at her back sent prickles up and down her spine, but she tried to believe that Midas was going to play fair. "What do you think we can offer him that would be unique enough to keep him happy?"

Wyatt wasn't letting the *bjer* out of his sight. He remained facing outward but threw a whisper over his shoulder, "You can bet he's not going to get excited about coin or jewels. Someone will have tried that already. He doesn't exactly look like he's starving, but eating people has got to get old, right? Maybe if we promise to deliver up a couple head of fresh cattle?"

Siona shook her head. "If he wanted a cow, who would stop him from taking it from any field? We have to be able to provide something he couldn't possibly get for himself from anyone else in Mylena."

"Well, we aren't Mylean," Greta said. She looked at Wyatt. "There's got to be something we can offer that nobody else can?"

"Trouble?" he said with a grin. Her stomach flip-flopped, and she smiled back.

Siona cleared her throat. "Humans are certainly unique."

"I've got it," Wyatt said. "Music."

"What does he mean?" The princess asked, curious.

Wyatt looked at her, an excited gleam in his eyes. "Humans are born with music in our hearts. We sing and dance for pretty much every occasion you could conceive of. Music is entrenched in *our* culture in a way that I've never seen anywhere in Mylena."

"We have music," Siona protested.

"Not like *we* have music," Wyatt said. "And our music would be like nothing you've ever heard before."

Greta sucked in a breath as hope bloomed. "I sang to my pater when he was alive," she said, remembering how mesmerized Luke had been by the sound.

Dryden and Byron both frowned. They seemed to have the same opinion about this idea. "Should we believe that something so intangible as a song will be special enough to win us passage when others have offered the *bjer* gold and jewels, and perhaps even their firstborn children?" Byron said.

"This is the thing. This is what we have to bargain with," Wyatt said with conviction. He paused and looked at her expectantly. "You can do this."

"What?" She stepped back. "Why me?"

"You said that you used to sing to your pater and he liked it."

"Yeah, but he was probably tone-deaf," she protested, "and all I ever sang to him were bits and pieces of the lullabies and the stupid cartoon theme songs that I could remember from being a kid."

Wyatt nodded. "What you sing doesn't matter, because nobody in Mylena has ever heard it before. It will work," he assured her.

"Have you nothing to offer me, then?" the *bjer*'s voice boomed, making her jump. As if on cue his pet growled, poking its head out of the shelter.

"No more time for debate," Byron said.

Wyatt's hand slipped over hers and squeezed. She took a deep breath and turned to face Midas.

"Do we ever have something for you," Wyatt called up to the *bjer* like a ringmaster announcing the main event under the big top. Not that she'd ever been to the circus, but she had a feeling this farce would certainly qualify. "Something so beautiful…so amazing and unique it can never be duplicated. You won't believe your ears."

Oh, God. He was going to get all of them killed.

Midas crossed his arms over that wide, barrel chest and narrowed his gaze all the way down until he settled on Wyatt. They all swallowed, suitably intimidated. "Then by all means," Midas said, "present it now before I lose what is left of my patience and decide I will have no offer from any of you."

"Don't be so hasty," Siona piped up. "If you reject this gift out of spite, you are sure to regret it for the rest of your life. A moment's satisfaction in your belly is nothing compared to the loss you will sustain. Your heart will mourn with every beat because it will never know the beauty that could have been."

The goblin grinned at Wyatt. She waved her arm to present Greta to the *bjer*, reminding her of the tonic salesman who stood out front of his carriage at the village market and called one and all to experience the magic of his wares, claiming his fancy vials filled with bitter root juice and cow piss would make you stronger or prettier or healthier.

Dryden elbowed Siona sharply in the ribs. She coughed and her voice fell off.

Wyatt wrapped up the pitch. "You asked for a treasure, and we introduce to you the greatest treasure anyone in Mylena will ever experience."

He took half a step back and gave Greta a push forward.

"We would like to offer you the gift of song," she said slowly.

Midas gazed at her intensely, doubt pulling his pale forehead into deep crinkles like cracks across the permafrost of the western plains on the other side of the goblin forest.

"I promise you'll like it."

He crossed his massive arms, the muscles bulging like swelling balloons. "Then by all means," he said. "Present this offering."

Greta ducked her head and clenched her eyes tightly closed. She took a deep breath and started to sing the only song she was pretty sure she could still remember from start to finish. It was a lullaby her mother had sung at bedtime when she was a little girl. It was also the song Luke had liked best when he was alive, which is probably why it was still clear in her head.

"Whenever you are crying, I will hold you. Whatever you are doing, I'll defend you."

Her voice started out thin and weak as nervousness choked her. She was going to blow this. She couldn't hold the melody, her voice was cracking. The *bjer* looked as if he was going to blow a gasket, probably wondering what kind of cheap trick they were pulling on him.

"Wherever you are hiding, I'll find you. However you are hurting, I'll comfort you. Wherever you are, nearby or far, I'll follow the stars just to be with you."

The words suddenly meant more than they ever had before. Isaac's image rose up in her mind, and the hot saltiness of tears became another challenge to overcome as she fought to keep her shit together and not think of him.

Wyatt took her hand. Someone else touched her shoulder, probably Siona. They were telling her that they were right there. Believing in her, encouraging her.

"Wherever you go. Wherever you laugh. Wherever you sing and dance and sigh. Wherever you are, nearby or far, I'll follow the stars just to find you."

She kept singing, pouring more and more of her heart into each verse and each note as the words fell out of her like a fountain. Every time she repeated the refrain, the memory of Isaac's sacrifice replayed. She remembered his kiss, and his eyes, and his smile. It broke her heart over and over again.

On the last note she opened her eyes, part of her convinced that it could be true and the battle had all been a dream, but she found herself looking up into Wyatt's face, steady and confident and encouraging. She held his gaze as she held the last note, letting it ring out in the clearing.

There wasn't another sound but hers. Not a screeching Mylean bat emerging into the twilight or a shrieking hopper bug. It was like everyone stopped breathing as she held that final crystallized note…until it slowly, slowly faded into the gathering dusk.

There were no words for a long time. Not from the *bjer*, or Wyatt, or anyone else.

She blinked as a snowflake landed on her eyelash, then another on her cheek. She had no idea when it had started to snow, but the big fluffy flakes drifted down gently, almost reverently. It was kind of nice, actually. The snow felt kind of like a postcard. Pretty without being brutal.

Finally, she turned to look at Midas, whose mouth hung open at her eye level. At some point that she hadn't even noticed, he'd knelt on one knee in front of her. He was staring at her like she'd just performed the most amazing trick and he was trying to reason where she'd got the rabbit to pull out of her hat.

"How did you do it?" he asked. "How do you take something so simple as words and turn them into magick?" He held out his arm and she edged back, expecting him to pick her up and shake her until the music came out again.

"Do it again," he ordered in a booming voice, leaning forward until she could smell his rank breath and see the flecks of green in his milky eyes. He didn't shake her, but gave her a not so subtle poke to the shoulder to urge her to obey.

Wyatt and the faeries all closed ranks simultaneously. "You must accede. We met your terms and have made payment as requested," Siona reminded Midas gently. "Danem Greta's song is exactly what you wanted, a treasure you have never been offered before. In fact, you have been given a treasure that has no match anywhere in Mylena."

The *bjer* frowned, still staring at her.

"You *will* allow us access to the bridge. Now." The steel of Byron's position ran through his tone, daring Midas to renege on their deal.

A calculating light dawned in his gaze, making Greta's blood run cold as she imagined what it could mean. "The agreement was never intended to include passage for all," he finally said.

"That's bullshit!" Wyatt surged forward angrily, but she grabbed his shoulder. She wanted to say the same thing, but the situation was on the verge of turning very dangerous once more.

She started to tell him she'd sing another song. After all, it was just a few minutes of her life. If it made the *bjer* happy, what could it hurt? But the bright shine in his eyes stopped her. One song wasn't going to be enough. Ten, twenty, or a hundred songs—assuming she could even remember that many—wouldn't be enough. If Midas had his way, she'd find herself locked up in a human-sized birdcage singing her heart out day after day until she ran out of songs—and then he'd probably kill her.

Midas focused only on her. "I'm feeling generous and I shall let everyone pass...as long as *you* stay," he said. "You will stay and give me more of this treasure, and when your group returns they shall be guaranteed safe crossing a second time as well." Now he was the one negotiating. He sounded almost desperate.

"And then you'll let me go?" she asked.

He nodded eagerly. As far as deals went, it didn't sound so unreasonable—all except for the fact that she didn't believe him for a minute. Trusting him to keep his word had already proven to be a big mistake.

"Get going," she told everyone, pushing Wyatt and Siona toward the cliff's edge and the bridge. "You have to hurry before it gets too late to find shelter for the night."

She looked at Wyatt. *Please don't fight this.*

Siona gave her a loaded look and a slow nod. Greta let out a deep breath and nodded as well. Thank God Siona understood.

When Midas didn't stop them from going she let out a soundless sigh of relief.

Her heart pounded as she watched. They were almost at the bridge —

A large creature burst into the clearing with eyes of burning red, a face smeared with blood, and a roar that could bring an avalanche down the mountain.

Her breath caught. She almost didn't recognize the former goblin king. He was as much a monster now as any Lost creature she'd ever hunted — crazed and without a hint of the boy who'd teased her, kissed her, and promised her a future by his side.

Her heart cracked with grief and sadness, even as the magick took hold with a forceful explosion of fire that was strong enough to throw even Midas back.

It took him by surprise long enough that he was still reeling when Wyatt reached her side. Why wasn't he halfway to the bridge already?

He reached for her. She shouted to warn him, but it was too late. He hissed at the sizzle of flesh when he touched her, but clamped his hand on her wrist anyway and didn't let go.

"Come on!" He pulled her along, but she hesitated and turned back.

Isaac was running for them with a wolfish snap of his massive jaws.

A heat wave pulsed out from her core. She *pushed* it without conscious thought. In fact, it seemed to have a mind of its own. Isaac hollered in pain. She gasped at the smell of scorched hair and skin and took an instinctive step toward him.

"You can't help him now!" Wyatt yelled.

"I can try!" she cried out, chest tight with half hope, half dread. "What if— "

Wyatt shoved his red, quickly blistering hand in front of her face. "What if you kill us all trying to find out?"

She flinched. He was right. She couldn't risk reaching out to Isaac until she was safe.

She let Wyatt pull her with him. Behind them something howled, but she didn't dare turn to look again.

They took off running. Midas's enraged shout rent the air, and she put her head down and pushed herself even faster. Wyatt kept pace.

The faeries waited at the base of the bridge.

"Go, go, go!" she yelled, waving for them to move their butts.

They turned and started single file onto the bridge, and then Wyatt was shoving her ahead of him.

Eyna's Falls was another mile or so upriver from Solem's Bridge. It was the only free-running source of water in all of Mylena except for the hot springs beneath the Brimstone Caves. The rivers and lakes everywhere else had frozen long ago.

The frozen mist covering the thin boards of the bridge had made it slippery and it swayed back and forth, threatening to tip everyone into the deep chasm. She immediately scrambled to grab onto the rope rails with both hands.

Then she looked down. Bad idea. There was no bottom.

She knew it had just gotten too dark to see the bottom, but that didn't make her feel any better.

She took another step and her foot went right through a rotten board. She caught herself and spun around to stop Wyatt from barreling into her. He careened to a halt and gripped the ropes tightly.

Behind them, Midas roared, and she could just see him

pounding both his massive fists into the earth as he glared out at them. Vibrations ran the length of the bridge and set it rocking even harder.

She scanned the cliff's edge for Isaac and saw him battling the *rizos* and could only pray that he would be okay.

Surprisingly, Midas didn't follow them onto the bridge, and he didn't start tearing it down—both of which she'd feared but had strategically decided were risks they had to take.

"Why is he just standing there?" she wondered out loud.

Wyatt's gaze widened, and he pointed over her shoulder. "That's why," he said, alarmed.

Greta turned back around. Mylena's two moons peeked through a break in the cloud cover. Siona and the faeries were about fifteen feet ahead, but beyond them everything disappeared into the settling darkness. There was no way to tell what might be waiting on the last half of the bridge, or the other side of the chasm, for that matter.

She squinted, but there was nothing—

Swoop.

The dark couldn't quite hide what the night had brought along with it. Something had swept down from above, right for Siona and the others. Someone screamed, and they ducked en masse. When something in the darkness echoed the cry almost exactly, Greta swore.

"Crap. Harpies!"

Chapter Thirteen

She leaped over the break in the planks just as her own voice cried, "*Harpies!*" back at her from right above her left shoulder. She ducked in time to avoid the clawing talons of the winged creature and looked up to see the opalescent white of its under wings disappearing back into the night.

"One of you keep talking," she called to the group ahead. "Just one. Harpies are mimics. When it repeats the words back to you, you'll be able to hear where it's coming from. But too many voices and—"

"*Too many voices…*"

She ducked again, hands plastered over her head as she waited for the harpy to carry her off. The words echoing at them in Greta's own voice cut off abruptly with a scream. Nothing touched her, and when she looked up, Wyatt was peering over the bridge's rope railing into the depths below. He turned to her and held out his hand to help her up.

"What did you do to it?"

"Nothing permanent. It will be back soon enough. Let's get off this bridge."

They ran to the others, stepping carefully. Greta drew her sword as they neared. The princess was crouched low, with Dryden leaning over her for protection, while Siona and the others flanked the prince. She let out a relieved breath to see that everyone was still accounted for. It was impossible to know how many harpies were up there. It could have been just the one, but she somehow doubted it.

In the dark of night, harpies were practically invisible until they were already on top of you. With midnight feathers, black hair, and charcoal skin, the only parts of them that caught the moonlight were the shimmering undersides of their wings and the glow of their yellow eyes.

She cocked her head to listen for the rush of air. Wyatt and Siona looked up, turning around like chickens waiting for the sky to fall. "Are they still here?" asked Leila.

"Still here?"

"Down, get back down!" Everyone ducked, but Siona cried out suddenly.

A harpy had her by the upper arm. She gripped the rope railing with her other hand but couldn't do that and keep her dagger. It slipped and tumbled end over end into the nothingness.

Siona's face scrunched up in pain as the harpy tried to tear her off the bridge. The thing looked surprisingly like a girl, besides the pointed beak and those glowing eyes. It had a girl's shape and arms and legs like a girl, although wide wings spread out from its shoulder blades, and those spindly legs ended in curled talons like a bird of prey.

Greta lunged and slashed at the creature until it let go of Siona, but another two were already swooping down on them. One went for Wyatt and Dryden, while the other reached for Byron.

"No!" she screamed.

A chorus of *"No, No, No!"* rolled back at her. As one of

them repeated it, more and more continued the echo until it came from all sides.

Greta hacked at feathers, arms, and legs. She looked over to see Dryden grab a harpy by the throat and punch it in the face before throwing it over the bridge. She winced at the brutality of it...but then she was forced to plunge her blade into the breast of another, and there was no time for attacks of conscience.

Not only were they being overrun, but the bridge was rocking dangerously from side to side and it would only take a second for someone to lose their grip or their balance and tumble right off...and that was if the frayed ropes didn't snap first.

When the magick started to rumble up from the depths of her belly like a grumbling volcano, she panicked. "Siona!"

Her friend looked up in alarm.

"Siona, do whatever it is you do when I go off the deep end," she said, already scorching the ropes she had an iron death grip on. "You can't let me lose control here. If that happens, we're all going over this bridge."

The goblin hunter looked at Leila in alarm, and something passed between them.

"Siona, please," Greta begged.

Siona nodded. "I will do what I can, danem," she said.

She immediately felt better. Whether that was because Siona had already put the psychic clamp on, or just the idea of it relieved her mind, she couldn't care less. "We have to get off this bridge! Everyone hold on to something, but keep moving and don't stop no matter what happens."

"*Don't stop...what happens,*" the harpies repeated.

Dryden took the lead, with the princess and Byron right behind him. Wyatt stepped ahead next and put his foot through a board, dropping so fast she screamed. "Wyatt!"

She hurled herself after him without thinking. She

snagged the cuff of his jacket and held on so tight her hand cramped. With a tight grimace, she heaved, but he was too heavy.

Siona was on her knees behind Greta with an arm wrapped around her thighs.

"Don't let go," she called, not sure whether she was talking to Siona or to Wyatt.

The plank dug into her ribs. Her side screamed in agony, and the muscles of her arms shook with Wyatt's weight. The echo of the harpies was getting to her, making her want to scream—but if she did, they'd only send her screams back at her, too.

And she might lose it completely if that happened.

She squeezed even tighter and ducked her head over Wyatt as another wave of wings brushed her shoulders.

Dryden knelt down on the other side of the broken space and reached down to grab Wyatt under the arm.

She glanced up at him, but the faerie didn't look annoyed, impatient, or angry. Just determined. She reluctantly moved aside. She couldn't do it on her own, and there wasn't enough room for the both of them to lift Wyatt out. She had to trust him.

But she couldn't breathe again until Wyatt was safely back on the bridge. "Thank you," she said to Dryden.

"Move," he replied shortly, pushing everyone ahead of him. Peering forward, it seemed like they had to be past the halfway point, but she couldn't see the end of the bridge yet.

Suddenly it started shaking. She looked over her shoulder. The harpies had landed right on it, taking their hunt to the next level. If they couldn't swoop in, then apparently they'd close in.

When Byron and Leila careened to a stop up ahead, Greta knew more harpies blocked the way there, too. "What are we going to do?" Leila looked back, wincing when her words were thrown back at her amid the flurry of battering wings. Everyone clutched the rope railing with two hands for balance as the bridge canted back and forth violently.

The pressure inside her started to build again. That push of power looking for a way out was getting familiar now, welcome, even, but if she started flinging magick around here, all of them were going to end up going over the edge... literally.

Suddenly Midas's shout ripped across the chasm. Greta gasped but had already come too far over the bridge to see back to where they'd begun. And then she heard another sound. The sound of pure rage...and she didn't have to see.

She looked up at the break in the clouds, or the break in the shadows from the harpies flocking overhead. It took everything she had to ignore the instinct to fight her way back to Isaac. She couldn't help him, and she couldn't abandon Wyatt and Siona. In fact, going back wouldn't help anyone, least of all Isaac, since that might mean having to take him out. She wasn't prepared for that. Not yet.

She turned back around to find Wyatt watching her. "Go on and help Siona up at the front," she said through the tightness in her throat. "I'll pull up the rear and keep the harpies back."

They made slow progress crossing the bridge. Siona, Wyatt, and Dryden battled through the harpies in front, and Greta managed to hold her own at the back of the line, but every minute they spent on the increasingly unstable structure heightened her fear that all of them would end up falling to the rocky shoals below or drowning in the ice-cold, rushing river.

She squinted ahead. Hope bloomed. For the first time, she thought she could actually see where the land began again on the other side of the chasm.

But the bridge started bouncing wildly once more. She

lost her grip on one of the rope railings and pitched to the side, keeping her balance by the skin of her teeth. Byron let out a surprised shout, but thankfully everyone managed to hold on.

Something else had gotten onto the bridge with them and was coming up fast. There was still a gaggle of harpies between them and the newcomer approaching, but Greta's heart rate spiked. She knew Isaac had made it onto the bridge, and she would be forced to fight him here and now.

She held her breath as some of the harpies took off and seemed to swoop back. "Hurry! Everyone keep moving!" she yelled up to the front of the line.

"*Keep moving!*" the harpies echoed.

When a figure broke the thick darkness, she hitched a breath. Even though she'd expected it, the sight of him coming out of the shadows down that narrow gangplank like a freight train coming out of a tunnel was terrifying. She screamed.

"Greta!" Siona called.

"Keep going." She planted her feet and pulled her sword. "I'll hold him back. Get everyone onto solid ground!"

The good thing about the bridge was that Isaac would have to take her on before he could reach anyone else. She spared a quick glance back and made sure that Wyatt wasn't going to be stubborn and try to stay with her. But of course, that's exactly what he was doing.

"Wyatt, go with the others," she warned.

"Someone's got to protect your back." He turned until they were shoulder to shoulder. Dryden and Siona managed to push everyone through the throng of harpies blocking their way, but the creatures went back to dive-bombing their prey from above.

Greta braced herself and ducked as Isaac lunged for her. The magick was there. She assumed Siona was still holding it back, but it whispered in her ear like a lover, tempting her with power beyond imagining. It was seductive and practically irresistible now, and the only thing that stopped her from ordering Siona to release it to her was Isaac. *He* was the one who would suffer. Thankfully, her need for it was still not as strong as her desire to keep him safe, but she worried there'd come a time when that wouldn't be the case anymore.

"Grab on!" she called out, wrapping her arm around the rope railing as it wobbled. Wyatt grunted as the whole bridge teetered. His feet slipped and he scrambled for purchase, but he held on.

"Everyone is safe," Siona called. "Hurry!"

The harpies converged on Isaac. They echoed his growls of fury, and he stopped to swat at them. It would keep him distracted for a moment, hopefully long enough to get off the bridge. She scrambled to formulate a plan for holding him back once they were on solid ground again.

"When I step off this thing, everyone has to be ready to hold back the goblin king," she said without looking back. "If we all surround him, we should be able to immobilize—"

"Already ahead of you," Wyatt replied. "Just be careful."

Finally, she put her foot down on the edge of the last board. Wyatt was there on one side and Siona on the other.

As the whoosh of steel whistled past her ears, the harpies started screeching.

She realized they were echoing her screams.

"No! Wait!" She grabbed Siona's arm, tugging her back before her sword could cut the rope, but she wasn't able to stop both of them. Like a slow-motion movie, Wyatt's blade sliced through the old, already frayed strands like they weren't even there—first the rope railing and then the ropes holding the planks in place—and the bridge immediately collapsed on that side.

She couldn't look away from the bridge, and let out a relieved breath when she saw Isaac's hulking form clawing for purchase on the splintered planks. He was okay.

She whispered his name.

Dryden stepped in front of her and, without any hesitation at all, cut right through one of the two remaining ropes.

"No! You're going to kill him!" She screamed and lunged, but he shrugged her off. Before she could reach him again, he'd already cut the last rope and the bridge was sliding away from the edge.

Greta stupidly tried to go after it, but Wyatt pulled her back, both arms around her waist. "What are you doing?" he yelled in her ear, holding her against him. "Are you crazy?"

Sobs ripped through her as she watched the bridge swinging away across the chasm. It was too dark and the clouds had drifted back over the moons, making it impossible to see—

She yelled at Dryden, "You didn't have to do that!"

"I could not allow him to make it off that bridge."

"We could have contained him," she insisted, clenching her fists.

"Why would I risk it, when the alternative was more effective and safer for everyone?"

Siona touched her shoulder. Her eyes were full of sorrow and pity. "If he'd managed to get across, he would have slaughtered—"

"You don't know that," Greta snapped. He'd specifically followed them. Beneath all the rage, there must have been a reason for that. There must have.

Her emotions swirled like a raging tornado, pulling at her insides until she wanted to curl up on the ground.

"He was already Lost to us," Siona said gently. "Is it not better that you remember him as he had been?"

"No, it was better when I could remember him as being *alive*." She tore free and reached down deep, not waiting for the magick to rise up but searching for it. It answered quickly and eagerly, and she latched on desperately, but there was resistance when she went to use it.

"Siona, let go," she demanded with a glare.

The goblin hunter hesitated and Greta reacted instantly, instinctively ripping the mental shackle away like a bandage just as a thick, muscled arm reached up over the cliff's edge.

After that, everything was a blur of heat and darkness... until there was nothing at all.

CHAPTER FOURTEEN

She threw fire from her fingertips as effortlessly as breathing. It made her feel good…no, amazing. Every surge gave her strength and power. The living darkness inside her opened a great red eye, lit with sparks and electricity, making her more powerful, and it encouraged her to keep feeding it so that together, they would become invincible.

Sight and sound were flat, but she didn't care. None of her senses mattered.

Not until a wild shout split through the smoke and fog, becoming a howl that shook her to the core and brought her to her senses. There was an innocence and beauty in all that savagery and rage, enough to snag her attention and make her want to follow it.

So she did.

The goblin king. He bled from a dozen wounds, and his fur was charred in places. He'd been wounded so badly he crashed unsteadily through the dense forest. The part of her that was only Greta called after him, as if she could still somehow reach the boy behind the beast, but he never hesitated, never flinched, never showed for a moment that he was moved by anything, or cared about anything.

She kept pace as he ran and finally realized they were dreaming.

When he collapsed in the mud from exhaustion, her tears came. She reached out to touch his arm. She forgot about the magick, because her heart was being ripped to shreds.

His head tilted as if he were thinking how to react to her touch. His breathing hitched and his muscles bunched. He snarled and snapped, and she jerked back, afraid. Siona had been right. It would have been better to remember him the way he'd been. Seeing him like this was breaking her in a way that even watching him go Lost hadn't done. Her sobs increased.

She didn't want to see anymore and thankfully felt herself drawing away.

Isaac, please. Please be real. Please be alive. As if from above, she looked down on him now as the lure of consciousness tugged at her.

Please come back.

He jumped to his feet and spun around with a mad snarl. What was he looking for? Was it possible that he could…did he maybe sense that she was there?

His eyes widened, red and wild. His teeth gleamed in the moonlight. He dug his claws, already caked in dirt and blood, into the ground and howled.

There was no beauty in it this time, only rage.

• • •

Greta awakened with a start, jerking to a sitting position against yet another tree trunk.

She groaned with pain. Her head felt like hot spikes had been slipped through her eyes into her brain. Her muscles ached as if she'd been running for days, and her side sent constant shooting pain up and down the rest of her. She was a mess. A mess that only ever got messier.

A dream. But not like the kind she usually shared with Isaac. Those had always been initiated by him and controlled by him, with a carefully constructed atmosphere for them to interact in.

This had been like a walk through the fun house at the county fair, warped and unreal, more disturbing than fun.

Still just a dream. You have to stop thinking about him. She choked on a sob.

"Are you okay?"

"Wyatt?" Heart still pounding, she cleared her throat and turned toward the direction of his voice. It was still too dark to see clearly, but she finally noticed a Wyatt-sized shadow sitting against another tree not far away. "Are you watching me while I sleep?" She gave him a shaky laugh as she realized she didn't remember getting to that spot, or going to sleep.

"It wasn't sleep." His voice was sharp.

"What do you mean?" She squinted to see his face.

"We finally knocked you out." He leaned forward. There was a deep red stripe down the side of his face, and his jacket had been scorched black across the front.

She gasped. "Great Mother, what happened to you?" she asked, already feeling the answer in the sizzle of her fingertips and dreading it.

He held her gaze. "You had a bit of a meltdown."

"What did I do?" She closed her eyes. "Never mind, I think I have a pretty good idea. Did I hurt anyone…else?"

He paused.

Oh, God. "Wyatt, *did I hurt anyone*?"

Her heart pounded as she tried to remember. The first part was easy. Isaac coming after them. Big, mean, Lost Isaac. The bridge coming down. Him going over with it.

Gone.

The rest was hazy. Blood. Fire. Blood. Fire.

Wait, she remembered Isaac *after* the bridge went down. He'd somehow made it…hadn't he?

Not just a dream.

"You didn't *kill* anyone, so that's something." Wyatt sounded beat. He bent his knees to his chest and wrapped his arms around them.

"Is Siona…did she…?"

He nodded. "She's the one who finally put the lid back on your trick."

"What time is it?"

"Still the middle of the night. You've only been out for an hour or so," he answered, shifting closer. "The others have found shelter not far from here."

She ducked her head and took deep breaths, rubbing her hands over her face as if she could scrub the magick off, the dreams off, the guilt and the pain off.

"So why aren't you with them? What are you doing here?" she asked, tugging on the sleeves of her jacket to avoid looking directly at him. She didn't want him to see how rattled she still was.

"Is it so hard to believe that I'm here to look out for you?" he said. She didn't miss the implication that he was talking about more than just this spot in the forest at this exact time.

"After what I just did? You should have strung me up. I'm surprised the faeries didn't insist on it."

He glanced over his shoulder before leaning closer. "I don't think what happened was your fault."

"It would be easy to push all the blame on the demon trapped in a limbo dimension right now, but I can't do that. This is on me. Until I can get this magick out of me, I have to accept the consequences of it."

"That's not what I meant." He lowered his voice. "When

you lost control on the edge of that cliff, it was like that was exactly what the faeries had been waiting for. If there'd been popcorn, they would have grabbed a bowl and pulled up a chair."

She shook her head. "That's not possible. Siona has always reined me in when things got out of hand."

He frowned. "I don't know what her deal was. Maybe she couldn't, or wouldn't, but either way, it wasn't until you turned your fury on the faeries that any of them, including Siona, made any move to put a stop to the craziness."

"No, you're wrong. I remember Siona holding me back, but the darkness was overwhelming, maybe too much for the both of us." Not only the darkness, but her desire for *more* of it. As much as could fill her up. Even now, she felt twitchy and needy. She didn't know what scared her more—the idea of *wanting* that power, or knowing that when it finally took the last drop of her humanity, no one would be able to stop her from setting the world ablaze.

"It's getting stronger, Wyatt."

"I know." He sighed in resignation.

She may not have killed anyone tonight, but… "How bad?"

"Your Lost boyfriend was hurt pretty bad…and Siona is still unconscious."

"Shit, really?" She got to her feet and winced at the painful pull in her side.

Wyatt leaped up and blocked the way. "The others are watching over her, and you need more rest."

She crossed her arms. "Are you afraid I'll go off the deep end again and hurt someone even worse?"

He stepped closer and slipped his hands up her arms to her shoulders. "Does it look like I'm afraid of you?"

She melted at the warm surety of his touch. "Maybe you're just a little slow on the uptake," she murmured.

"Petty insults? You must be feeling really crappy."

"I'm sorry," she whispered suddenly, looking into his face.

He tipped his head with a quirky grin. "Not for calling me slow, I assume?"

"For leaving you alone after the eclipse." His skin was dry, his hands callused, but she didn't pull away immediately. Instead, for the first time since seeing him again, she let herself remember everything. His smile and his laugh. How those young boys had hung the moons on him, and the way he'd completely accepted her into the group, trusting her with all their lives. "For disappointing you."

"You didn't disappoint me."

"What a liar you are." She shook her head. "But I'm not going to argue with you right now."

"First time for everything," he teased. Then his smile faded and he pushed aside a lock of hair from her forehead. She bit her lip but didn't move. "If I'd gone back and gotten the boys and waited for you, would you have really stayed away? Would you have really remained here for *him* and let us go alone?"

"I didn't decide to stay *just* for him." She took a deep breath. "But yes. Yes, I would have stayed."

"But now that he's gone, you can't still believe there's a place for you here?"

"I don't know what to think right now. It's been a pretty long day." She refused to get talked into more promises. "All I know is that I can't trust myself *anywhere* when I'm like this."

And she still couldn't bring herself to believe that Isaac was really gone. He'd survived Solem's Bridge, and he might have survived her explosive attack. Was he out there somewhere licking his wounds? Maybe…asleep? Could the bond they'd shared before he went Lost still be connecting them?

Did it matter?

Just because he's alive doesn't make him Isaac. He hadn't

shown any signs of the boy she'd fallen in love with. *Am I supposed to be bound to a rabid monster?* She shivered.

"Are you okay?"

She focused on Wyatt, who was here in front of her now. Wyatt, who was whole and sane and cared about her. "Yeah, I'm fine. I should go check on Siona." She took a step around him, but pain shot up her side all the way to her chest like it was splitting her open. She stumbled.

He put his arm around her. She gasped and jerked back, and he looked down at his hand. It was covered with blood.

"Jesus, you're bleeding." He was right. Her wound definitely should have started to heal by now, but she could feel the wet stickiness of it coating her skin like paint. "Is that still from the fight with the gnomes?"

She forced a shrug, even though she'd broken out in a cold sweat. "I must have torn it open again during the fight with the harpies," she said. *You can't tear it open when it never closed to begin with.*

Concern creased his forehead. "Sit down and let me rebandage it."

"I don't think—"

"Come on, Greta. Are you really that stubborn?"

She sighed. "All right."

He helped her back to the ground and pulled the supplies Dryden had given them from his pocket. By the time she leaned back against the tree, she was gritting her teeth and taking deep breaths.

Slowly, he stripped off her coat. Gently, he lifted her shirt. She couldn't even tell whether the air was chilled or not, because she was so hot. Fever? Or was it the magick building up inside her like a pressure cooker with the lid screwed on tight? If she didn't release the heat, would it burn her right up? And if she *did* release it, would the whole world burn instead?

"Why didn't you say something about this sooner? You're an idiot, you know that?" Wyatt's voice sounded hoarse and gruff, but his hands gently cleaned the blood from her ribs before wrapping a fresh bandage around her torso.

"Thanks," she said, covering his hand with hers when he was done. "Thanks for being here. Thanks for caring."

He swore and pulled his hands away, roughly wiping her blood off with the edge of his shirt. "Damn it, of course I care. I wish to hell I didn't right about now, but I can't seem to turn it off. I can't seem to walk away."

"Maybe you should." Her throat was thick with tears.

"Maybe," he admitted. "But it isn't going to happen. We're in this together until the end."

"The end might be too late for you to get out alive. I don't want you to be hurt because of me. You have to get the boys back, take them out of here."

He cupped her chin. Their gazes locked. He seemed to search her face for...something. "Don't worry," he said, caressing her cheek with the pad of his thumb. "I'm not leaving anyone behind."

Her heart pounding hard, she tore her gaze away and drew back. She pushed herself to her feet and brushed off her legs and butt. "It's getting late. We should probably get back to the group."

He sighed and got up with her. Greta held her breath and cocked her head to listen to the sounds of the forest. Wyatt looked at her with a raised brow, but he didn't speak, noticing the tension that had stiffened her limbs right away.

Finally, she put her hands on her hips. "What are you doing skulking around in the shadows, Siona?"

The female goblin stepped into the gently moonlit path. "I wasn't skulking. You are simply not the only one who happened to need some time alone."

Greta stepped closer but held back from touching, afraid

of herself. "Are you okay? Did I hurt you? I didn't mean to…"

"I'm fine. I was overcome, but next time I'll be better prepared for how powerful you've become."

Greta shuddered. "There can't be a next time, Siona. I refuse to put you in that position again." She took a deep breath and looked at both of them pointedly. "If it looks like I'm going to lose it, you both have to promise me you're going to take me out. For good."

The words hung in the air between the three of them, but neither Wyatt nor Siona responded.

Finally Wyatt said, "I'm going to go check on the… thing…over there." He walked away.

"I guess that's a big *no*," Greta mumbled, propping her shoulder against the trunk of a gnarled old tree with a groan.

"You can't ask something like that of him. His heart would never allow him to hurt you."

She glanced up. "But you know I'm right, don't you?"

"It won't come to that," Siona said with a frown.

"If it does," Greta pressed.

"I promise to do what must be done."

Greta let out a long breath of relief and nodded. "Thank you."

"Don't thank me yet."

CHAPTER FIFTEEN

"So where is everyone?"

"Come with me."

She followed Siona to the base of a massive tree. Wyatt had stopped to wait there for them, arms crossed and a militant look of stubborn determination on his face. He was such a fierce protector. A smile tugged at her lips. It must have thrown him off, because he stopped scowling and frowned at her.

She looked up into the tree. A small house had been built high up in the branches. In fact, a makeshift ladder hung from a thick limb off to her left. It was short of the ground a good five feet or so. High enough to discourage wild animals, but still low enough for a regular-sized person to reach it and pull herself up.

The trunk was so wide that everyone holding hands might still not be able to close a circle around it. It had actual leaves instead of needles, plus there wasn't any snow on the ground around it. All of this suggested that the tree formed the center of a sprite's sacred circle — and humans usually couldn't cross the magick boundary into a sprite's sacred circle.

Luke had told her that sprites and faeries shared many intersecting paths in their histories. But while the faeries had abandoned the Great Mother in her time of need and claimed magick from unnatural sources, the sprites devoted their gifts to the earth and were one of the few species still able to claim a tangible connection to Mylena's divine in the present day.

A sacred circle was where a sprite connected with the Great Mother to renew his natural energy. It was a very personal place and a powerful spot where magick was strong. A smart sprite rarely kept his circle where he lived, because he wouldn't appreciate others crossing the boundary and defiling it.

"This is someone's home. It looks like it's been protected. I don't think—"

Wyatt touched the tree without any resistance. "The circle's broken. Whoever lived here is dead. It must have happened pretty recently, because the leaves are still green, but they're already starting to fall."

Now that he mentioned it, she looked down and noticed quite a few leaves in various states of decay littering the ground.

She tried to shake off the sadness that suddenly seemed overwhelming.

She could hear the murmur of low voices and shuffling sounds of movement from above. "All right, I guess this should be safe enough for the night."

Siona started up the ladder first, followed by Greta. Wyatt took the rear, pulling the rope ladder up behind him and tucking it onto a hook beside the doorway, which looked like it was there for exactly that purpose.

The walls were made of oiled, hand-hewn planks, the cutout windows trimmed nicely. The only thing missing was a hearth, but that was understandable considering how much damage a fire would do if it happened to get out of hand up here.

There was a real door, a real roof, and real furniture. A rocking chair with the arms worn smooth from use, a narrow cot against the far wall with a threadbare blanket folded on top of it, and a knotted throw rug on the sanded floor that looked as if it had seen better days. She ran her hand across the wood grain of a small square table.

A quick check of the cupboards didn't turn up much, not that she was surprised. But when she saw that the table was laden with berries and roots and greenery, she realized the faeries must have been foraging throughout the day along the trail, and gathered whatever they happened to come across. Her cheeks flamed hot. Normally, she would have done the same, but she'd apparently been embarrassingly ignorant of her surroundings for most of the day and had nothing to share.

She was fingering a soft green leaf when Siona came up beside her. "I saw a lot of new growth popping up out of the snow today, and it wasn't half as cold as it usually is."

It was almost as if she felt saying the word "spring" out loud would jinx it, but the bright thread of hope was there in her voice.

"When I was young, spring was my favorite season, because it meant my dad would get my bike out of the garage," Greta said softly. "After a long winter—or what had seemed long before I got dumped in Mylena—spring meant that the sun would stay out longer, so I could ride up and down the street after dinner, and he would always be there, standing at the end of the driveway watching me go."

Since her birthday was in late April, it had been a tradition to get a new one every other year just in time for bike-riding season, and her outgrown model would get passed down to Drew.

Traditions had been big in her family. Every birthday had been a rite of passage worthy of chocolate chip pancakes in the shape of the first letter of her name. And Christmas had meant new footie pajamas, even after she was way too old for footie pajamas. Sunday evenings had been family game night. And Monday mornings her mom had always driven her to school so they could hit up Starbucks for coffee first—it had been hot chocolate for Greta until that last year—and have twenty minutes or so of what Mom had called gearing up. They'd both named the one thing that they thought would be challenging that week, and—

She shook her head. She glanced down and realized she had a handful of pine nuts squished in her fist. She popped one into her mouth. It was hard to swallow, but now that her entire life had become a Monday morning with endless difficult moments stretching in front of her, she'd probably need the sustenance.

Even though it had snowed today, just like every other day, the precipitation had felt lighter, the winds not as biting. There'd almost been a hint of something in the air, something she'd never felt in Mylena before, like maybe the land was waking up.

Then again, it wasn't called the never-ending winter for no reason, and she didn't want to get her hopes up over a day or two of temperate weather.

Still, the image of those baskets filled with fresh flowers filled her head, and Isaac's eyes as he'd handed her a bouquet. She mourned the loss of her pack, wishing she had *something* of him.

The prince and princess were sitting on the threadbare rug in the middle of the room, probably because Dryden had wanted them somewhere that he could protect from all sides. They didn't speak. In fact, none of them did.

She realized with a start that throughout the day, the only time any of the faeries had said a word was when they were talking to her or Wyatt—which had made for pretty intense nonconversations.

She grimaced and glanced over her shoulder. Siona had slipped off to the far side of the room and stood gazing into the darkness through one of two small cutout windows. There was nothing to see outside, but whatever she was seeing in her head had put a harsh, absorbed look on her face.

Wyatt had also drifted away from the group, toward the opposite side of the little house. He looked stiff and unapproachable. His hair stood straight up in places and had been mashed flat in others like a harassed scutter rat. The shadow of scruff across his cheeks seemed heavier, as if he'd gotten three more years older in the span of an evening, and the circles under his eyes were more pronounced.

He looked up and his expression cleared when he saw her. He motioned for her to join him. She shrugged and complied but almost regretted it as he followed her progress across the room with a look that made her blush.

"Don't do that," she muttered, stopping in front of him and crossing her arms until she realized it was the same pose as his, and so she put her hands on her hips instead.

He didn't pretend not to know what she was talking about. "I can't help it," he answered with a grin that made his eyes sparkle and her breath catch. He hunched his shoulders and stuffed his hands in his pockets. "You're gorgeous, or didn't you know?"

He'd said something like that to her once before, but it was even funnier now than it had been then. She looked down at her torn, bloody clothes and snorted. Her hands were dirty and callused, not to mention dry and cracked, and right now she could feel every one of her aches and pains. Her lips were chapped, and her hair was coming out of its braids, and...the list went on.

"Don't make me laugh," she warned. "It's bad for the gash in my side."

"I've discovered recently that I have this thing for strong, capable women." He waggled his eyebrows, and she let out a chuckle. He had to be teasing her.

It felt good to laugh. Laughing reminded her of the day she and Wyatt met. She'd almost gutted him with her dagger, but he hadn't batted an eye. In fact, he'd taunted her and ended up inviting her into the secret sanctuary he'd made to keep the boys safe.

She would never have had the balls to do that, could never have trusted him so easily. But he was always able to find the good in people, and he brought it out of others, too.

He slid his finger across her cheek so gently it was like a feather's touch. She went still, lifting her gaze to his. Even though the look he gave her was still trying to be light, she saw what lurked beneath and was humbled. She was unworthy of such feelings. She wasn't the person he thought she was.

She stepped away and looked out the window. The fluffy snowflakes had stopped at some point, and shafts of moonlight cut through the breaks in the trees. It was actually kind of pretty, but the hair on the back of her neck stood up. Something was out there.

"What was that?" she whispered, raising her hand.

"I don't see anything." He leaned through the window opening and looked down. After a long moment, he added, "I don't hear anything, either."

"Neither do I," she admitted. "But I feel it." There were no night sounds at all. That brief moment right before the eclipse when the whole world had seemed to hold its breath—this was like that.

Both of them peered out. Greta's uneasiness grew.

Suddenly, Wyatt put a finger under her chin and tilted her face to his, his other finger over his lips in warning. His forehead was tight as he deliberately looked all the way down.

She followed his gaze. At first she didn't see it. It was hard enough to get an unobstructed view of the ground through the tree's thick branches, and the pale moonlight wasn't strong enough to be an effective source of illumination.

But the longer she looked, the more she knew he was right. Even if she still couldn't see it, something was there.

She flicked her gaze back to him without really moving her head, conscious of the need to be quiet and still. He leaned a little closer until his breath tickled her ear as he whispered, "Don't try to see what moves in the shadows. Look to the shadows themselves."

What is he talking about? She frowned and turned back, and before she could try to refocus in order to see what he saw, something shifted just out of the corner of her vision. Beside her, Wyatt stiffened. She narrowed her gaze but it was no use, she lost whatever she'd almost been about to see.

Trying it his way, she looked at nothing in particular, the way you looked at a painting by one of those impressionist artists her mom used to like. If you focused too closely, it was just globs of swirly paint, but if you stepped back…there it was.

She sucked in a gasp. "Blood wraiths."

Slithering like a snake, darker than the darkness. At first there was only one, but she knew she just wasn't seeing them all. She tried again and realized the forest floor was covered with them.

Wraiths were faeries who had lost their magick. Without it they became husks of their former selves, barely alive. Amorphous and insubstantial, they wandered Mylena looking to replenish what they'd lost. They were mostly harmless. Sometimes they'd manage to knock over a cup or rustle your hair about as hard as a weak breeze, like one expected from a ghost, but if they happened to gather, they could sometimes manifest enough energy to hold you down and feed. And wraiths with a taste for blood were a whole other problem.

They became addicted to the momentary surge of power and obsessed with making it last longer.

Slowly, very slowly, she turned to warn Dryden and the others, but he must have spotted them, too. His shoulders were stiff.

Siona let out a sharp gasp.

"That's why this place is all the way off the ground," Greta muttered under her breath.

"No," Siona answered in a carefully modulated tone. "It may have protected the inhabitant from a variety of other threats, but height will not save us from blood wraiths." She raised her arm and pointed over Greta's shoulder, out the window. "In fact, locking ourselves up here has only made it easier for them."

Greta's brain was still processing how to pick the creatures out of the shadows. It took her a second to see what Siona was pointing at. When she finally did, the thin sliver of hope she'd been holding onto died, and her throat closed in panic.

It was right there in the tree outside her window. Right at eye level, staring at them.

Even though her vision had adjusted, she still couldn't tell where the wraith ended and the shadows began, except for a hint of softly wispy edges, like smoke drifting on the breeze. But she definitely saw beady red eyes and clawed hands clutching the tree's thick bark.

Oh, God, and teeth. Lots of teeth.

There was a scratching sound at the door. Dryden glided over to it soundlessly. He looked to her in expectation. She nodded, muscles tense and ready. As smoothly and quietly as possible, she drew her sword.

"This is not a foe you can best with steel, danem," Siona whispered. She nodded to one the faerie warriors. "Check in the cupboard for salt."

The warrior came back with a small container. "That

won't be enough to hold them back."

"Spread whatever is there in front of the doorway," Dryden ordered. He picked up a small table and upended it, grabbing a leg and snapping it off. He pointed to a ratty old blanket draped over a chair. "Tear that into sections to wrap the end of each of these legs."

Realizing what he intended, she gasped. "Do you think that's really a good idea? This place is old, the wood is dry. One stray spark and the whole thing will go up, taking us and the entire forest along with it."

"If you have a better idea, you are encouraged to share it."

The door of the little house rattled against its frame. Everyone jumped.

With shaky hands, the faerie finished lining the floor in front of it with the small supply of salt and darted back on his hands as the door was ripped right off its hinges completely. She heard it crashing through the branches on its way to the forest floor.

Well, that was one way to alert every blood wraith on the ground to their presence. The tree house entrance was filled with red eyes and sharp teeth.

"Death by fire it is," she muttered. The wraiths really had no shape or substance, only smoky, ghostly shadows. Still, there had to be four or five of them—maybe more—crowding the doorway. They rushed forward to get inside but crashed into the salt line and couldn't cross. That was something, at least. Only…there was no salt at the windows.

Both Wyatt and Siona each grabbed a table leg from Dryden. Wyatt immediately headed for one window. "Anything?" she called.

He shook his head. "They're out there, but they haven't made a move yet."

She turned back to the door and shivered. Her magick stirred, but she gritted her teeth. She would *not* lose control again.

Skeletal, clawed hands reached out, testing the barrier, but the wraiths hissed painfully and jerked back. Thank the Great Mother, the salt seemed to be holding them at bay.

Siona held two table legs, torn fabric already tied up into a ball on the ends. Wyatt had a flint but the sparks it generated weren't enough to light the fabric. Her fingers twitched.

Byron looked at her. "You can light the torches."

She didn't realize until he said it that she'd been thinking the exact same thing. The temptation to do it was strong. So strong her mouth went dry as a desert and smoke clouded her eyes.

Horrified with herself, she shook her head and held her hands up. "No, I can't."

He looked at Siona. Her mouth pressed into a thin line. Desperate, Greta grabbed her friend's arm. "Don't let me do it, Siona," she begged.

Byron pulled out a small tin flask from his pocket and threw it over. "Fine. Then a couple splashes of this will help," he said.

She gasped. "If you had that all along, then why—"

"No time." Siona stepped in and grabbed the flask. The strong scent of Mylean whiskey permeated the room as she poured alcohol over the torches. Wyatt scraped the flint again and again, but it was as if fate had decided to screw them over.

Across the room, clawed hands curved over the window frame. A blood wraith pulled itself up to look inside.

Instinct took over good sense as she lunged forward with her sword, slashing and cutting through the foggy threat.

The shadows shifted like a gust of wind blowing dead leaves around, but when it settled the wraith was still there. It growled. How did something like that even *have* a voice?

She turned at the distinct whoosh and crackle of a fire catching, feeling the rush of warmth at her back and an overwhelming relief that it wasn't coming from her. "I need one of those," she called out.

Siona tossed a torch right at her. Greta fumbled. Her heart stopped beating and she caught her breath, but she bent and caught it. Thank the Great Mother for good reflexes. The inferno that would have engulfed them all if she hadn't…

Siona shook her head. "That was too close, danem."

She didn't dare respond, turning to jab her torch at the wraith in the window.

Wyatt was headed to the other window, where two more wraiths were now climbing through. Dryden and his warriors manned the doorway. Wraiths hissed and cowered but didn't seem interested in going anywhere. Suddenly, one of the faeries screamed. Greta twisted around in time to see Siona standing with Dryden over the fallen warrior as a throng of wraiths piled inside. The salt line had scattered, leaving the way open.

Both Leila and Byron were breaking more table legs. All the faeries had torches now, but there were too many wraiths. They surrounded Siona.

The only substantial part of the wraiths were those teeth, and Siona cried out as a set sank into her arm. Greta's stomach heaved, and the magick heaved along with it. Another wraith latched itself onto Siona's throat. Her eyes rolled back into her head, and her lips moved in a soundless cry.

Wyatt was closer to Siona than anyone else. "Watch the window!" he called to Byron and crossed the room in two long strides.

He waved his torch in front of the wraiths that had started *feeding* on Siona. It was obvious that he was trying not to hurt her, but the wraiths practically ignored him. The threat of fire wasn't enough to scare them away now that the blood was flowing.

Without thinking, Greta started wiggling the imaginary

cork she'd been using to keep the magick contained. Just a little, just enough to let a tendril slip out for her to test.

She drew back with a gasp, disgusted that it was now instinct to reach for it for any little reason.

It was addictive in the worst way, and she was horrified to realize she'd been scheming against *herself*, looking for reasons to use it. If it didn't kill her this time, she *would* find a reason to use it again. And again. She would keep setting it free until it claimed her completely.

It swelled against her, pushing outward like a bloated stomach. *Oh, no.* She gritted her teeth. Her heart thundered with fear and loathing. How could she have been so stupid? So weak? So blind?

The cork wasn't as effective as it used to be, or maybe it had never been under control to begin with and she'd only been deluding herself.

The urge to blast the wraiths with every flame her body could generate was blinding. The only thing holding her back was the knowledge that she'd lose control of it all. Wyatt would have to help Siona.

"Do it." Siona told him, her voice a broken croak that Greta could barely hear.

Wyatt's jaw clenched. He nodded. Greta bit her tongue to keep from screaming at him to be careful.

Siona's fists tightened, but her knees wobbled. She was weakening. Wyatt jabbed the flaming torch through the wraiths, holding the end right up against her side. The sound of the wraiths screeching threatened to crack Greta's eardrums.

The creatures finally let Siona go. Wyatt threw an arm around her before she fell to the floor, but it looked like she was unconscious. He beat the wraiths back with his torch as they threatened to converge again.

More of them crowded through the window. They were going to be overrun and there was nowhere to go but all the way down. She considered it, but even if they survived without broken bones, the blood wraiths were on the ground, too. In the dark, they could walk right into a pack of them and not even realize it until the first drop of blood fell.

"There are too many," she called. The wraiths were even starting to tear at the walls to get in. They were on the roof, too, and she could only assume they crawled over every branch of the tree as well.

An ominous crack rent the night, and one of the outside walls was torn away. Countless pairs of glowing red eyes filled the dark space, clawed hands reaching inside as another spot in the corner of the room was opening up.

Greta frantically ran scenarios through her head and came up short every time. Except for one. One shot. If she was stupid enough to risk it—and risk everyone else, too.

The air crackled with more than just the flaming torches. The beast with its claws in her spirit cracked that great eye open.

CHAPTER SIXTEEN

Someone shook her.

Wyatt. He shook her so hard her head snapped back, making her realize she had no idea when he'd crossed the room, when he'd started shaking her, or how long he'd been calling her name in that high, frenzied voice.

The fine hairs on her arms stood on end as if she'd been zapped by electricity. Her skin was tight and ultrasensitive, and Wyatt's hands were almost painful.

"Greta, dammit!" he yelled. She blinked and shook her head as the black cloud receded and she felt that waking eye in her mind close to a thin slit, watchful but restful.

"Greta!"

"What? What happened?" She gripped Wyatt's arms to stop him shaking her. Her mouth fell open. The wraiths in the tree house were gone, but the entire place was ablaze.

He gripped her face with both hands and shouted her name again, still begging her to snap out of it. Oh, no, oh, no, oh, no. She'd lost control again.

She held onto his forearms, desperate for an anchor.

"Okay. I'm okay," she muttered, totally *not* okay. "What the—"

"What the *hell* was *that*?" he yelled. He shook his head and tugged her forward. "Never mind. We have to get out of here."

Oh, God, he wasn't wrong. She pulled back, but he let her go only after a long look into her eyes.

The blood wraiths screamed all around them, their inhuman wails echoing in the night and ringing in her ears. Dryden beat back the flames near an emergency trapdoor that had been uncovered in the center of the floor.

Siona was on the floor. She looked weak and cradled her arm close to her, but at least she'd regained consciousness. She stared at Greta with an intense look of focus.

Greta ran forward and fell to her knees in front of the hatch.

Blood wraiths immediately swarmed the door, but when they got to her they hissed and seemed to back away. Wyatt shoved his torch through the opening. Fire had already started to eat away at whatever happened to be supporting this structure, at the tree itself. She coughed, thick smoke searing her lungs.

The whole house shook. Wyatt threw himself over her. His body flinched and tightened as a shower of sparks and burning wood crashed down over them both from above.

When there was a break in the chaos, she pushed him aside and quickly brushed the glowing embers from his back, then tried to focus on finding clean air to breathe. "Everybody out," she called, holding the trapdoor open and gesturing for Wyatt to go first with the torch. She wanted him to help Siona, who was still looking pale, maybe even close to the breaking point.

Wyatt grabbed Greta's hand. "Not without you," he yelled over the roaring fire.

"I should remain with you as well," Siona said with a

frown that put deep grooves in her forehead.

"You can barely move," she yelled, shaking her head. All this was her fault, even if she couldn't remember exactly how, exactly what, had happened. She had to make sure everyone got out. "I'll be right behind you."

Neither of them liked it, but she shoved them toward the opening, and there wasn't time to argue. Wyatt helped Siona, carrying a torch at the same time, being solicitous of her injuries as only he could be. The surprise in Siona's eyes as she looked between him and Greta was just as obvious. She wasn't quite certain how to react. Was this the first time anyone had shown such outward concern for her well-being?

"Keep each other safe," Greta ordered. Wyatt looked like he wanted to say something, but she couldn't let him. If they were all going to get out of this thing alive tonight, she had to keep him strong and focused on something other than her.

One hand on the trapdoor, Greta was already ushering out Leila's handmaid, Jessa, who'd been standing close by, her eyes wide and fearful. Next came one of the faerie warriors. He'd been injured and slowly lowered himself through the opening, leaving smears of blood across the wood grain. A wraith suddenly charged forward, drawn most likely by the scent of the faerie's blood.

She automatically swiveled to face the threat. The wraith hissed and snapped, but surprisingly, it did not take another gliding, misty step toward her.

She grabbed a long piece of burning wood and swiped at the creature, but got the distinct impression that the fire wasn't keeping the thing away now, not when the fire was everywhere.

No, it was scared to come closer. Scared of *her*.

On the edges of her attention, she heard the faerie tumbling through the branches. Had he been attacked by wraiths in the tree? The blood would almost certainly draw more of them to threaten her friends—assuming they weren't surrounded down there already.

The prince and princess had to still be here somewhere. She searched the smoke for them, coughing like crazy, lungs burning. Her chest hurt and her eyes watered. She couldn't see anything but a blurry, twisting inferno of red and black. Something grabbed her.

Hold onto me, said a voice in her head suddenly. She gasped and jerked back, but Byron gripped her wrist. He was right in front of her. His jaw clenched and his gaze bored into hers.

Hold. On. It was him. She glanced down at his hand on her arm and realized the connection was allowing the damn faerie to get inside her head.

If she'd ever thought that having a goblin king in her mind was disconcerting, this was a thousand times worse. As soon as he was there, she had the eerie feeling that every faerie in existence was listening in as well. There was a definite sense of being left out in the middle of an empty stage, knowing that the seats in the audience were full but being unable to see any of them.

She shook her head, and Byron's touch eased. The feeling abated.

He dropped Greta's wrist altogether to heft his sister into his side. Leila was bleeding from a gash to the head. Greta started to go to her, but another coughing fit stopped her cold. Byron nudged her in front of him and put a hand on her shoulder. *Don't shake me off or you will not be protected.*

She nodded and realized that when he touched her she could breathe. She squinted and noticed Dryden by the hatch. He was surrounded as a few wraiths dared try to come back into the tree house. She started for him but he shook his head weakly. The wraiths were making a meal of him.

He pressed his lips together in a grimace. "Get them out,"

he said.

Taking a deep breath of air that tasted surprisingly fresh, she jerked away from Byron. As soon as she let go, the heat and smoke suffocated her once more.

Dryden scowled. "Take the prince and the princess to safety," he ordered sharply.

"This may come as a surprise to you," she snapped, "but I don't take orders from anyone, especially not a pathetic warrior like you." It was a cruel thing to say, but she was hoping to motivate him into action. Byron was going to have to put his sister down for either of them to climb the ladder, and Leila wasn't going to be able to do it on her own. They needed him.

She pushed forward, lifting her arm to shield her face from the heat, but there was really no escaping it. The flames licked across the floor under her boots, over her head. They singed her eyelashes and smoke filled her lungs, leaving no room for actual oxygen.

But every step she took toward Dryden was one less wraith attached to him. They hissed and shrank away from her. One even screamed when she swiped at it. She wondered who was more scared of the thing she'd become: them or her.

Dryden wobbled as the last wraith detached and skittered away. She reached out to hold him upright. He frowned down at her, searching her eyes, his flinty gaze filled with all the questions she had no answers to.

She gritted her teeth and shoved him toward Byron. "Time for *everyone* to go!"

She followed and pushed everyone toward the trapdoor, but it was hard to find amid the destructive chaos, and she realized that was because it had fallen shut again. Flames and smoke licked up through the floorboards. If she dared open it, would the blaze explode through?

They needed to find another way out.

She spun around and locked onto the window. It wasn't going to be much safer, but at least she could see some night air through the smoke.

The window was the only shot they had left. She cleared the way of debris and wraiths as best she could. Byron stopped and whispered something into his sister's ear. She blinked and opened her eyes.

Greta did her best to beat back the flames on one side of the window while Dryden did the same on the other side until Byron had helped Leila through and the two of them managed to make it onto the thick branches of a neighboring tree. It too was on fire but not yet burning completely.

"You will go next," Dryden yelled.

She shook her head. "If I go, the wraiths will swarm you again before you have a chance to get out."

"That was not a request."

She grabbed his hand and had to bite off a gasp at the ice in his touch. He *was* like Lazarus…or he could be if given enough time to mature. She didn't want to be around when that day came. In fact, she might actually be doing Mylena a favor if she left him here, now, just like he suggested.

She might have killed her fair share of the Lost, but she'd never killed anyone else unless there'd been no other choice. Dryden might have the potential to become a monster, but so did everyone else. So did *she*, apparently.

"Come on, we'll go together."

He moved with her to the window. The fire had already spread more, banishing the sliver of night that had been visible when the prince and princess escaped. Greta raised one arm to protect her face as she climbed onto the hot ledge. Dryden squeezed in beside her and they both jumped through the flames. She couldn't see for shit, but when her chest hit something hard, she frantically scrabbled to hold on. Beside her, Dryden grunted.

She coughed and coughed, almost losing her grip on the branch and feeling consciousness waver dangerously. She locked her arms and took a deep breath. The smoke was still heavy, and the fire scorched her back, but she blinked.

"Greta!" A voice from below. Oh, thank God. *Wyatt*. That had to mean he was okay, right? That they'd been able to hold back the wraiths on the ground?

She and Dryden clambered down through the branches as if the devil was on their heels. Finally, she hung from the last limb of the tree, and the blaze crackled at her back. Her grip slipped and she was barely holding on. She was running on empty, no strength left.

Dryden let go, and she tried to follow his progress to see how far she'd have to drop. It felt like a long way.

"Go ahead," Wyatt called. "I've got you."

There was nowhere to go but down. She let go with a whispered prayer. Wyatt's grip closed onto her hips and slowed her fall. Then he moved up to her waist and then under her arms, until her body was sliding down the length of his.

She couldn't *not* feel every inch of him against her, and when her feet touched the ground he didn't let go, only lifted her again and carried her away from the fire. She wondered if she could have stood on her own anyway.

Her cheeks burned, and it had nothing to do with the fire. He stopped and laid her down, holding her close. For a minute she lost herself in it. She hid her face in the curve of his shoulder, filling her lungs with the scent of sweat and smoke and, beneath it, the subtle hint of warm breezes and cool water that always reminded her of Wyatt, and of home.

But even though it should have felt comforting, she instinctively pulled back, and then she coughed, wincing against the chain reaction of painful scratchiness that went all the way down her throat to her lungs.

"Wait a minute," she croaked. She reached for her sword

and spun around frantically. "What happened to the—"

He squeezed her upper arms. "The wraiths are gone. I assume they'll be back once the fire burns itself out, but for now, at least that's one less thing for us to deal with."

That wasn't as comforting as it might have been if the fire hadn't still been such a major concern. She'd never seen anything like it. The tree was engulfed completely, raining debris and sparks, and the fire had already spread to all the trees directly adjacent to it. She couldn't believe she'd been in the middle of that. Her skin was still tight and painful from burns she hadn't even seen yet, and the scorched ends of her braids scratched the nape of her neck.

"What are we going to do?" A fire this size would spread quickly.

With one arm huddled close to her body, Siona put her other hand on Greta's shoulder. "There's nothing you *can* do," she said quietly. "The fire is too strong. It must burn itself out."

"It'll destroy the goblin forest." This was still Isaac's land, and there were countless creatures—big and small—who called it home. Isaac himself was somewhere out there. "I can't let that happen. I'm not leaving until it's under control."

"How do you plan to get it under control when you are the cause of the blaze?"

Byron was right. She had done this, which was why she had to make sure it was contained. Warily, she looked at Wyatt for support, but his expression was tight, worried. "We don't have so much as a blanket to beat back the flames with, Greta."

Leila straightened. She seemed to be recovering quickly from her bash on the head. "You're weak. You can barely stand. If you stay here, you'll die," she said.

Greta looked at the fire, feeling desperate and useless. What good were these powers of hers if all they did was destroy?

Siona looked at Dryden. Greta followed her gaze. After

a moment, his lips compressed, and he shook his head. Then Siona was looking at the princess. Leila frowned, but after a pregnant moment, she nodded. And finally, Dryden squared his shoulders and stepped forward.

That's what had been bugging her about the faeries; they never spoke directly to one another, only to her and Wyatt, and sometimes Siona. At first, she'd thought they were just quiet, but now it was clear that conversations between them were happening, just on a level humans weren't supposed to hear.

That was something she'd have to think about later. Now, Dryden came forward. "I will share my power with you, and you will use it to snuff the flames," he said matter-of-factly.

"I'm sorry, but what power do you have, and how exactly does one go about lending it out?"

He only looked at her like she was missing something obvious.

Greta crossed her arms, defensive.

He came closer. "Take my hand and open yourself to me."

Wyatt opened his mouth to argue, but Siona put a hand on his chest to hold him back. "It will work, and it might be the only chance we have to save the forest."

"Why do they care about the goblin forest, anyway? This isn't their land." He spoke to Siona, but he was looking between them all with growing suspicion. It was a reasonable question. One she'd been about to ask herself.

Byron opened his arms wide. "This forest provides as much protection and security to our borders as it does for goblin lands. None want to see it razed to the ground." He nodded to Greta. "And considering all of the progress that has been made between us already, if we have the ability to assist the future goblin queen in order to maintain good relations, it shall be done."

She winced at the word "queen" and noticed that Wyatt

had a similar reaction. He didn't respond otherwise, making her wonder if his tongue was bleeding from biting it.

She focused on Dryden. "What will happen if I do this? If you have magick that can help, why do you need to share it with me to put out the fire?"

His gaze shifted for just a second, and she thought she saw Leila sending him a loaded look. "I'm not strong enough," he continued. "But your ability can amplify my power."

It's not my *ability*, she wanted to say, but that wasn't an important distinction to make now. He might be right. She'd sensed how greedy the darkness was, always wanting more freedom and more strength. But if she gave it Dryden's power, would that amplify the insidious effect it was having on her?

Beside her, Wyatt was getting more tense by the moment. A live wire of angry volatility. He was telling her not to do it, not to risk it. The words hung in the air even though he hadn't said it out loud. Whatever she'd done up in the tree house earlier must have been bad. Really bad.

She shuddered as that blinking, knowing eye in her mind fluttered. The last thing she wanted to do was give the darkness more of a hold on her…and yet she also wanted it so much she trembled.

The forest was full of dry timber. If she didn't try to do *something*, how far would the fire travel? At this deepest time of night, how many Myleans would wake up surrounded by it, with no time to escape? How many of them wouldn't wake up at all?

She held out her hand. "Let's give it a shot."

Dryden took it. She refused to look at him, or Wyatt or Siona, and closed her eyes.

The rush of power was immediate. Dryden's ice crashed against the wall of black, smoky magick inside her. For a minute she thought that was it, a stalemate, but then the eye snapped open completely, making her body jerk. Instinctively, she tried to shut it back down, but it was already too late—there was no escape. Dryden's ice started to crack. Her power penetrated it, like oil that flowed into all the fissures, until it was everywhere, consuming everything.

Her mind flowed right along with it, and in the back of her subconscious she knew she was losing herself again. Not that she cared. The strength of it was intoxicating and pervasive. She was so focused on it, she didn't automatically notice the sliver of light entering her consciousness, like a blade slicing through mist to clear the skies.

Somehow, she felt more in the moment and realized that she actually had some control. Her magick was still awake, still soaking in Dryden's power, but she wasn't lost in it.

Siona. She had to be helping.

It didn't take long to understand exactly what Dryden's power was—or to realize that he was indeed a descendant of Lazarus. The knowledge was there, like seeing every gene and chromosome that put him together. It would have been distracting if she wasn't still hyperaware of everything else. Smoke. Heat. Flames. For once the urge to cause fire was less than the greedy urge to explore this new ability at her fingertips, so she started to put out the flames.

It was easy. So easy. Every time she reached for the magick it responded eagerly, and this time she'd fueled it with a limitless supply of perfect, extreme faerie cold instead of the blistering heat. She blew ice across the flames, sucking the oxygen right out of the air. In no time, the fire couldn't breathe. It sputtered to embers that glowed weakly under the thick sheet of new ice coating the branches and the ground.

And yet…she didn't stop. *Why would I stop?* Her grip on Dryden's hand tightened. He tugged against her, but she wouldn't let go. Not with all that power still at her fingertips.

Seize it. Use it. Keep it. The urge became a savage growl of possession until she was screaming into Dryden's face as he fought to be free of her.

Arms around her waist, jerking her back hard, even as she stretched against them like she was still bent over the branch up in the tree.

She fought to stay in contact with Dryden. *Mine. Mine. Mine.*

And then everything just stopped, like snuffing a match. For a moment all her senses went dark. She couldn't hear, couldn't see, couldn't taste the blood in her mouth.

When the world rushed back in, the pulsing darkness had retreated, but there was more ash coating her soul...and this time it hurt with the frigidity of ice.

"Wake up, please wake up." Wyatt held her. His voice filled her ear, startling her out of the furious haze.

This time she remembered exactly what she had done.

She pulled air into her lungs so hard and fast her heart couldn't catch up. "Get him away," she bit out through clenched teeth. She went from desperately reaching for Dryden to putting her hands up to ward him off. "Get everyone away."

Wyatt squeezed her closer and tucked his chin into the curve of her neck, like letting her go would be letting a tornado loose.

"Get them all away from me!" Her knees buckled so that the only thing keeping her upright was him.

Siona watched. Her gaze was guarded and sad, but she almost looked guilty, too.

Not your fault, Greta wanted to say, but the lump in her throat was too big. Her own guilt and disbelief overwhelmed her. *I wanted to save Mylena. Instead, I just unleashed another monster on it.*

"Wyatt," she sobbed, fingers clenched tight.

"Shh. It's okay." He murmured into her ear and brought them to their knees on the forest floor. "Just rest."

None of the others could touch her. She couldn't risk it

again. Only Wyatt was safe. And oh, God, that was a lie. Her teeth chattered. Her vision blurred. Her body was a pulsing mass of agony. Nothing was safe, nobody. Not from her. The darkness inside was wide-awake and salivating with hunger. It had a taste for power, she didn't think she could keep it down even if she wanted—

And that was the worst part.

She didn't want to keep it down.

"Rest, Greta," Wyatt whispered, rocking with her. His breath warm on her neck. "You'll be safe. I'll stay with you."

She closed her eyes. She didn't want to, but the cascade of pain and exhaustion was too much, and she couldn't keep them open for a minute longer.

CHAPTER SEVENTEEN

"Isaac!"

She knew she was in a dream. She had to find him, even though it was going to hurt like hell to see him like that again. "Please," she croaked.

Crashing footsteps sounded through the woods. Tears choked her as she ran in that direction.

Everything was so wrong. She was never supposed to be the one responsible for Mylena. She was never supposed to burn down the forest or traffic with faeries. And she was never supposed to have magick, especially magick so terrible it made the deadliest of creatures cringe in fear of her.

She was just supposed to be the ordinary, loner human who stayed mostly on the sidelines hunting the Lost, maybe offering advice or her sword arm every once in a while. Isaac was the one who needed to rule the goblin kingdom…because that's what he'd been born to do. That was his destiny. Not hers.

She felt his presence. He had to be close.

The morning sparkled, sunshine filtering through the branches of the trees and bouncing off the snow dotting the ground in melting little patches. When she looked up she even had to squint.

It was warm enough that she didn't need her coat. Granted, it was a dream, but either way, she stripped it off and left it behind, walking into the woods without looking back.

After what felt like an hour, she bent and pressed her fingers into the pads of a massive footprint in the mud. *There you are!*

Now she had real evidence that she was on the right track and picked up the pace. She covered his footprints with her own, going as fast as she could, but jerked to a stop when she came through a thick copse of evergreens and found herself in a secluded glade. *Their glade.*

The snow here was all gone. The ground was brown with mud and crispy, dead grass, and the sunshine that had felt so good now seemed to make everything look stark and barren. This wasn't anything like the romantic spot the goblin king had always brought her to in her dreams. But it was still the place, and if he was here that had to mean he remembered what it meant to them. He had to remember her.

"Isaac!" She spun around, searching, but faltered as she caught the scent of freshly spilled blood.

Something large had been dragged off to the edge of the clearing, into the shadows, leaving rivets in the ground that had softened with the thaw. The blood trail smeared with the muck, creating dark puddles before disappearing ominously into the bushes from where the distinct sounds of sloppy, greedy chomping emerged.

Slowly, she took a step forward. She rested her hand on the hilt of her sword. Her instinct was to draw the weapon, but she spread her arms out at her sides instead. "Isaac?" she whispered now, pulse racing, muscles tense.

The sounds halted, and she could imagine him in there with his head tilted to listen, maybe readying himself to launch out at her with claws pointed and sharp. Not for the first time, she wondered what would happen to her sleeping body if she got herself killed in one of these all-too-real dreams.

This is Isaac. No matter how far gone he was, if he could bring her to the glade where they'd had their first kiss, she had to believe there was a way to reach him.

One more step closer. She crouched a little, squinting to make out the shapes in the shadows. A hulking figure shifted, leaning forward over its kill. Eyes gleamed red, staring out at her.

Isaac?

She didn't say it aloud, but his head snapped up. Was that a line of blood trickling down his chin? She shuddered.

Isaac, it's Greta. Recognize me. Please. You know me.

His lips pulled back in a snarl, showing off just how sharp his teeth were. Wasn't there anything of the boy she knew in this...creature?

Come out. She didn't go any closer, staying at the edge of the tree line where the sunshine still reached. *Wait, stay there.*

Weak knees. Thin breaths. She didn't know if it was anticipation or fear that she felt. "Tell me I'm not wrong about this," she whispered.

Greta.

Her hopes skyrocketed like fireworks. Was it real, or did she just want it to be so badly that she'd started hearing things in her head? Fabricating the dream to fit her expectations?

He didn't move forward, but he didn't shrink farther into the darkness, and he didn't attack. He didn't move at all, as if he was going to wait her out and see if she would give up and leave. But she could wait a long time. For Isaac, maybe she could wait forever.

Her thighs burned holding the crouched position. She reminded herself that this was a dream and she was in control of it, and felt better immediately. The only thing she couldn't control was her own emotions. *Patience is a virtue.* Every hunter knew that.

As if they were tethered to each other through sight, Isaac never once took his gaze off her, and she refused to look away from him, either. If she did, it would be over. His entire body was a coiled spring, waiting to release and leap onto her.

"You *know* me."

She willed him to remember—

"You said my name." He rolled a lock of her hair between his fingers, his gaze fixed on her mouth. "You invited me in. You gave me the power."

"You can put up walls, Greta. But sooner or later I'll break down every last one. There won't be any secret you can keep or any part of you I don't know…intimately."

"The truth is right here." He kissed each of her eyelids, flattened his hand over her heart. "And here—"

Memories. All her memories of Isaac cascaded through her, pouring out in a river she couldn't stop—

"I know who and what you are, and I've already told you it doesn't make any difference—"

Did he know those were the very words he'd said to her? It seemed fitting that they should echo in her head now.

Finally, a paw inched forward. Her heartbeat tripled. Was he tired of waiting? Was he moving to tear her throat out? Or had she reached him, and now he was coming forward, hoping she would give him a chance?

He slowly uncurled himself from his…breakfast. She blanched as a hunk of mangled flesh that must have missed his mouth plopped from his fur to the ground between them.

He lunged out of the shadows.

She scuttled back on her hands as fast as she could, but he loomed over her, bloody paws in the ground on either side of her head, his jaws snapping less than an inch from her nose.

"Isaac, you don't want to do this," she stammered, the

pulse point in her throat hammering madly. His gaze dropped right there, saliva gathering on the points of his teeth. She shoved against him, warding him off.

The contact was as physical as anything could get. It slammed into her like a horned bull coming at her full tilt.

"Remember. Please remember," she begged. She pushed the memories at him, praying for something to work—

"It never mattered what you are, or what I should have done. Not since the very beginning. I fought my own uncle to keep you safe. I've fought my own people. I have no intention of letting the demon have you now. You're mine—*"*

He stopped midgrowl and tilted his head—

He reached through the rift, grasped hold of her arm. His eyes blazed with purpose. They held her as surely as his claws and with a final squeeze he pulled. She screamed as the portal tried to suck her back in, not wanting to give her up. "I won't let you go," he promised—

Her heart burst. He had to feel it, too. That raw, honest bond that had been between them since the very beginning. It hadn't broken. Not yet. If a demon couldn't break it, and a portal to another world couldn't break it, Isaac going Lost wasn't going to break it.

She flattened her hand over his chest. As she looked up at him, his eyes cleared.

His muscles were tense under her fingers, but the red film over his eyes faded a little more the longer she held the contact, and she could see the familiar amethyst tint in his pupils—

He sits beneath a snow-covered tree as Greta cuddles in his lap. Her mouth is soft. She's still asleep. He gently traces the curve of her jaw, the roundness in her cheek, waiting for her to embrace the reality of the dream and come to him. She arches her back, and a groan breaks from her parted pink lips. He watches her with both love and agony plain on his face.

"You are such a jumble of contradictions," he murmurs. "All that ferocity in such a tiny, vulnerable package. If only you knew that the moment I glimpsed the depths of pain beneath that gruff, prickly exterior, I'd have fought all of Mylena for the right to be the one you would let down your guard with—"

Another memory, but obviously it wasn't one of hers. This had to be his.

Isaac. It was Isaac.

"It's me," she whispered. "I'm here." Optimism and hope made her heart beat in choppy, irregular patterns. A constant, low rumble barreled out of his throat, but he remained still. Slowly, she dared slip her hand up his chest and along the tight cords in his neck, watching as his muscles twitched and jumped wherever she touched.

Her fingers trailed across the harsh line of his jaw. His fur was coarse and scratchy, coated in mud and dried blood, but she ignored all that, looking for *Isaac* beneath it all. The boy whose cocky grin could melt her heart, whose laughter knocked the pain out of her heart, whose whispered promises gave her hope for the future. He had to be there, somewhere.

Surprisingly, he let her touch him, and the longer they stayed in contact, the more he seemed to change. She realized that where her fingers touched, the fur covering his face had slowly started to recede, and she could actually see skin now.

"I knew—"

She felt dizzy. Her gaze focused on those jagged teeth. She hesitated and another memory ripped through her—

She looked down the rock face to the monster growling up at her. His claws dug into her ankle and he pulled. Her knee buckled and she scrabbled to hold on.

His nails went deeper, and she screamed. The savagery in his eyes was cold, making him seem like nothing more than a vessel for all of nature's violence and rage.

"Isaac, don't do this," she begged, pressing her cheek to the

frozen rock. He yanked harder. Her grip slipped—

Suddenly, the Isaac looking down at her now promised just as much violence, just as much rage. Maybe more. His lip curled and he reared back.

An arching pain in her side. Her head swam. The glade wavered before her eyes.

She drew her hand back with a hiss, but as she severed contact, Isaac's roar shook the fabric of the dream itself.

No! She jumped to her feet, stumbled, and went back down to one knee in the dirt.

Her head spun.

"I'm not ready!" she yelled, throwing her head back. She couldn't wake up yet. She might not get another chance like this!

Pressing her fist into her side, she pushed to her feet in time for Isaac to swipe his arm wide, striking her in the sternum and sending her flying across the glade.

She hit with a grunt and a thud and hurriedly rolled to avoid the fist coming down at her from above. It smashed into the ground right where her head had been.

Nausea and dizziness overwhelmed her. Isaac looked as wild and dangerous as he'd ever been.

"You're not getting rid of me. I'm not giving up!" she yelled at him, hoping the words penetrated that thick skull of his. She dodged his deadly claws and steeled herself to reach for him again.

She didn't get a chance.

Isaac's enraged howl was like a shrill denial echoing in her ears that followed her all the way to wakefulness.

CHAPTER EIGHTEEN

Siona's hand was on her shoulder as Greta jerked awake with the image of Lost Isaac barreling toward her still vivid in her mind.

"I think I can save him," she said, turning around and gripping her arm tightly.

Siona didn't have to ask whom Greta was talking about. "Danem, I know it is in your nature to want to try, but after the vicious attack earlier, you must finally accept that the goblin king is still Lost to us all."

"What if I could do it? Isn't it at least worth a shot?" She jumped up to her feet, but faltered as her pains kicked in. Siona stepped forward to help, but she shook her off, impatient. "He came to me in my dream. I touched him. I *made* him remember, I know I did. If I just had more time…"

"No," Siona said firmly. "We can't risk your life on a fool's errand."

"But if he's still reaching for me in sleep, then—"

"Have you considered that maybe he isn't the one initiating the dream connection? That *you* search for *him*?"

Her mouth dropped open. She shook her head. "That's ridiculous. I don't have that ability, Siona."

"Were you not able to appropriate Dryden's magick and use it for your own?"

Greta opened her mouth to object, but the words got stuck in her throat. "You think that's what I did with Isaac's power to enter my dreams, without even realizing it?"

Siona didn't answer. She didn't need to.

She might be right, but it didn't change her mind. Isaac might not control her dreams any more, but if she could control *his* instead, then there was still a chance to reach him again. "What if we've been wrong all these years, and a person who has gone Lost isn't completely irredeemable?"

Siona let out an exasperated snort. "Danem, you're reaching at nothing but air now. After hunting them as long as you have, you know as well as anyone that it's not possible to come back once Lost."

"You only say that because no one ever has before."

"The Lost are the Lost, nothing more, nothing less. You do yourself and his memory a disservice by ignoring this reality."

"I guess that makes more sense, doesn't it?" she said flatly. Sure, magick sounded more plausible than believing that a poor Lost creature had managed to retain some semblance of himself within the moon madness.

She hadn't realized just how high her hopes had risen until they plummeted right back down.

Wyatt approached, and Siona looked at the ground, her features pulled tight. "The faerie group will want to be underway shortly," she muttered and quickly left.

Greta stayed at the back of the group with Wyatt, watching the sky lighten as they walked and analyzing her dream, searching desperately for reasons to hope when all the evidence said there was none.

For once there wasn't a cloud anywhere to be seen. The

air was crisp and clean, tasting of springtime. They were traveling north, and the farther they went, the farther away from the small gnome and goblin communities they got, too, into territory she was less familiar with.

Whereas Isaac's lands made up the western counties and Leander's lands took up most of the southern counties, the section between Mount Laos and Mount Lunas where the faerie queen claimed dominion was relatively deserted and unmapped. That might be part of the reason why the Glass Kingdom was so difficult for curiosity seekers to find.

Greta glanced up at one point to find Siona looking at her over her shoulder with an expression that seemed to alternate between sadness, confusion, and pity.

Greta caught up with her. "You know, as a human in Mylena, I've had the great privilege of being treated with dismissal, hate, suspicion, and revulsion, and I manage to throw it off most of the time." She leaned in. "But if you don't wipe that look of pity off your face, I'm going to—"

"Danem, I meant no—"

"I won't accept it, not from you, Siona."

Her friend swallowed. Dryden called her, and she bolted for his side, looking relieved for the excuse.

Heart heavy with disappointment, Greta watched her go. She didn't blame Siona for feeling sad about Isaac. Maybe she should lay off the talk about bringing him back, as it seemed to upset her more. If that's *all* that was bothering her. Unfortunately, Siona hadn't opened up to her since before they joined the faeries, and Greta herself had been preoccupied with her own problems, but it seemed like there was some heavy stuff weighing on the goblin hunter's shoulders.

"We have to talk." Wyatt didn't even look at her when he spoke. He continued to stare straight ahead at the faeries' backs.

She groaned. "Do we really have to?"

Now his gaze jerked to her, anger and disappointment warring for mastery over his features. "So I should just shut up like the good little human and ignore the fact that you're killing yourself?" His forehead creased.

"I'm fine."

"That's bullshit," he snapped. Yep, he was definitely pissed. "Do you think because I don't wield a sword like I was born with it that I'm helpless or stupid? Maybe if I had some magick powers, too, you'd listen—"

"Be glad you don't." She stopped in her tracks. The prospect of the same overwhelming darkness being forced into someone good like him scared her stupid. She'd already seen him change so much, harden in a way that put sharp little chips and cracks in his optimistic confidence and sweetness. She hated to imagine those cracks continuing to spread. "Protect your humanity, Wyatt. Don't ever let anyone take it from you."

"Don't say shit like that." He grabbed her by the shoulders. "Every bit of you is human. Every bit of you is worthy. Whatever got hold of you is just a kind of sickness. We're on our way to making you better, and then we're going to get the hell out of here, okay?"

He was so fiercely determined. "No more crazy eclipses. No more human persecution. No more demon magick and black portals. We need to go back where we belong and live normal lives." He shook her gently. "Lives with safety and sunshine and baseball, where camping is just for fun, and the only scary monsters are the ones in movies."

Tears pricked her eyes. Not for her, but for him, because it was obvious that he needed all those things. This world was close to breaking him. He'd been so strong for so long, but without the boys to focus on, he was wearing down.

The urge to tell him a lie that would make him feel better was overwhelming, but he deserved better. "I want to say you're right and we'll get through this. That we'll find the boys, find a portal, and be completely happy far away from Mylena." Her voice was reed thin. She cleared her throat. "I want to make you all kinds of promises, but…I can't. I can't do that right now. Do you understand?"

"Just don't say no altogether, okay?" The determined light in his eyes didn't even flicker. "Don't do something stupid to save everyone else just because you think you're already on borrowed time. I'm not giving up on you, and you'd better not give up on yourself."

She laughed. "Since when have I ever done anything stupid?" She raised her hand at the look on his face. "Don't answer that."

He smiled and dropped his arms from her shoulders. They started walking again, but movement was agony for her, and she bit her tongue trying to keep in the cry of pain.

He noticed the stiffness of her gait and pulled her back again. "That gash in your side should have knitted together by now."

She pressed her arm across her midsection. Waves of heat radiated from the wound, but she didn't think she was coming down with fever.

He put an arm around her shoulder. "I don't like this. The more often you use that magick, the stronger it is, and the more damage it does to you."

"It couldn't be helped."

"How do you know for sure? The faeries have to know what it's doing to you, too. They could even have purposely looked for ways to bring that magick out of you, to make it stronger."

"They couldn't have known Isaac would follow us and attack, or about the blood wraiths."

"How can you be sure? They knew about the *bjer* and still insisted on taking that route. They could have known about the pack of blood wraiths, too, and purposely led us there. They could have engineered everything that's happened from the moment we met them."

"I'm the one who flipped my lid at Solem's Bridge. I'm the one who started that fire," she reminded him. "And they offered to help put it out."

"Yeah, by putting you in more danger."

"The entire forest could have gone up if we didn't do something quickly." Her head ached. A thick, pulsing ball at each of her temples.

Wyatt's frown deepened. He didn't like that answer, but he couldn't very well argue with her, either. The choices had been unequivocally clear: either risk her life to put out the fire, or risk losing hundreds of other lives, *innocent* lives, in the resulting carnage. She'd made the only choice she knew how to make...the only choice she knew how to live with.

"I don't trust them," he said, flexing his hands open and closed as if he didn't know what else to do with the tension inside him.

She knew how he felt. That kind of helplessness was the worst. "I don't trust them beyond a point, either, but they've saved our lives more than once now, and they haven't given us a reason to believe their agenda is anything but what they say it is."

"I still think something isn't right. And don't forget that I was there when Lazarus tried to kill you. He was merciless and brutal. How can you trust any of them when they're capable of such violence?"

"You think they're the only ones who are ready and willing to do violence?" she asked, stomach clenching. "Jesus, Wyatt, have you got any idea the kinds of things I've done in the last four years? It isn't being faerie or goblin that makes people monstrous."

"You were fighting for survival. That doesn't make you a

monster." He looked up the path where the rest of the group had all but disappeared from sight.

She shook her head. "Listen, if Siona trusts these faeries, then so do I. Unless something happens to challenge that, I have to."

"And what if I can't?"

She ducked her head. "Then maybe you should go."

Her chest hurt just thinking about sending him away, but maybe it was the best decision for both of them. There was a decent chance that he was right about the faeries. She might be putting his life in more danger with every step they got closer to the Glass Kingdom.

"Is that what you want?" he said. "It would be easier for you, wouldn't it? After all, if I left, you wouldn't have to choose."

She frowned. "What do you mean, choose? I want you safe."

"That's not what you're worried about, and you know it." He stepped closer, his gaze moving across her body like a physical touch that left her feeling breathless and uncertain. "If I leave, you don't have to keep pretending that you haven't already given up."

"I haven't given up on anything."

"Oh, I know you want to protect Mylena, find the boys, and save the goblin king from his own madness." He touched her cheek. "But you've given up on the idea of having a life that you choose for *yourself*." He leaned in and whispered in her ear. "And that's why you can't allow yourself to think of me as anything but another responsibility you have to manage."

"That's not true," she croaked. "Who says this isn't the life I wanted?"

"Is it? Or is it just the choice that's become easiest to bear? Believe me, you're not the only one who wonders if they've changed too much to ever fit in at home. Do you honestly think it's going to be easy to return to high school and contemplate life as an accountant after all this? That's what I thought I would be, you know." He laughed harshly. "You think you're alone, but you're not. I know you. I know you better than your long-Lost boyfriend, and as much as we both have doubts, we can find our way back together."

"You don't know me as well as you think you do," she muttered.

"Want to bet?"

That was a bet she'd win, hands down.

"I know you have nightmares every night. Not about the monsters of Mylena, but about being turned away by your own parents. I know you think loneliness must be better than that."

"That's where you're wrong," she scoffed. "Those nightmares are exactly about Mylena's monsters…because I'm one of them. Come talk to me about change and loneliness when you've done something so bad you can't get the blood off your skin for days, or when you've done something that haunts you even when your eyes are wide-open during the light of day. Something you can't ever take back." She shook her head. "You haven't crossed the line between good and evil, Wyatt, so you can't pretend to know what it feels like."

"And you think that you have?"

She *knew* she had. If not in the desperate years when she'd been willing to hunt and kill any poor Lost creature for a bag of coin, then surely what was inside her now was evil. That dark, oily magick couldn't be anything else…and the worst part was that, even knowing it, she wanted more.

Before she could move away, he slid his hand to the back of her neck and held her. His fingers delved into the fine hairs at her nape that had come free of her braid, making her shiver.

She put her hands on his arms, but she didn't know if she

meant to push him away or hold him close. She was confused by all the feelings choking her. "Are you going to leave?"

"Do you want me to?"

She refused to make a decision like that, but as he stepped into her like she was a doorway he could walk through, she wondered if maybe this was the real reason she'd told him to go, this topsy-turvy apprehension in the pit of her stomach whenever he got too close.

And he was getting closer more often, becoming bolder, as if he was trying to force her to acknowledge that he had just as much of a claim on her heart as anyone else.

He didn't wait for a real answer, maybe because he didn't want to know what she would say, either. He bent over her, and his breath teased her skin, his lips grazed her temple. Then he tipped her chin up and pressed his mouth to hers.

Everything stopped, even her heartbeat, as she held her breath and clenched her fists in the fabric of his coat.

She didn't know how to respond. Didn't know what to do. But as he pressed his hard body against her and his tongue slipped into her mouth, instinct took over. She pushed him away so hard that she knocked him off his feet.

It wasn't fair to compare him with Isaac, but she found herself doing it anyway. In her old life on Earth, Wyatt would have been perfect for her. He knew exactly who he was and accepted it with a grace and patience she truly admired. Maybe in part because she had no such patience, and was short on trust and optimism as well.

But she wasn't part of that life anymore. And it wasn't fair to lead him on. Her heart was spoken for, even now when everything was spinning down the drain and it hurt so bad she could barely breathe through it. But in their darkest moments, Isaac hadn't given up on her, and so long as there was the slimmest possibility of saving him—real or imagined—she wouldn't give up on him, either.

She winced. "I'm so sorry, Wyatt. I don't know what to say."

He stood up and straightened his shoulders. "You don't have to tell me. It was clear as soon as I saw you in his castle." He paused. "You love him. Maybe I just didn't want to accept it until now."

"It's not that I don't care for you—"

"I know. But it's not the same." He looked down, considering, then said, "But don't think this means that you can get rid of me." He smiled, and to his credit, it seemed genuine. "We're still friends, and I'm not going anywhere."

Siona's voice rang out. "If you're done, we've got bigger things to worry about." She sounded impatient.

Greta looked up to see her coming back along the muddy path toward them. Her gaze was shuttered, as if she'd seen Greta and Wyatt together.

"What is it?" Greta said.

"We are nearing the gates of the Glass Kingdom."

CHAPTER NINETEEN

Siona seemed nervous, wringing her hands together, her expression drawn tight. This was her first time returning to her mother's home since she was just a kid, right? It wasn't hard for Greta to imagine what that would feel like.

"It'll be okay," she said, taking Siona's hand. It was cold. She was reminded of Dryden and what she'd learned about his connection to Lazarus. "When did you know that you had some faerie magick?" she asked, suddenly curious.

Siona seemed to catch her breath and hold it, then glanced at Wyatt nervously.

"We don't actually have to talk about it now if you don't want to. I didn't mean—"

"No, it's obviously not a secret any longer." She gave Wyatt a shy smile before turning back to Greta. "Truthfully, I didn't realize I had any ability at all until I was able to help suppress the portal magick that I sensed in you. Before then, I simply believed I would never manifest any faerie magick of my own."

"Because you're only half faerie?" Wyatt asked.

She nodded. "Not all full-blooded faeries have magick. I assumed my goblin blood would cancel out whatever ability was contributed by my mother's blood. Besides, my skill with my blades has always been more than enough for me to do my job, so it never became an issue."

"But your mother did have magick, right? What was her gift?"

"I don't remember her demonstrating her power to me at all before she died."

"I'm sorry." Greta felt worse for asking in the first place.

Siona shook her head. "It's nothing." But it wasn't nothing. Greta was starting to be able to read Siona better, and she recognized the anguish gleaming in her eyes. The wounds of her past must still hurt like hell, and maybe it was harder for the strong goblin hunter to brush them aside because they were getting so close to the Glass Kingdom.

She decided to change the subject. "So what's the deal with the faeries talking to each other telepathically?"

"How did you—"

"It's pretty obvious if you pay attention," she said with a grin. "Can you do it, too?"

"No, of course not," she answered quickly. "Not since I was ejected from the Glass Kingdom."

"How does it work?"

"You remember I told you that every faerie mind is connected through Queen Minetta, and that this allows her to see through the eyes of any of her subjects?"

"Sure."

"The same gift also allows all faeries to communicate with each other along this same connection."

"And you're not part of all faeries?" she asked.

"Not for a long time." Siona looked her in the eye, and any pain or sadness she still felt about *that* was hidden well.

"But you were, at one point?"

She nodded.

"After having just one person thinking he can poke his way into my head whenever he wanted, I can imagine you must have been glad to be rid of it, right?"

Siona paused and a shadow passed over her features. "You don't realize how much you'll miss something until you have been barred from ever receiving it again." That sounded a lot like regret, but Greta wouldn't have pegged Siona as the type to pine for acceptance from people who'd turned their backs on her. She was too strong for that, too independent.

"If we're getting close to the Glass Kingdom, there are a few questions I want to ask the princess," Greta said. She stepped ahead and left Wyatt and Siona alone together.

As she jogged up the path, it became obvious that Siona had come back for her, not so much to tell her the news about the Glass Kingdom, but because she and Wyatt had fallen quite far behind and the faeries had probably wanted to check on her. Probably still had half a mind that she was a flight risk.

A rumble in the bushes made her pull up short, and she immediately drew her sword. She looked back to warn Wyatt just as something flew out at her.

She knew what it was even as she flew off her feet and crashed on the ground beneath all three hundred or so pounds of goblin king gone Lost.

Her sword was between their bodies, and she held him back by bracing it against his massive chest.

Blood dripped from his muzzle onto her cheeks, proving that this wasn't his first attack of the day. She didn't dare scream because Wyatt and Siona would come running, but her side was shrieking with pain and her arms were already shaking. She wouldn't be able to hold him off for long.

Isaac, please remember.

Could that work here? In the "real" world?

His jaws snapped less than an inch from her nose.

She shifted her hand and deliberately spread it open over the dirty, matted fur covering his chest. In her dream, they'd been touching.

Nothing happened.

In her dream, she'd been able to make him see her memories. How to do that here?

"Isaac, it's me, Greta," she said between teeth clenched tightly together. The more pain she felt, the stronger her need to let loose the black cloud of magick. Already it twisted and writhed like a storm that had pulled a field full of dust up into a funnel. "You know you don't want to do this."

He growled and curled a clawed hand around her throat, squeezing until she choked. Her arms buckled and she struggled to push him back before he could tear her to pieces, but she was failing very fast.

She blinked through the spots in her vision and saw Wyatt running for Isaac's back with her own dagger held high. She tried to scream but couldn't. Tried to throw Isaac off, but he wouldn't budge.

She felt the impact of her own weapon sinking between his shoulder blades and sobbed, but it didn't stop him. He reared up and spun around to face Wyatt. She jumped to her feet. The hilt was still sticking out of him, and she pulled it out before throwing both arms around his neck.

"Do it, Greta," Siona called, standing with Wyatt. "You must."

She didn't know what they were talking about until Siona pointed at the dagger still in Greta's hand. Isaac growled and spun, trying to throw her off.

The faeries were going to join the fray any second now. She needed to show him a memory that would shock him out of the moons' grip quickly, before they decided he needed putting down.

She closed her eyes and prayed there would be enough

time. "Remember what you said to me when you wanted me to say your name, Isaac?" She spoke as closely into his ear as she could and tightened her arms around his neck. "You said...you said we..."

It wasn't working. The memory wouldn't stick with her long enough to...

She was getting fuzzy and didn't think it was from pain. The storm of magick was so strong it swept away the words and thoughts and images she wanted to project before she could latch onto them, as if it didn't want her to remember.

He wasn't responding. She caught sight of Dryden out of the corner of her eye with an arrow cocked and ready.

Her breathing was shallow and raspy, and her lungs hurt. Her fingers slipped through his fur, losing purchase. A coughing fit overcame her, and she let go of him, collapsing on the ground. Blood-tinged spittle flew from her mouth into the muddy snow.

Before she could recover, Dryden let his arrow fly. Another joined it, both thwacking into Isaac so hard *she* winced from the hit.

He roared and turned to the faeries, but they dodged as he rushed them. When Isaac would have come back around, Greta stood and lifted her hand. She didn't have the strength to go after him with her sword, even if the magick wasn't battering away at her rib cage and her skull.

Siona was right. It was too late. The Lost couldn't come back, and she was only hurting everyone—including Isaac—by holding out false hope.

She should be the one to do it. She should—

Her fingertips sizzled. She was horrified by the eagerness that overcame her and scrambled to cut it out.

"I can't." She tucked her hands into her abdomen and bent over. Her whole body shook. "I can't. I can't." She looked up at Siona through a veil of tears. She couldn't save him. And she couldn't let him go free again, either.

But she couldn't kill him.

From the corner of her eye, she saw the arrows fly. Dryden and two others hadn't hesitated.

Isaac snarled and spun toward them, but the faeries were already nailing him with more arrows, and suddenly Dryden's icy power filled the air, too.

Greta jumped forward, but Siona held her back.

Siona shook her head. "Please, Greta. This is a kindness. He deserves to die honorably."

Isaac had fallen to his knees. His head hung between his hunched shoulders as he wheezed for breath.

"This isn't honorable, Siona." Greta sobbed. "This is the most unhonorable thing I've ever done."

Dryden stepped forward with another arrow. He looked to Siona, and she gave him the all clear.

No. She couldn't let him do it.

She opened herself to the magick, and a wave of heat hit the faerie warrior like a broadax to the midsection. He grunted and froze to the spot, a wide burn mark appearing across his chest. Mercilessly, she threw out another wave, and another. He put his head down and braced himself against the onslaught, but the storm swept him up, and he was caught in a vortex of ice cold. She was using his own power against him, because it was her power now, too. Of course it was. The beast was greedy, not willing to give anything back. It took, and took, and took.

Just as the maelstrom filled her completely, she felt a tug. Siona was clamping down, shoving the door closed. Greta instinctively rebelled, but this time Siona was ready for the pushback and was able to reclaim control.

Dryden recovered and with a shaky hand, he let his last arrow fly. Isaac shifted, but it still got him in the chest. He rose up with a howl that shredded her to the core.

Her heart broke, and with her last shred of control, she turned everything that was still Greta completely off.

She wiped all emotion from her heart. After all, hope hadn't worked to bring him back from being Lost. None of her cherished memories had worked. And if this was truly the end, she didn't want to mourn him. It already hurt too much.

Finally, she felt blessedly detached.

When Isaac collapsed into the muck and didn't move again, Greta turned and walked away.

CHAPTER TWENTY

They got moving immediately, Siona on one side of her, Wyatt on the other, and the faerie warriors completely surrounding them…much like a prison escort.

Greta stopped a few minutes later.

"I'll be leaving now," she said. "I've decided not to continue to the Glass Kingdom."

Two of the warriors immediately pulled back their bows and aimed them at her head. Byron and Leila looked at one another before Leila said, "Danem Greta, I thought we had a deal?" Her voice dripped with geniality.

"A deal that I've decided no longer benefits me."

"Why is that?"

"Because I don't want to rid myself of the demon's magick," she said simply.

"But what of your duty to the goblin kingdom?" said Leila. "Have you forgotten that war is imminent, and you do not have the resources alone to protect the goblin king's people?"

"The goblin kingdom is no longer my concern. I think all

would agree that they would fare better without me anywhere near."

Leila motioned to Wyatt. "Then think of your human friends. Who will help you rescue them?"

"That, too, is no longer relevant to me." Her needs were simple now. Power. Then nothingness.

Love, hope, responsibility, honor. Those were born of emotion and sentiment, none of which mattered. She only cared about amassing enough magick to give the demon what it wanted so there would be an end to the pain.

Wyatt started forward. "Greta, think about this." Gone was the Wyatt who'd wanted her to leave with him and forget about the Glass Kingdom. She didn't blame him. She'd gotten steadily weaker and stronger at the same time. More volatile, less reliable. In everyone else's minds there was no doubt what had to happen—at least in everyone's minds but hers.

"Without the faeries you don't stand a chance of withstanding the—"

"It doesn't matter anymore, Wyatt," she said, tired. She wasn't even sure the faerie queen *could* remove the magick, it was so entrenched in her every vessel and vein and cell.

The avaricious monster in her thought about daring them to try, though.

Byron crossed his arms. "I don't believe that we can allow you to leave our protection."

Her laughter was hollow and tinny. "*Allow?* You don't get to allow or deny me anything. I don't belong to the Glass Kingdom, the goblin kingdom, or any other part of Mylena."

He frowned. "You don't actually believe that you—*a mere human*—could best any one of my warriors if it came to that?"

"You've got to be kidding me, right?" She looked down her nose at the four who remained in the group, including Dryden. "Human or not, I can take you all on with my eyes closed. Even if you happened to have some decent powers to use against me, you've all seen what I can do with my own. You don't stand a chance and you know it."

She thought that would shut him up, but he actually smiled. "Can you really be so certain of your power?" He raised a cocky brow. "Or that we are so lacking in same?"

Byron's sister put a hand on his arm. He glared down at her, but it hadn't escaped Greta that she was the one in charge. He backed down from the hard line.

"Don't make a decision that you will regret when the smoke clears," the faerie princess warned.

Greta almost laughed again. She was the one with all the power here, and they knew it. Since they'd helped her unlock it, maybe she should thank them.

"Think what the goblin king would expect you to do."

She snarled. "You know what? He isn't here, and where he *is*, there are no expectations anymore." She didn't feel the connection to him now. He must surely be dead.

The idea of it threatened to make her crack all over again, but she tightened the noose keeping out her emotions and focused on Siona, who was very obviously standing with the faerie warriors. She was starting to realize that she'd been played. Not only by the faeries, but also by the one other Mylean she'd thought she could trust.

With a sneer she said, "Are you going to try reminding me about my responsibilities again, or maybe appeal to my gentle nature? Because I'm pretty sure I no longer have one, and truthfully, I never wanted any responsibilities."

"No, I understand why you're doing this. I can feel what's going on in there." She nodded in the general vicinity of Greta's heart. Greta imagined it was clogged and shriveled, suffocating from the sooty black magick that had invaded every single cell. Was she even pumping blood through her veins anymore, or if she looked down at the festering wound in her side would she find her blood was as black as tar?

"It hurts all the time now, doesn't it?" Siona said. "There's no room for anything but the pain…and the craving. The craving for *more*." Siona leaned closer, voice dropping to a whisper. "But just imagine the supply of magick available to you in the Glass Kingdom. All of it yours for the taking."

The idea had merit. The darkness craved more power, and she was beyond denying it now. Besides, taking magick from the faeries would help guarantee that they couldn't use those weapons against the goblin people. Even without her emotions, she could see the benefit in that.

"All right, I'll continue to the Glass Kingdom as long as it's clear to everyone that I'm no longer interested in having Queen Minetta relieve me of the magick. I only want to find the human boys for my friend and facilitate negotiations between the faerie race and the goblin race."

That was a lie, but she didn't actually care.

You still care, a weak little voice whispered. *If you do this, you're not the only one who's going to die. You have to care.* The monster sank its poisoned teeth, made of darkness and smoke, into her soul until that voice fell silent.

The terrain climbed steadily for the next hour or so. Large pieces of jagged, ice-covered rock jutted all over the place. There was something about the formations that creeped her out. As they passed one particularly rounded boulder, she reached out and chipped away at some of the ice with the heel of her hand. When it fell away, she found herself looking at a perfectly shaped mouth held open in a silent scream.

She jerked back. "What the hell is that?"

Siona stopped beside her, lips pressed together in distaste. "The Lamia have long cowered within the caves of Mount Laos," she said.

The Lamia? Agramon had made a deal with the Lamia to bring humans to Mylena. Twelve of those humans had been needed to open his black portal. To make sure nothing happened to those twelve until he was ready to initiate the spell, he'd compelled the assistance of the Lamia once again to turn the boys into stone.

She glanced up and examined the almost sheer rock face as inconspicuously as she could. High up the side of the mountain, at a height that made her want to throw up just tipping her head back to look, was a narrow outcropping and a series of cave openings that were really just cracks in the stone. But a body could fit through there.

"We must continue," Siona said.

She filed the location away but continued on.

Greta looked up again a little while later and gasped.

The Glass Kingdom. It had to be. But it hadn't been there a minute ago. The only thing she'd been able to see was more mountain, but then they'd turned a corner and there it was, hidden in plain sight.

The castle grew into the sky. So many towers, as if there'd been a hundred architects and each one had had a corner of the castle to work on, all of them needing to outdo the others. Some of the towers were tall and skinny, stretching to where the suns' pale light could bounce off pointed tin roofs prettily, while others were wide, as if daring the high winds coming off the mountain to do their worst.

And there were windows everywhere. Big ones, small ones, oddly shaped ones. But also crystal and mirrors. It wasn't hard to picture what the place must have looked like a week ago when the endless sea of white snow had covered everything, reflecting off all of those surfaces. It would have made the entire place look like a glittering ice palace...or a kingdom of glass.

Granted, it wasn't made completely out of glass. There was enough stone, timber, and iron incorporated in its structure to make it as sturdy as anything else she'd ever seen. But it was certainly a sight to behold. If Greta hadn't blocked out all emotion, she might even have found it beautiful.

Soon, they approached the gates. Monolithic carved barriers on massive posts the thickness of concrete pillars that looked strong enough to hold up the Golden Gate Bridge, they were made of some kind of burnished steel that shouldn't have existed in the backward civilization of Mylena, but she wasn't really surprised that the faeries had somehow found it. The gates towered overhead and looked ridiculously heavy, and no one person could possibly push them open to get either in or out.

Across the front something had been carved in a Mylean language Greta hadn't ever come across before...then again, she'd never come across faeries until recently, either.

"What does that say?" she asked Siona.

"Ever seeking."

"Seeking what? That doesn't make sense."

"Seeking all things. Wealth. Power. Strength." Siona's features pulled tight.

"Are you okay?" Greta asked out of simple curiosity. "It's got to be hard coming back here after the way they forced you out." She might have reached for Siona's hand before, but now felt no need to do so.

Siona looked as if she didn't know how to respond. Finally she said, "My concern now is for you."

Greta snorted and turned away. She noticed that the gates were actually open. Just enough to let people in and out—if they could pass the army standing guard, positioned at all angles and armed to the teeth with steel and arrows, which she supposed was in addition to whatever magickal weapon each one of them happened to be packing.

Did any faerie ever get a nice ability? Like maybe creating flower arrangements in the blink of an eye, or turning tubers into cupcakes? Not that it mattered. The seething monster inside didn't seem to care what ability it could snag. It salivated over them all, like walking up to a mile-long buffet table with plate in hand for the first helping.

She looked around, blatantly ignoring the fact that hundreds of pairs of eyes had immediately focused on her. She held her head high as they passed through the gates, but when extra faerie guards fell into step ahead of and behind her until she was completely surrounded, she started to get suspicious.

Her skin itched, and her fingers twitched with every step.

The prince and princess hadn't exaggerated the situation inside the Glass Kingdom. Greta could see why they would have petitioned the queen to open the gates. The faeries were seriously running out of space. Everyone was living on top of one another.

Up ahead, the castle that gave the kingdom its name cast a jagged shadow over the small portion of land that had been allocated for crops. The rest of the space within the walls was taken up by ramshackle housing, buildings so close there was no break between the walls, and the narrow streets were more like walking paths. Every available space was being used.

Faerie kind had always been reclusive, yes, but these close quarters would make anyone go stir-crazy. She wondered how Queen Minetta had managed to keep them all in here without a massive revolt long before now.

Not to mention, how many faeries had been left out in the cold when the doors shut? There must have been more than just Lazarus and Siona. Had they gone underground? Did they know they were the lucky ones, or were they like Siona and yearned to return?

Leila and Byron led the way. She felt like the virgin being paraded through town before getting carted off to the dragon's lair as a sacrifice. They kept picking up stragglers until the group that stopped in front of the castle doors had to be hundreds strong.

Although she'd generally liked to avoid busy villages for obvious reasons, Greta had been in her fair share of crowds, even mobs, usually after bringing in a particularly nasty Lost creature for execution. She'd never understood why everyone wanted to be there to see something like that. She could never look into those dying eyes and see anything remotely entertaining in it. Lost or otherwise, everyone deserved to meet the Great Mother with dignity.

That's why after the first few times, she'd made it a point never to bring in any of her bounties alive if she had a choice. Sure, it sounded cruel, but at least those creatures got the chance to meet their end on their own terms, and if they happened to best her in the process—never happened, but there was always that chance—then they'd buy themselves another day of freedom before the next hunter came along.

She did it that way not only for her and them, but for the families left behind when a father, brother, mother, or sister went Lost. They didn't need the double whammy of having to stand by while an entire village of their friends and neighbors cheered for their loved one's death on top of having to see that person in their Lost state.

So with her, at least, they had a better option. Instead of fighting *to* the death, she liked to tell herself she was giving them the opportunity to fight *for* their death.

That's the way she wanted to go when it was time. Fighting. Not strung up, helpless as the blade came down. Not with the din of a crowd of jeering strangers screaming obscenities in her ears.

A sliver of awareness broke through her haze as she took in the expressions on the faces of her "escort." Was that where she was headed now? To her own execution? With all these people eager to watch? Her battered soul didn't even flinch at the idea. Would her head roll, or would they hang her instead? Did they expect her to beg? Cry? They'd be disappointed in that.

This particular crowd was different than the others, if only because it was so quiet you could hear a pin drop on the cobblestone. There was no noise from anyone besides the shuffling of footsteps and the banging of weapons against hips.

The silence must getting to me if this is what I'm focusing on.

Suddenly, she looked ahead and realized that somewhere between the gates and this point, Wyatt had disappeared. Where had they taken him?

One glance at the strained look on Siona's face and Greta suspected two things: first, the eerie silence was only on the outside—the faeries' mental broadcast must be humming along at a deafening level—and second, Siona's avowal that she was no longer part of the telepathic highway had been a lie. It was so obvious.

Siona glanced over and saw Greta's frown. "What is it, danem?"

"Oh, nothing." She shook her head. "I was just wondering how many more lies you've told me."

Her face froze. Guilt flushed her cheeks just as the faerie procession stopped in front of the grand entrance to the castle, and Greta had her answer.

"I don't know what you mean."

Greta laughed and had her sword drawn before the sound could fade, but she didn't get very far. As she brought her blade down she was met with a clash of familiar-looking daggers crossed right in front of her face.

She met Siona's gaze across the gleaming steel. The goblin hunter's expression was dark and unreadable.

"So much for friendship," she said bitterly.

"Greta, you don't realize how much rests on—"

"You know what? I think you can go back to calling me danem."

Siona winced, but Greta didn't care. Had the hunter been lying from the very beginning? How long had she been colluding with the faeries? What did they really want from Greta? Or was this about Isaac? Had they planned to make him go Lost all along to leave the goblin kingdom vulnerable?

Once the idea took root, she couldn't let it go. Maybe Siona had been planted as a spy when she was still a child, with orders to wait patiently for the right moment.

Man, that took some serious patience and dedication.

That took a heart of stone.

She recalled all the times she'd gone to Siona for advice. Siona had been the one to advise her to give the faeries a chance. Every time Greta showed any uncertainty, Siona had been there to reassure her that this was the only way, that she was making the right decision going to the Glass Kingdom. She'd been the one who told her over and over again that there was no hope for Isaac.

The screech of steel against steel echoed between her and Siona as they strained against each other, arms trembling with effort, but so far no one had intervened.

Was that because Siona knew Greta couldn't win and had mentally ordered them to stand down? Well, the goblin hunter hadn't learned all of Greta's tricks these last few weeks.

"Don't try it," Siona warned as if sensing her thoughts.

"You're right," she said with an exaggerated sigh. "We're too evenly matched…"

She relaxed her stance and started to lower her blade. Siona reacted slowly, trying to decide if Greta was really giving up or…

She grabbed Siona's wrist and twisted, angling the hunter's own dagger toward her midsection. Siona jerked out of Greta's grasp in time, but Greta had expected that and was already stomping on the goblin hunter's instep, following that up with a knee to her face. Siona stumbled back, but she shook it off quickly and her blades came back up.

The faerie warriors had closed in, but Greta didn't engage them. She knew she was outnumbered, and her actions hadn't been about getting away.

She'd just wanted to see Siona bleed.

Her sword was plucked from her fingers as the warriors drew her arms behind her back roughly, but Greta kept her gaze on Siona and let a brittle smile twist her lips.

Greta glanced to the front of the crowd, where the faerie prince and princess stood in front of the door to the castle. They had known that Greta trusted Siona more than anyone else, and they'd used it to lead her exactly where they wanted her to go, just like a rabbit with a carrot on a stick.

She'd pretty much decided that this must be part of a plot to seize Isaac's lands, but didn't doubt that either way, she wouldn't have long before finding out for certain.

"It didn't have to be this way," Siona muttered, touching a finger to her lip and nodding at one of the faerie warriors standing guard. Greta's smile vanished as he gave Siona her sword and the goblin hunter slipped it under her own belt.

"Tell me one thing," Greta said. She winced at the tug on her arms as someone wrapped a length of rope around her wrists. The faeries obviously saw no more reason to pretend that she'd been brought here to negotiate.

She instinctively flexed, knowing the small swell of her muscles could theoretically leave a little bit of give in the bonds. Probably not enough to slip free, but it might be worth a shot at some point. "After all Isaac did for you...how could you purposely drive him over the edge and make him go Lost?"

"No, danem. We didn't have to do any such thing." Siona squared her chin, looking more like a faerie with every passing second. "You did that all on your own."

The faeries shoved her forward roughly until she stood

directly between the prince and princess in front of the gate.

The doors were shut.

"I guess no one's home," she shouted. "Or maybe queen bee just isn't in the mood for visitors."

She was getting lippy. It had been bound to happen. Something disconnected between her mouth and her common sense in times of stress. Sometimes she could get it back together before getting clocked in the face or punched in the gut, but maybe not after all she'd been through today.

Yep. Unsurprisingly, someone cracked her in the back of the head. She pitched forward, balance being one of those things that usually required the free use of hands and arms.

Someone else—assuming it was someone else and not the same person who hit her—grabbed her shoulder to keep her from tumbling face-first into the castle wall. With stars dancing behind her eyes, she snatched her arm back even before realizing it was Siona.

The door began to groan, and all the faeries seemed to hold their collective breath. Maybe she was about to get lucky and they would just forget to breathe altogether and keel over. A girl should be able to hope for something, right?

The groaning turned to a loud creak that echoed in the sudden silence, and the door swung open slowly.

By. Itself.

She glanced left and right. Good to know she wasn't the only one surprised by this, although she got the impression that the shock on the faces of the faeries was less about *how* the door opened and more that it was opening at all.

As they went inside, she looked around. It wasn't anything like she'd expected. The brilliance of the building's outer architecture certainly wasn't reflected within. She'd kind of pictured sunshine and color and the hustle and bustle that always came with a large demesne, but it was dark in there. Dark like no one was home. Like no one had been home for a long time. Maybe years.

Arms holding torches high shook just a little, and there was a kind of global hesitation. But then the faerie guards entered first, and others followed, flowing around her like she was a rock moored in a streambed.

Siona pushed Greta inside.

"You know your chance to get me to cooperate is long gone," Greta snapped. "I don't give a damn what your faerie bitch queen wants with me, there's nothing that could make me give it to her now."

Siona jabbed Greta between the shoulder blades with the butt end of her dagger. "You would do well to behave yourself," Siona warned in a low voice.

"Like I'm ever going to take advice from you ever again." She twisted halfway around and made sure Siona could see the disgust in her expression.

Siona shook her head. "I did warn you not to trust *anyone*."

She snorted. "And are you satisfied in knowing that you were absolutely right?" She quickly faced forward again, feeling no desire to look at Siona.

"I find no satisfaction in any of this, danem. You will not believe it, but this was the only choice."

"You keep telling yourself that," she muttered.

More faeries came into the castle. They started unboarding the windows and pulling open heavy, dusty drapes. Light finally filtered in, looking just as miraculous through all that glass as she'd thought it would. But the place still felt empty, cold, dead. It gave her the shivers.

"What's going on? Where is the queen? Why does this place look abandoned?"

Siona looked around with wide eyes as if she, too, had expected something different.

Greta snorted. "This place is big enough to house the whole damn village. What kind of queen lets her people live on top of one another like rats in the sewer when this place is here, sitting completely empty?"

Dryden approached with ice in his gaze. "Shut up," he said.

She huffed and would have crossed her arms if they hadn't been tied behind her. Five faerie warriors surrounded her, and she laughed.

Dryden frowned. "What could you possibly find amusing?" he asked.

"The fact that you faeries are supposed to be the most feared race in Mylena, and you're all scared of one human girl."

"If that's all you were, you would not be here. You would be dead." He made it sound so simple. They'd kill her. No qualms. No second thoughts.

She wanted her damn sword back so bad and played out different scenarios for taking it from Siona. Her jaw clenched with determination. It wasn't going to do her any good to try now, but there would be a moment. It would come soon, and she wouldn't let it pass her by. When that moment came, God help the goblin hunter if she tried to stand in Greta's way.

The faeries took her up a flight of stairs. She had a flash of hope and started to plan, until she saw that Siona was accompanying them, too. It might have been worth making a break for it against five of these faeries, even tied up like she was. But with Siona's magick-canceling power and combat skills in the mix, her narrow margin of success bottlenecked down to nothing.

The steps got narrower, the walls closed in. They were ascending one of the tall towers and didn't stop until entering a room at the very top.

She was shoved and stumbled to the other end of the room, mentally taking stock of her options.

When only Siona remained in the room with her, she made a run for the door. "Hey," she yelled, kicking it. "I won't try anything if you just take this lying, worthless *faerie* with you."

Nothing. She booted the door once more in disgust and spun around. It wouldn't do to leave her back exposed to a traitor.

"What did you do with Wyatt?" she demanded.

"He is being kept separate from you, but he will remain unharmed if you cooperate."

Siona knew her well if she was using such threats against her. What she didn't realize was that Greta still didn't really care about anything.

The hunter crossed the room to look out the only window. "The least you could do is untie me," Greta muttered.

Siona glanced back at her with raised brows. "I think not," she replied. "I plan to keep my head attached to my body."

"So what, then? We're supposed to just stand here staring at each other for how long? I don't think I can stomach your presence another minute."

Siona huffed with impatience. "You are making this more difficult than it has to be."

"*This?*" She sneered, leaning against the door with as much insolence as she could with her hands bound behind her back, partly to be forewarned in case anyone else decided to try and get in this room. "Did you really expect that I would just fall in line and help the faeries destroy Mylena?"

"No one is going to destroy Mylena. I won't *let* them," she said in a diamond-hard, determined voice. "You and I are here for my mother, and that is all."

She shook her head, epically confused. "Your *mother*?"

Siona crossed her arms. "My mother is the faerie queen."

"You said your mother was dead."

"That was a misrepresentation to protect myself after I was banished from the Glass Kingdom. If the rest of Mylena had known that I was Queen Minetta's daughter, I would have been used as a weapon against my own people."

"Calling it a misrepresentation still makes it a *lie*. You *lied* to me, to Isaac, to the only people who ever actually cared about you." Her stomach rolled. She should really be used to getting lied to by now, but it still sucked ass. "And if you lied about that, what other lies have slipped off your tongue?"

Her nostrils flared. "It's true. I wasn't cast out of the faerie kingdom because of my half-goblin blood, but I certainly wasn't welcome to stay, either. Once my magick manifested and everyone learned what my ability was, I became a threat to every faerie…including my own mother."

"If you do that canceling-out thing with everyone, I can see why the faeries wouldn't have wanted you around messing with their mojo. So why would they risk letting you back in now?"

"They didn't have much choice. I was the key to getting to you."

"Maybe the better question is, why would you *want* to come back?"

She didn't answer that.

"Well, then, what can they possibly want with me? Obviously, it isn't to *help* with my problem."

"The magick you inherited from Agramon is the only thing that might be able to save my mother." Siona's voice dropped to a whisper and she glanced toward the door. "If there were any other way—"

"I don't understand what she needs to be saved from. And why wouldn't you just ask for my help instead of this elaborate farce where you pretend to actually care? And"—she was on a roll now—"assuming there's something I could do, how am I supposed to manage it when I'm stuck in here with my hands tied behind my back, arguing with you?"

Siona gave Greta a piercing look. It was becoming obvious there was still something she wasn't telling. "Come on, Siona," she said, at the end of her patience and ready to drive her knee into the half goblin's stubborn nose just to hear the satisfying crack. "If you want my cooperation, prove to me that you didn't set Isaac up and throw the goblin people to the wolves just because you missed your mommy."

Siona lifted a hand in defense. "That was never supposed to happen."

Greta snorted. "Maybe it was always supposed to happen, but your new pals just didn't tell you that part."

Siona looked guilty and devastated, but Greta clenched her teeth. She couldn't afford to feel sorry for her. She had her own problems to worry about...*because* of her.

"If he hadn't rejected the faeries' offer of allegiance at the banquet, none of that would have happened. They would have invited him to attend before Queen Minetta in the Glass Kingdom as an emissary for his people, and he would have brought you with him."

She thought about that night and the gnomes who'd caused a scene—just in time for the faeries to swoop in and break it up, then offer an alliance with the goblin king. Isaac had turned them down flat. Even after their assistance, he hadn't trusted them. Maybe they hadn't expected that, and without an excuse to remain close by, they'd been forced to figure out another way to draw him away from the goblin castle, where he'd be more vulnerable.

Greta had been the bait. "He trusted you, and you set him up," she accused. "If only he'd known there was a traitor in his midst."

"I'm no traitor," she protested.

"Right. Because everyone who's completely loyal to their friends lies repeatedly and plots with murderous faeries campaigning to take over the world."

"You don't know anything."

"I don't need to know, nor do I care. Why don't you untie me, give me my sword, and make this a fair fight?"

"We aren't going to fight," Siona said, edging backward. "And we certainly won't accomplish anything useful arguing with one another. You need to listen and trust me."

"Okay, don't even untie me," she snapped. "All I need is my sword."

"We aren't going to—"

"You're out of luck, *faerie*. The opportunity to earn my trust was before you went and threw your lot in with a bunch of conniving—"

"Listen to me," she urged again, making a big show of putting her dagger away nice and slow. Greta raised her brows. Bold move when the only other person in the room was tied up. "Leila and Byron are the queen's first children, born hundreds of years ago when she was wed to the faerie king. He was an evil man, and his children are cut from the same cloth."

"Seems to me that's not a trait exclusively reserved for *his* children," Greta sneered.

Siona didn't rise to the bait. "My mother fled this place to get away from him, and that's when she met my father. Unfortunately, after his death she was forced out of the goblin kingdom and, alone and expecting a child, she had no choice but to return to the faeries."

"What did the king do to her?"

"Nothing, as it turns out. He was killed the very night she arrived."

"Convenient," Greta muttered, gritting her teeth against the pins and needles running up her arms. "So, what's the big deal? She's still the queen, which means the faeries didn't find that overly suspicious and hang her for his murder."

"Few mourned his death," she admitted, "and before his body cooled, Leila and Byron were already scheming to seize control. My mother wasn't about to let the Glass Kingdom fall into their hands. Her magick was stronger, and she successfully claimed the throne, but when I was born a short time later and it became clear what my power was, it was also clear that I would make her vulnerable. I was young, I had no control, and it was only a matter of time before Leila and Byron would find a way to capitalize on it, so she sent me away and locked the gates so no one could come after me."

"After I was gone, I learned that she was attacked by Leila and Byron. Everyone outside of the Glass Kingdom believed she was dead."

"Then what happened?"

"She retreated deep into the catacombs beneath the castle to heal, where she has remained locked away from the rest of the world and her people ever since."

Was she supposed to feel sympathy for Siona's messed-up family life? "So now you're going to help them finish the job they started trying to kill her all those years ago? Is this some way of getting back at your mother for kicking you out?"

Siona glanced at the door nervously and waved at her to keep her voice down. "I've let them think that, because I needed access to the Glass Kingdom," she said. "The gates are finally open after all these years, but they remain heavily guarded. I could never have walked in on my own."

Greta recalled how close they'd had to get before she could even see the castle walls, as if someone had gone to a lot of trouble to try hiding the whole kingdom. And then there'd been the hundred or so warriors manning the gates. "Nobody wanted you here, Siona. Even the faerie queen." Was it small-minded of her to take pleasure in pointing that out? She shrugged. Maybe she'd feel bad about it later.

"She's my mother." Siona said it without apology, like that was enough justification for her betrayal and lies.

"If she's been locked away all this time, how does anyone even know she's still alive?"

"I feel it," she said. "I've felt it since the eclipse. I think the shock that rocked Mylena when Agramon was banished from the world penetrated enough to bring her some awareness."

"Your *feeling* is not exactly proof."

Siona took a step closer, but Greta still wasn't ready to let her come near and took a corresponding step away.

"The gates opened. That, too, must mean she's awakening," Siona said stubbornly.

"Great. So then she can take care of herself."

"She's awakening, but not awake," Siona clarified. "Her consciousness remains trapped in the limbo state that kept her trapped all this time. But the deeper she went into it, the more it slipped out of her ability to control, and now she can't lift it. She is unable to return completely."

"How do you know this?"

"The same way every faerie knows it. She's been whispering in our minds." Siona's hands clenched into fists at her side. She didn't look happy for someone who'd just heard her mom was coming out of a coma.

"You actually think she's gone insane after all this time," Greta guessed. "That maybe this is the start of the end. She's getting weaker, maybe even dying."

"That's exactly what the prince and princess believe, and they think they can use both of us to strike against her now," Siona answered.

"If she does wake up, they're screwed, right?" A powerful faerie who'd lost her marbles would cause them as many problems as a faerie queen who'd simply wanted to reclaim her position and had no use for them. Either way, Leila and Byron weren't getting their hands on a throne unless Minetta was dead and gone for good.

"What does any of this have to do with us?"

"The dark magick Agramon called upon to open the black portal resides in you now. Leila and Byron will force you to use it to open the catacombs, and they think they'll use me to block Queen Minetta's ability if she rises and tries to retaliate against them."

"But that's not all, is it?" The scope and variety of all the lies Siona had told—not only to Greta, but to *everyone*—was staggering, but her true motives were starting to fall into place. "You want me to give them exactly what they want, but when your mom is free, you're going to *let* her blast them both to kingdom come."

She shook her head. "No, of course not. Leila and Byron will be dealt with mercifully."

That lie wasn't even a good one.

Greta had to know one more thing. "Are most of the faeries still loyal to the queen, or has everyone been taking orders from Leila and Byron?"

"They have a small following, but Queen Minetta is much loved among her people," Siona said with a smile. "You witnessed the procession as we entered the Glass Kingdom. Even though the faeries have spent many years imprisoned here as surely as their queen has been imprisoned within herself, they have not abandoned her now that the gates are open. They would go to the ends of Mylena to do her bidding, because she protects them. She keeps them connected to one another, and that connection is more valuable than food or water or air to breathe."

Greta had never known Siona to express anything with so much emotion. The always cool and collected goblin hunter was *desperate*, and desperation was a dangerous thing. A thing that could turn loyal friends into unwitting enemies.

Siona was telling the truth about Queen Minetta's predicament, and she was telling the truth about Leila and Byron's plans to take her down. She was telling the truth when she said she wanted to help her mother…but she was also telling the truth that the faerie race would do anything for its queen, that *she* would do anything for her *mother*.

It had made sense that Leila and Byron were behind all

the plots and conspiracies, setting gnomes against goblins and pushing the goblin king closer to the edge until he went Lost, so that when they were ready to claim the faerie throne and go after the rest of Mylena, their work would be half done for them.

But Leila and Byron weren't the ones Greta was worried about.

If it was true that Queen Minetta had been whispering to her subjects, getting them ready for the moment when Siona would eliminate her opposition for her and release her from her prison…it was because she had plans for Mylena.

And Greta shuddered to think what they might be.

"What if I just refuse to do it?"

Siona shook her head calmly. She didn't look worried about that at all. "Why do you think we crossed Solem's Bridge and made camp in a blood wraiths' den? Every moment of the journey was calculated to tempt you into using the magick more and more often."

Greta blanched. "Because you knew that once I started, it would be impossible to stop."

She nodded. "And because it needed to be *much* stronger in order to be able to free Queen Minetta."

By the Great Mother, none of them were sane. "You're all playing with fire, you know that, right?"

Siona flinched but stood her ground. "We didn't completely lie. When the queen is awake, she will be able to relieve you of the magick."

"As long as everything goes as planned," she said. "But you realize that nothing *ever* goes as planned, right? You're a hunter, you know I'm right."

"If you trust me, all will be well," she said stubbornly.

"Never going to happen again."

Siona frowned and drew one of her daggers and stalked across the room to stand before her. Had she decided that if

Greta wouldn't cooperate, she was too much of a liability?

The hairs on her arms and neck stood up, and she balanced on the balls of her feet, ready to defend herself even without the use of her hands.

"Turn around."

Greta shook her head. "I'm not going to make it easy for you. If you want to kill me, you're going to have to stab me right in the heart, not in the back like a chickenshit little—"

Siona hissed and grabbed her by the shoulder. "Turn around so I can cut your bonds."

Surprised, she'd let Siona push her almost all the way around before she reacted, but by then it was too late. An arm slammed across the back of her neck and shoved her face-first into the wooden door.

As she squirmed, Siona did exactly what she'd said she would do…she cut the ropes around her wrists.

Greta lashed out immediately, but Siona quickly retreated halfway across the room. Greta rubbed the feeling back into her hands and arms, contemplating her next move.

She decided to play it cool. For now.

"When are Leila and Byron supposed to come for us?" she asked carefully.

Siona let out a long, thin breath. "You'll help me?"

"You haven't given me much choice, have you? You fed the monster until it was out of control, and you know I won't be able to deny it. I just don't think you realize how big a hole you've dug yourselves. All of you."

"I apologize for deceiving you, my friend"—hearing the word "friend" from Siona's lips was like being gutted by a rusty iron spoon—"but when this is all over and the queen is freed, she has promised that I shall sit by her side. And I promise that you and your human friends will be free to leave Mylena, and we will aid the goblin kingdom."

The door opened and Dryden entered. He looked at

Greta's unbound hands with alarm, but Siona stopped him from drawing his weapon. "She has agreed to help the prince and princess."

"You believe her?" he said, skeptical. This guy might just be the smartest one of the bunch.

"Whether I believe her or not makes no difference," she answered. "I control her power, and she knows that even if she manages to escape this room, she will never make it out of the Glass Kingdom with her life unless she does what is required of her."

"What exactly am I going to be required to do?" she asked, crossing her arms.

Siona went to the door with Dryden. When she turned around, the desolate, unvarnished truth shone from her eyes. "You know that magick was never yours to control, Greta," she said. "All we're asking you to do is let it out."

CHAPTER TWENTY-ONE

Pacing never got her anywhere, and whenever she was shut in somewhere like this, she couldn't seem to stop. She was naturally restless, and with the dark magick throbbing and straining for action, she felt even more so now.

Part of her still wanted to believe that Siona wouldn't just walk her into something like this, something that had every indication of being the end of her. But the masks were all stripped away now, and there was no mistaking where Siona's loyalties truly lay.

Greta didn't even know if she could be mad…yeah, she could. But she wasn't. She was surprisingly calm.

Siona thought she was doing the right thing to save her mother. Trouble was, that kind of motivation couldn't be reasoned with. The goblin hunter honestly believed she was going to help Queen Minetta rise from this coma thing and her family would welcome Siona back with open arms just like they were all in a sweet fairy tale. She believed all the promises she'd been given and didn't even realize the irony that she'd broken her own promises every step of the way getting here.

Promises were like that. They were great big flashing neon arrows pointing the way toward heartache and disappointment, and Greta was done with them. She was done accepting them, done making them, done relying on them. If she'd learned anything since meeting Isaac, it was that life had been a heck of a lot easier when she'd only been out for herself.

Luke had died on her, Isaac abandoned her, Wyatt wanted what she couldn't give, and now Siona had betrayed her. All the people she'd opened up to, let under her skin, dared to care about, had left her alone over and over again.

That's why she'd rejected emotion. It had been a relief.

At first.

Without emotion she could look at the situation impartially. It would protect her from heartache and put a barrier between her soul and the evil that wanted to claim it.

But she was starting to wonder now if that same barrier was actually blinding her to something really important. Something she should have seen before now. Without her emotions she felt disconnected from her humanity.

Your humanity is all you have left.

It's what had kept her going. It's what had given her an edge. Those killer hunting instincts hadn't just manifested naturally like faerie magick. They'd come from sweat and tears and a *human* determination to stay alive and be the best.

"Protect your humanity. Don't ever let anyone take it from you."

She'd said those words to Wyatt and had believed it to be the most important thing she could tell him. Maybe she should start taking her own advice.

She looked around the bare tower room. It probably hadn't been used for anything in a very long time—much like the rest of the castle, it seemed—but chairs and tables and other furniture would have been wasted here. The windows went all the way around the perimeter. That vista was the only decoration the room needed.

She stopped pacing and went to look out one of them, but that only hammered home just how screwed she was. It was a magnificent view from up here, but she could see no escape. Faerie guards manned every tower. They were stationed on the walls and patrolled the grounds.

She gazed farther out. She could see more of Mylena here than from any spot in goblin lands. The mountains loomed to her right, and to her left was…everything else. In fact, she could almost trace the path they'd taken to get here. There were Eyna's Falls, and down from that somewhere would be Solem's Bridge. And there was the goblin forest.

She strained to see more than just the landscape. The evergreens themselves were tiny from this height, nothing more than a great blob of green and brown with large patches of white. Impossible to pick out anything in particular…like an individual.

Something had been stuck in the back of her mind for a while. Something she'd been trying to ignore because, well, she and hope apparently didn't play well with each other.

But now that she was standing around with nothing to do but wait—likely for the last battle of her life—hope had started poking its head back into her business. If there was any time to give it one last chance, that time was probably now.

But could she do it? She still hesitated. There'd been very good, sane reasons for shutting away all her emotions in the first place. Opening herself up to that again could be a brutal mistake. If she opened herself up, she'd have to deal with what had happened to Isaac.

Isaac.

Just his name was enough to shock her out of her daze, as if the real Greta had been waiting for any opportunity to escape the dead, empty place she'd been shuffled off to.

She bit her lip and everything tumbled back, all the anguish and the pain she'd been trying to leave behind. But with it came a niggling feeling that Isaac was still out there somewhere.

Guessing. Hoping. It was all part and parcel of relying on emotion. And maybe it was only her imagination, but it felt like their link snapped back into place. Maybe it wasn't his death that had severed it for a while, but her own decision to reject her love for him. In denying her emotions, she'd denied their bond.

She pressed her forehead to the cool glass. The hot tears flowed. She couldn't stop them. The arrows. The blood. Isaac's crumpled form. She shouldn't keep hoping—it would only hurt more.

Even if he lived, he's still Lost.

Greta had been in Mylena, hunting the Lost, for four years and had never once heard of anyone coming back from it.

And yet...

And yet.

She needed to sleep if she was going to know for sure.

Yeah, like that's going to happen.

This wasn't exactly the place to purposely put herself in such a vulnerable position.

Dare she risk it anyway?

She had to. Not only because she couldn't bear to sit here just waiting for the faeries to come back, and not only because this could be her last chance to see him.

I won't let you go. He'd said those words to her in Agramon's lair right before he pulled her out of the black portal. *I would bring you back from death itself if I had to.*

She turned away from the windows and slid down to the floor, then tipped her head back against the stone wall and closed her eyes. Being able to doze at the drop of a hat wherever she happened to be was a necessary skill when you spent your days and nights hunting, and she'd never had any problem before.

Her eyes were open again a second later, though. She watched the door, listening for movement on the other side. Her mind was a locomotive, rushing along, pulling train cars behind it. All of them were filled with another problem she was trying not to worry about. There was the Isaac car, and the Wyatt car, followed by the car with all the rest of the boys. Then there was the Siona car, and the faerie car, and the magick car, and—

She drew her knees up to her chest and folded her arms over them. The only way to get to sleep was to clear her head. The only way to clear her head was to make sure it was focused on only *one* thing.

"Isaac," she murmured. Her throat tightened until all she could taste were the salty tears. Shame and self-loathing overwhelmed her. Had she really let them kill him and not even felt an ounce of remorse? If the cost of escaping her own heartbreak had been at the expense of his life, she might never be worthy of love again.

She swallowed and closed her eyes again. It was easy to picture his face. The harsh angles in his cheeks and chin, the intensity of his amethyst eyes, the unrepentant quirk in his lips when he grinned—which he seemed to do only for her. She imagined that he was there with her, that she could feel his body radiating heat like a gigantic oven right beside her.

She let out a long breath and tipped her face to the side, as if he was sitting there and would lean in and plant his lips on the vulnerable pulse point beating in her neck. She could almost feel his arm curving around her shoulders and drawing her closer, his hot breath against her skin, his whispered words tickling her ear. *I'll never let you go.*

Her breathing evened out, her lashes fluttered.

When she opened them, she was still locked in the room at the top of the faerie tower, but she was asleep. She knew this because he was there.

Not beside her, not kissing her, not holding her. Of course not. He was still Lost, crouched on all fours across the room, his face a mask of wild, violent hunger as he snarled. Although he looked around the small, enclosed room, one eye was trained on her.

This might not have been such a good idea. She didn't really want an answer to the question of whether or not her physical body would die in the waking world if she were killed in a dream.

Making no sudden moves, she slowly put her hands on her knees, shifted her weight, and pushed herself to a standing position.

"Isaac." She had his full attention now. He went so still she could see the tense muscles in his torso quivering. Did that mean he'd recognized his name, that she was reaching him?

He didn't immediately try to rip her apart, but she wouldn't say he was exactly lucid. He was little more than a cornered animal, ready to strike, eager to strike, as soon as she showed him an ounce of vulnerability.

Neither of them moved. They stood staring at one another for what seemed like forever, with Isaac maintaining a constant, low growl. She kept talking, calmly telling him who she was and who they were to each other, but it wasn't working, and something had to give.

She had to make contact. Last time, it was touch and memory that seemed to give him that tiny moment of clarity.

The tower room was a circle. She edged along the wall as slowly as she could. His growls increased in volume, but she pushed another step. He lunged at her with a brutal snap of his jaws an inch from her nose, and she froze, heart slamming.

He circled her, and she shifted her back to the wall. "Isaac," she said again. "Don't let the moons control you. You're stronger than this. You can overcome it and come back from it. You can come back to *me*."

Big mistake. Her voice had risen with her agitation, and he reacted with a roar. He swiped at her, showing every intention of taking her head off, and she raised her arms to block, but that left her side exposed.

His claws went into her like knives sliding through butter. She screamed, the pain immediate and excruciating, every bit as real as she expected it to feel in waking life. Her legs collapsed under her, and her hands clutched his arm for support, even though his claws were still embedded in her gut, coated with her blood.

Her vision blurred, but he was right there. He leaned over her. How did she get on the ground? She blinked and squinted up at him.

She was touching him. *Touch.* Her fingernails dug into his forearm. Was it working? His face was so close to hers, but her vision was too blurry to know if his eyes were still red.

I won't let you go. I won't let you go.

"Isaac," she whispered, but even one word was hard to get out. She finished on a gurgly cough. That couldn't be good. She let her head fall to the side, feeling the grit from the stone floor clinging to her cheek just as her blood was sticky on her skin.

The memory that came to her was from a late afternoon shortly after the first time they'd met, before they really even knew each other, definitely before there was anything between them other than suspicion and mistrust. She almost ignored it and tried to think of something else, but it was the one sticking with her as her blood splattered onto the floor—

A farmhouse. Deserted because the goblin mother and two babies who had lived there had been slaughtered the night before by the goblin husband and father, gone Lost.

These were the scenes that horrified her the most. Thankfully, they didn't happen often. She chased a lot of bounties into the woods, into the mountains, into the Brimstone Caves. After all, the poor souls got the name Lost because something in their lives had caused them so much distress that they couldn't deal, and they wandered away, both physically and metaphysically. Giving in to the moons left them free to bask in the freedom the Great Mother offered with her wild embrace—or so she'd heard.

But sometimes the Lost lingered—they didn't seem to want to leave their civilized lives behind—and Greta had often wondered if the ones who stayed somehow still felt something for the people they left behind and were trying to find a way back.

Of course, it had always ended in bloodshed and screams... and a doubling of the bounty.

When this bounty had come down the pike there'd still been time to stop him from killing. If only she'd been quicker, but it had taken her a full day to track him here. She hadn't expected him to return to his home.

She'd crept across the field leading up to the house as quietly as she could, ducking behind fences and boulders on the way, to stay out of sight.

The creature stood outside the house, howling his heart out. It was haunting and horrible. There was no way to miss the blood coating his fur and smeared across his jaws.

A shadow moved near the side of the house.

Crap! Who was stupid enough to get near one of the Lost? Besides herself, of course.

The creature broke off midhowl and snarled before taking off...right for whatever had moved near the house.

She gave up the pretense of stealth and started running.

With her back pressed against the stone wall of the building, she took a deep breath and peered around the corner. The thing about being a bounty hunter, you always ended up doing the job in the dark. That just seemed to be how it went, and this time was no different. That didn't make it any less unnerving, especially tonight when the moons were barely visible through a thick cover of clouds.

She shook her head. Who would have thought the same girl whose bedtime had once been a respectable nine thirty on weeknights would, only four years later, be out scouring the land for monsters at all hours of the night?

A soft noise made her shiver. She adjusted her grip on her sword and rounded the corner ready to take down the Lost…

Only to find herself face-to-face with the goblin king.

"What are you doing here?" She hissed in an impatient whisper. "Do you realize the danger you're in right now?"

"And good evening to you, Danem Greta," he murmured in a low voice that sent tingles up her spine.

She shook them off and scowled. "If you know what's good for you, just stay here out of my way, and don't move."

His raised eyebrow said exactly what he thought of her giving him orders, and when she spun away, he stepped in close behind her. Way close.

She fought to put his presence out of her mind as they slowly made their way around the perimeter of the house. Where had the Lost creature gone?

The goblin king's hand fell on her shoulder. She turned, and he held a finger to his lips. She couldn't help but stare, but then he pointed over her head, and she looked up, steeling herself against everything except the job.

Open window. The creature had gone inside the house.

It was about three feet too high for her to reach and climb through on her own. She looked at the goblin king. She looked at the window. She looked at the goblin king.

He grinned, and it tugged at something inside her despite

her determination not to pay any attention to him. "Would you like some assistance?" he asked.

Her gaze narrowed in warning. "No funny business. Keep your hands to yourself."

His forehead creased. "Then you do not *want me to lift you up?"*

She sighed. "Yes, I want the damn boost. Hurry."

She turned to face the wall and he came up behind her, his hands closing around her waist. She was immediately warm all over, immediately distracted. Focus on the job, Greta. *She bit her lip and looked up at the window.*

He lifted her and she wobbled. Startled, her hands flew down over his for balance. He quickly readjusted his grip. She wasn't touching the ground. The front of him was plastered all against the back of her, and he held her at just the right height to whisper close in her ear. "I've got you."

Her heart thumped wildly, but she nodded. "A little higher," she murmured. "I still can't reach the window."

He pushed her up another foot. His strength was impressive. She was tall and far from dainty, but he hadn't even grunted against her weight. His breathing was a little hurried, but hers was, too.

She gripped the windowsill and pulled herself up, pausing to make certain she wouldn't be ambushed halfway through the opening. It looked like a bedroom. Mostly empty except for a small cot in the corner. A child's room? After climbing inside, she turned around to call down for the goblin king to wait right there, but his big body was already squeezing through the window. Impressive.

"Do I have to tell you not to get in my way?" she asked impatiently.

He looked down his nose, but obviously felt her comment didn't deserve a response.

A noise drew both their attention. It sounded like something scratching in the walls.

They made their way out of the room. The floor of the hallway was covered in wet, dirty footprints the size of pontoons, leading to a set of narrow steps.

The attic.

She and the goblin king approached slowly and carefully. She started up, sword in hand, thankful that he seemed willing to let her take the lead.

At the top of the stairs, she readied herself to attack, but what she saw froze her and she didn't know what to do.

The Lost goblin knelt before a closed door, his hand spread open over the thick wood, claws scratching, scratching, scratching. He'd almost scratched a hole right through, but surprisingly he probably could have just bashed the door in and been done with it if that's what he'd wanted.

Beside her, the goblin king cocked his head. She caught the sound at the same time.

Crying.

On the other side of that door, a baby was crying.

Shock and alarm flooded her with cold, and she took an instinctive step forward.

The creature spun toward them with a snarl. She had a half second to catch the bunching of its muscles before it sprung for her.

She shoved the goblin king back so that he was forced to take a couple of steps down the stairs, out of harm's way, and then she positioned herself protectively in front of him.

The close quarters worked to her benefit. The Lost didn't have anywhere to go, no way to avoid her blade. It was over in moments.

The goblin king pushed past her and went to the door. She looked down over the dead creature and murmured her apology like she always did when forced to take a life. When she glanced back up, the goblin king was coming back out of the attic room with a bundle cradled in his arms. Her chest tightened.

She looked back down at the thing that had once been this child's father. "Do you think he knew?" she murmured. "Even in that Lost state, could he have remembered?"

His brow furrowed. "You hunt them. Have you ever known one of the Lost to retain knowledge of anything once the moons have taken them?"

She shook her head. Of course not. "But what if—"

"For one so accomplished, your heart is soft." His gaze seemed to probe just a little too closely for her peace of mind.

"We should get out of here."

He stepped forward and reached for her hand. "Thank you for your assistance this evening, Danem Greta. This child will live because of you."

Was that supposed to be a good thing? All of her family was gone, and she would be completely alone in the world—something Greta wouldn't wish on anyone. "I was just doing my job."

"Isaac."

She started. "I'm sorry, what?"

"My name," he reminded her.

She crossed her arms. "I know what your name is. And now I also know you tricked me into saying it the night we met." Maidra's tavern. A cozy table in the corner. Hours of talking. He'd made her believe in the possibility of friendship in this crazy world…only to realize she'd been duped.

He only grinned. The damn goblin had no shame.

She stomped down the stairs. "I'm out of here."

"I'll see you in your dreams," he called after her with a chuckle that made her blood boil—

Maybe this wasn't the way to bring him back. If there'd been a window of opportunity, maybe she'd already missed it.

"Greta."

She gasped and glanced back up into his face, her heart skipping a beat. His voice. *Isaac's* voice. Raspy and guttural like he'd been swallowing knives for the last several days, but beautiful to her ears. "You—" Cough. "You said my name."

He looked at her, his red eyes clearing.

"Isaac," she whispered. She reached up to touch his cheek, but nausea and dizziness hit her suddenly like a ton of bricks. "No!" She clutched his arms desperately. "No, I can't go yet," she cried.

"Greta!" His voice took on the snarl again.

He held her tighter, but she was already half gone. His face faded and his roar was muffled, and all she felt was his fury and the claws digging deep into her skin.

Chapter Twenty-Two

It was not surprising to find Siona standing over her when Greta awoke, but the concern and worry in her expression wasn't what she expected.

"What? Did you think I was dead and you had lost your sacrificial lamb?" she snapped. "I needed a nap."

Isaac. Hope and fear warred. Had he really beaten the odds and escaped the pull of the moons? Could she already have pushed him back over the edge by leaving him?

Siona eyed her pityingly. "He can't return to you, danem. You won't find him in your dreams ever again."

She ignored the hunter and got to her feet.

Siona finally said, "It's time."

Greta glanced out the window. Night had fallen, the moons were full. "Oh, goody." She crossed her arms and cocked her hip. "So that's it? I don't even get a last meal? You're here to escort me to the gallows?"

"The process may not result in your death." She had the good grace to at least look ashamed of herself.

"Gee, don't sound so confident."

Siona didn't blink. "It will go easier if you cooperate."

"I'm sure that's what you tell all your helpless sacrifices."

She crossed her arms. "Don't profess to say that you have ever been helpless in your entire life. I have never met a stronger, more capable…or more honorable person."

She opened her mouth, but the snarky comeback she'd planned wouldn't come. Why give her a compliment now? Did Siona really think that would compel her compliance?

Greta swallowed back the bitterness that threatened to become a tidal wave of regret.

Even if Greta could overcome the prejudices of the Mylean people and force them to accept that she wasn't weaker or inherently evil or whatever bullshit they got it into their heads to believe about humans, it would never change a thing. They would never see her as one of their own. If Siona could so easily sacrifice Greta when she was supposed to be one of the ones who cared, then why should anyone else feel differently about her?

The more she'd fought for her place in Mylena, the more she seemed to be losing everything she'd decided to stay here for.

It was time she stopped trying to be all the things that everyone else seemed to want her to be and showed them that she was a force to be reckoned with all on her own. It was time Mylena realized just how strong humankind could be.

And if that left her alone again when all was said and done…so be it.

The door opened and Dryden stood outside with lots of backup. Greta lifted her chin and went to meet them. One of the faerie warriors moved to tie her hands again, but Siona stopped him. "Don't bother. She isn't going to try anything."

But Greta returned the warrior's wary look with an evil grin. "Do you really want to risk it?"

Siona pushed her forward. "Do not antagonize them,

danem," she hissed in Greta's ear.

Greta was led back down the long staircase. She'd expected to be escorted to some kind of great hall, so when they actually left the castle and started wandering along a meandering path on the grounds, she was surprised.

"Um, this is a nice tour and everything, but where exactly are we going?" Had someone decided to have her taken out back and shot?

Of course, nobody answered, and she got a jab between the shoulder blades when she slowed down.

Finally, they entered a courtyard with a large stone structure at the opposite side of it that looked like some kind of mausoleum. Leila and Byron stood in front of it. For the first time since she had met them, they were dressed in something other than gauzy, flowing robes. Both of them wore leather and steel just like real faerie warriors.

She lifted her brows at the blades strapped to their waists. "I hope you actually know how to use those. It would be such a shame if you hurt yourselves," she said, dripping sarcasm. "Let me give you a tip. Keep the pointy end facing up, would you? It'll save me time later if you've already stabbed yourselves."

Greta was glad to see the smug complacency on their faces waver just enough to be noticeable.

She looked over their heads at the monstrous tomb. The double doors were two stories high, made from solid granite. They'd been polished and etched, and something was written above them in an ancient Mylean script.

"What does that say?"

Siona said, "It's the equivalent of 'None shall pass.'"

She turned back to Leila. "It doesn't sound as if your queen wants to be disturbed."

"Our queen has hidden herself away on the other side of these doors for too long. She has abandoned the faerie race, consigned all of us to rot right along with her, and no longer has any right to the throne."

"The faerie people aren't going to let you just take over as long as there's a glimmer of hope that she might kick this thing and return some day."

"They will if that hope is removed." Leila glanced at Siona.

"So why do you need me to open the door?" Greta prodded. "And how do you even know I can do it? If none of you have been able to get the job done…"

"All our efforts to overcome the barrier spell have failed," Leila admitted. "The only magick that has a chance of working is that of the black portal, which is so powerful, it opens doors to other worlds."

She crossed her arms. "I'm not going to do it."

Byron glanced up over her shoulder. "For their sake, I suggest you rethink your position," he said. She jerked around at the sound of shuffling steps.

Wyatt, Ray, and all the rest of the boys were being led into the courtyard by a contingent of faerie warriors. Ray's face was pulled back in a tight snarl, and his face was covered in bruises, but Wyatt looked worse. His eye was swollen shut, and he had a long, nasty gash cutting through his coat across his chest. Blood stained his clothes, making her wonder how deep those cuts went.

Thankfully, besides being put in chains, the others looked mostly unharmed. She drank in the sight of them with a heavy heart before turning to Siona with an accusing glare. "You promised Wyatt wouldn't be hurt. And you *knew* the boys were here the whole time, didn't you?"

Then again, maybe not. Siona looked bewildered and winced at the cold, dark look in Wyatt's gaze before he pointedly turned away from her. She turned to Dryden then, her expression accusing and betrayed.

"It's time." Leila stepped forward, nodding toward the big

mausoleum with a beatific smile. Greta was getting so sick and tired of that fake sweetness. If the opportunity arose before the end of all this, she wouldn't think twice about wiping it off her face.

"I won't do it," she repeated.

"We have no quarrel with humans, Danem Greta. If you fulfill your promise to give the queen your dark magick, we would be happy to release your friends and ensure that all of you are returned to your world."

Siona stepped forward and shoved Greta until she stood in front of the massive chamber door.

"Don't do it, Siona. I can't stress how very bad this is going to be," she begged in a low voice. "If the magick gets out of hand and my friends are caught in the middle, make no mistake, I *will* come after you," she warned.

It was already crawling up her throat, sensing danger, sensing opportunity. She tried to tamp it down, but it wouldn't be held back. It was stronger than ever…stronger than Greta.

"You have to trust me," Siona murmured. "The queen will set everything to rights once she has been freed."

She couldn't bring herself to trust the faeries, but she wanted to trust Siona.

She had no choice. It didn't take much now, and the magick would not be denied. She focused on the mausoleum as the least deadly option. The massive doors had no handles to grip. No visible lock to pick. Nothing was getting through until the right person said, "Open sesame." She flattened her hand over the seam and stood there for a long moment.

There was…something. Some kind of resonance coming up from the ground, infusing every stone that had been used to build the faerie queen's tomb. The vibration compelled her, taking all of her concentration. It was a little like music—there was a beat to it. It traveled up her arm into her chest and became the beat of her heart, connecting her to the rhythmic thumping coming from the other side of the door.

It called to that other consciousness inside her and sent it rolling up from the pit of her stomach into her throat and her head until her whole body shook.

She understood somehow that it wasn't really the door that was locked, but the queen herself. The frustration and rage coming from the other side was almost as oily and black as the thing inside Greta. The queen was definitely alive. Alive and angry enough to punish the world. To rain fiery destruction over everyone.

Did Siona realize that her mother had gone insane? Did she realize that the thing that had awakened inside that chamber had no ties to family, to the faerie race, or to Mylena? This creature only cared about escaping this prison and making sure that no one could *ever* lock her up again.

She couldn't do it. There was no way she could let her out. She'd rather hand over the faerie kingdom to Byron and Leila.

As she pulled back, the queen's impotent fury bowled Greta over both physically and mentally.

She barely registered the hands on her arms. They were the only thing keeping her on her feet, but the jolt against her mind left her vulnerable to the black cloud that clogged her throat. She choked on so much dark black magick that she tasted it in her mouth. She tried to push it back, but it became obvious that Siona was actively preventing her from doing anything other than overloading the spell.

The queen was drawing the magick out of her now. It felt like razor blades dragging through her veins, and she couldn't even slow it down. Hopelessness brought hot tears to her eyes, but then she sensed something else.

It was powerful and fierce. Familiar.

It fortified her, infused her with added strength. She felt as if she could actually do this.

Greta could see the spell now, like a coating over the inside walls of the tomb, with deep claw marks everywhere as if a caged animal had been let loose within. Perhaps the queen would be able to break the spell down all by herself if given a little more strength and a little more time, but Greta understood why Leila and Byron couldn't allow that to happen.

Queen Minetta might have been a good mother and a decent leader at one time, but that person was gone now. This was no loving mother who just wanted to be reunited with her child, no unfortunate faerie who was only grateful to be free. Queen Minetta was crazy. Homicidally crazy. The kind of crazy that made mass murderers.

How could Siona not sense it? Was she so blinded by guilt and the fantasy of getting her mother back that she refused to see what the seclusion and incarceration had done to her?

She hated to take Leila and Byron's side, but they'd been right to want to end her, no matter their motives. Now it was up to Greta to take down Queen Minetta before she opened those doors.

A crash of steel filtered through the struggle going on inside her. The sense of reinforcement heightened. Exhilaration pumped through her veins, fighting off the darkness.

Thank goodness, she wasn't alone anymore.

Isaac.

Isaac was here.

The thing inside her took advantage of her distraction. The eye opened wider, glowing, eager, its endless blackness threatening to swallow her up again. Then it surged full speed ahead, a runaway snowball that continued to grow as it rolled over onto itself again and again.

Her chest constricted with shock and worry. *Nothing* would stop it now—not even Siona could get in the way of this.

It was stronger than ever before. It had fed off her long

enough to build enough strength not only to free the faerie queen, but to free itself. It didn't want to hide inside her anymore, it wanted to seize control once and for all.

Of her. Of this world. Of *every* world.

Agramon.

She screamed as the truth became obvious, desperately throwing barriers up as fast as she could, but it was no use. They were torn right back down again.

"Siona, stop." She couldn't speak above a whisper, but the goblin hunter heard. She just wouldn't allow anything to put a lid on the magick until her mother had been released.

"Don't do it!" Every word was torture to get out, and in the end there was no time to warn her about the epic firestorm that was about to be unleashed on Mylena.

Because Agramon was already here.

CHAPTER TWENTY-THREE

"Siona," she called again, struggling weakly to claw her way out of the darkness. "We have to stop it." Even while saying the words, she knew it was impossible. Siona could no more put a halt to the black storm anymore than she could. Agramon had all the control.

How could she have known? She'd left the demon helpless and alone in the nothingness between worlds. And yet, she should have known. This oily black magick had come from the portal spell he'd created. She shouldn't be surprised that he would find a way to use it against her again.

He wanted to turn Greta into the instrument of his rise to power, just like the faerie queen. Except this time he wouldn't simply kill her...he would eradicate her soul and defile her body by taking it for his own.

Energy continued to flow from her through the stone of the mausoleum. Inside, the queen paced back and forth, silk robes slipping across the floor. Greta could see it as if the walls were made of glass. Suddenly she stopped and looked up. Her silver eyes were threaded with ice blue—nothing like Siona's eyes—and they stared right through the stone. Then she smiled.

Greta bit her lip. She wanted to call for Isaac so badly, but refused to do it. He was almost here, fighting his way to her, but if she distracted him, he could be in more danger.

Siona squeezed her hand. "I was wrong. Very wrong," she whispered. "The woman in there is not my mother."

The pain and grief in her eyes spoke volumes about what she must have been hearing, seeing, or feeling from Queen Minetta as the cracks in the spell keeping her contained widened. "There's no saving her, is there?"

Greta shook her head. "I'm sorry. I wish there was, but—"

Pain slashed through her belly, bowling her over. She fell to her knees. Siona still had her hand, and Greta gripped it tightly.

"What is it?"

She clenched her teeth, fighting for consciousness. "Agramon," she spat. "The source of the portal magick. The demon's inside me, and he…*wants…out.*"

Isaac howled. He sounded so close.

And then he was there. Big and alive, and kneeling at her side. He pulled her into him, and not a single claw dug into her skin. Her whole body melted at his gentleness.

She looked up. His eyes were beautifully clear and full of pride, faith, and love.

"You're here." She sobbed with relief, thankful to see him again before…

He squeezed. "This is not the end," he promised with a growl that brooked no argument. "If your love can save me from the moons, then mine will protect you from the demon."

Leila and Byron were busy fighting for their lives as Isaac's soldiers flooded the courtyard.

Goblin warriors, dwarves, sprites, even ogres and gnomes,

they had all come. He'd led an army against the faerie gates!

She glanced up just as Wyatt spun around and wrapped his chains around the neck of one of the faerie guards. The look in his eyes chilled her to the bone.

What have I done to him? The lengths he'd been forced to in such a short time, all because of his association with her. She shuddered.

Siona stood over them, hand covering her mouth, shock and guilt etched on her face as she looked at Isaac. "How is this possible?"

Isaac turned to her with a snarl, but Greta clutched his hand. "Don't," she whispered. "She's suffered enough."

Agramon flexed inside her skin…*pushing*.

The pain ratcheted up again, and she gasped, holding her stomach. It was happening. He was seizing control, cutting her off. She felt it in every organ of her body, every nerve and vein and blood vessel. Would she simply wink out of existence, or would she remain trapped inside her own shell, unable to do anything about it? No, she doubted Agramon would allow any part of her to remain. He wouldn't want to share his new body.

"Isaac," she gasped, afraid.

"I'm here." He sent reassurance and strength through the bond. "I came back for you. You must fight this for me." He glanced up at Siona. "Can you do anything?"

It must be so hard for him to ask her for help. He was still so angry with her. Greta should be angry, too, shouldn't she? But it didn't matter. She couldn't waste energy feeling hate when these could be her last moments.

Isaac would *hate*. He would *hate* to hear her think like that. He would *hate* to think she was giving up. He would *hate* to say good-bye. She had to make sure that didn't happen.

"She's human," Siona said. "She was never built for the kind of power the demon burdened her with. If she could focus long enough and hard enough, her body's natural reaction would be to expel it from her body…"

"And he'll follow. He'll go where the magick is," Greta choked out, certain of it. "Agramon won't bother taking over a body that has no power."

The trick would be regaining control of it long enough to get the job done, and hoping she didn't kill herself in the process, since the more she opened herself up to the magick, the more Agramon's evil spread into all the nooks and crannies of her being.

Then the double doors of the mausoleum creaked open… and there was no more time.

She looked up to see Wyatt and Ray herding the boys in her direction. Both of them had divested themselves of their bonds and procured weapons. Greta leaned on Isaac as she struggled to her feet.

"We may have a small window of opportunity to take down two birds with one stone," she said to everyone.

She couldn't do it alone, but she could do it with them. Her friends supported her. These people cared whether she lived or died today. These people accepted her for the flawed but determined fighter she was, and didn't care where she'd come from, only that she was here now, working with them to preserve the goodness in this world.

"I can help," Siona said in a tight voice.

Greta nodded. "Okay, good. Because I'm going to need you to help me focus."

"I will not leave your side," Isaac said, as if he expected her to make him go.

She nodded and squeezed his hand. She couldn't imagine him being anywhere else. "The magick has always reacted to threats against me. If the demon thinks its replacement body is in danger, it will be too busy fighting off the threat to realize that I'm siphoning everything I've got into the faerie queen behind its back."

He frowned. "How do you propose to put yourself in such danger?"

She glanced over his shoulder. "I don't think it's going to be a problem."

He turned around in time to see Leila and Byron bearing down on them, flanked by the icy Dryden and a retinue of faerie warriors.

Isaac roared and engaged Dryden before the faerie could raise his bow. Greta urged Wyatt and Ray to get the boys behind her. "Keep them far back," she said. "I'm going to let the faeries come at me."

"Screw that," Wyatt snapped.

Siona glanced at her in shock. "Danem, the king would never—"

"Isaac won't let me be hurt too badly," she assured them. "But he understands that the demon needs to see the threat as real."

Reluctantly, Wyatt nodded at Ray and they all retreated. Byron and Leila stopped in front of Greta and Siona. "You will finish what you started," Byron demanded with a desperate look in his eyes. "The queen cannot be allowed to exit the catacomb."

"Come over here and make me," she said with a grin.

He did just that, socking her in the face so hard her head snapped back.

Shit. That *hurt*.

Byron pulled his sword this time and came at her again. Siona tossed her one, too, and she dodged. She didn't need to get stabbed to feel like she was in danger. She *was* in danger.

"Wyatt, get out of here with the boys," she called back to him, worried. There was a distinct and very real possibility that this could go very wrong.

He settled at her side. She glanced back in shock. Ray

and Sloane had positioned themselves in front of the younger boys, a thick wall of rock at their backs. So far, they were being left alone.

She snapped the gold chain from her neck and thrust it at Wyatt. "Go."

"Forget it."

"I'm not saying this is it," she yelled, blocking Byron. "But you're going to get back home to North Dakota and give this to your sister when you see her again."

His shoulder bumped against hers as he took on one of the faerie warriors, the chain still dangling from his fingers. "Greta, I'm not—"

"No, don't say something ridiculous like you aren't going anywhere without me. If you get the chance, you *go*. Do you understand?" She threw him a hard look. "You *cannot* become like me," she said, breathing heavily with exertion.

He finally stuffed the chain in his pocket. "Don't you want me to give it to your parents?"

"God, no," she laughed. "It's probably better if my parents never find out what happened to me."

Isaac dumped Dryden's body, but Greta noticed that the faerie warrior was still breathing. She took a deep breath and locked gazes with Isaac. His expression was grim, but she felt his strength and confidence flowing through their bond. He would never let her say good-bye.

She dropped her sword and faced Byron. Isaac gritted his teeth but didn't move. The creak of the mausoleum doors snagged her attention, and she saw the faerie queen's hands slipping between the crack. Those skeletal white fingers gave her the shivers.

Byron could easily have run her through with his blade, but she was betting that he wouldn't risk it. If she died, the magick inside her would be useless.

He hit her again, and Greta went down. Isaac wasn't going

to stand for more. She saw him leap for the faerie prince. She gazed at them through blurry vision. Her skin tingled with heat.

"Siona!" she cried. Siona clenched her jaw and came closer. They clasped hands tightly and faced the stone mausoleum together, but she sensed the surge of magick hurtling outward.

She tried to ignore everything that was going on around them. For weeks, Agramon had been busy setting hooks into every part of her, and now she methodically went to each one of them and pulled until she screamed. She tore them out of her heart, out of her head, out of her soul...and she shoved it all outward just as the mausoleum swung all the way open and a tall, emaciated figure with long white hair emerged.

A massive thundercloud of oily, writhing darkness poured out her mouth, her ears, her eyes, and Siona helped her send it hurtling toward the faerie queen like a wrecking ball.

The queen stopped in shock and surprise, but as it hit her she laughed and spread her arms wide, welcoming it in. Her gaunt features started to fill out immediately, the wrinkles in her skin smoothing out. Soon her skin was glowing and healthy looking. Her brittle white hair turned lush and black, her lips reddened, her eyes glowed. She was sucking in the portal magick like a balm, looking more and more like her daughter by the second.

Could they have made a mistake? Would Siona falter now? Her mouth was set, her expression tight, and she was mumbling under her breath. It was impossible to hear above the sounds of the battle raging around them, but Greta could read Siona's lips.

I'm sorry. I'm sorry. I'm sorry.

Greta mumbled the same thing and squeezed her hand tighter. Together they kept pushing, funneling all the darkness outward until a giant cyclone twisted around the faerie, trapping her within it. As Greta's arms lifted, she watched the queen's gleeful grin twist into a grimace of pain and her eyes widen. She must have realized that the barrage wasn't going to stop, and now she was being overwhelmed with more power than she could safely absorb.

Suddenly, the demon rebelled, blinding her with immediate, epic pain. She lifted her hands against the mental walls dropping down on all sides of her psyche. They moved in like the walls of a booby-trapped tunnel, tighter and tighter until she couldn't move, the air was thin, and the light was all gone.

This was it. She'd failed.

The faerie queen had regained her strength and would lay waste to Isaac's kingdom before moving on to all the others. Even worse, the demon was making his move. He was squeezing her out so that he could rise again. And this time he wouldn't be confined within the depths of a mountain. He would be free to terrorize countless worlds.

No! She'd brought the goblin king back from being *Lost*, damn it. She could *do* this.

Because of you I will never truly be Lost. You can always call me back. Just like she made Isaac stronger, he made her stronger, too. And she could not…could *not*…lose this fight.

Not when she'd finally realized how rare and special what they'd started together was. No king and queen anywhere were going to be as good together as they would be. She was finally going to prove that not only was she good enough for Isaac and good enough to stay in Mylena, she was good enough to *rule* Mylena.

Greta sucked in a breath and felt for the source of the pain. It was deep inside where her lifeline lived. She grabbed hold of the last thread of black magick still hooked in her, like a sticky tentacle wrapped around her ankle dragging her down into the dark, cold depths…and she pulled.

CHAPTER TWENTY-FOUR

Consciousness returned in a rush of heat and screams, but she didn't have to wonder who'd caught her when she fell. She'd know that possessive touch anywhere.

An agitated Isaac snarled and snapped at Wyatt, who was bruised and shaking, brandishing Greta's own sword—where had he found it?—like he was ready to run the goblin king through to get to her.

Funny enough, if she had to choose which one of them looked closer to the edge, she was more worried about Wyatt.

She tried to lift her hand and play referee, but all the relevant muscles protested. It made her stop and take stock. Agramon? Was the demon gone?

"We have a problem," Isaac said. He squeezed a little too hard, making her cough and groan, but he got her attention.

Her heart leaped, and she twisted in his arms. "Oh, crap."

The demon had left Greta, all right. She didn't have to search inside herself to know for sure…because all she had to do was look into the eyes of the malevolent creature glaring both ice and fire down on them from the doors of the faerie queen's tomb.

Siona stood guard, facing off against her very own mother. Greta hadn't counted on that.

She couldn't let her stand alone. She found reserves of strength in the deepest parts of herself, places Agramon hadn't been able to reach, and pushed herself to her feet.

Isaac and Wyatt flanked the two of them with the boys huddled behind, and they stood against a fearsome faerie demon with so much power it sparked from her fingertips and turned her eyes cloudy with black smoke.

She shuddered as Agramon grinned at her through Queen Minetta's fine-boned features. Was any part of the crazy faerie queen still alive, or had he succeeded in doing to her what he'd tried to do to Greta?

"I've tread on your soul, human, and left my name carved on it," she said with a grin that made Greta feel soiled and violated.

But it wasn't Queen Minetta. It was the same taunting, insolent voice that had promised she would give her life to fuel a demon's portal. The same voice that had set up twelve helpless human boys in a circle and laughed as they bled from every opening and started tumbling to the stone floor like dominoes. "Even in your very imminent death, you'll never be rid of me."

Fury the likes of which she'd never known rushed in. Yes, she *was* human. There was nothing special about her. She had no magick. She was not immortal. She should have died in this world years ago. She should have been hunted down and cast in irons.

But she'd survived. In fact, she'd *thrived*. Because being human was to be strong, even when the odds were against you. It was to stand tall, even when everyone else fled. It was to be brave, even when fear knew your very name.

This guy might know her name…but he didn't see her. He

couldn't tame her. He'd never *own* her.

As if she'd choreographed it for weeks, Greta snatched her sword from Wyatt's hand and lunged for Queen Minetta/Agramon with all the confidence, skill, and agility she'd learned in four years of training with Luke. Four years of hunting the biggest, baddest creatures that Mylena could sic on her. She went straight for the long slash across the neck.

Agramon reacted, but Greta had already played this out a bunch of times in her head, and at least two of her four or five scenarios resulted in her sending the faerie queen's head—that looked so much like Siona—sailing through the air before the demon was able to roast her with black magick.

"No!" Siona cried out, hurtling forward to put herself between them.

Horrified, Greta pulled back a split second before cutting Siona.

She missed her chance. Agramon gathered his magick. In the hands of the queen, it was less like a cloud and more like a thousand pitch-black, writhing snakes bursting forth from her fingertips and arching through the air right at Greta.

Siona raised her arms and closed her eyes, and the snakes dispersed like smoke.

Wyatt jumped in and dragged Siona aside. Isaac roared and tried to protect Greta, but she wouldn't give up.

She lifted her sword again. The demon inside Siona's mother screamed with rage and tried again. Thrown off balance, this time Siona couldn't completely neutralize the next attack and the squiggly serpents, instead of dispersing, morphed into a black void right in front of them all.

It was too late to pull back this time. Greta's momentum carried her right into the portal.

And when she spun back around…

Mylena was gone.

CHAPTER TWENTY-FIVE

She stuffed her knuckles in her mouth and bit down hard to stifle her scream, twisting around wildly. She looked for a door, a window, a sliver or a crack…any way out, but it was already gone! It was too dark to see anything, and she was stuck here, alone.

"No," she sobbed, collapsing to the ground and curling into a tight ball. "Please, no." She couldn't be trapped in the dark void alone. Not again.

The nothingness between worlds. The place where nightmares lived, became flesh, and stalked her memories until she had none left, until she was nothing but a shell for the fear and the doubt.

Greta.

Isaac, where are you? She hiccuped, fingernails digging into her palms. She used the small pain to ground her. Was she dreaming?

Come into the light and find me.

The light? What light? "Stop freaking out and breathe," she muttered, planting her hand in the dirt floor and—

Wait a minute. Dirt floor?

Her fingers curled, testing the gritty, dusty stuff, letting it coat her skin. Dirt? It felt real.

She slowly stood. Her hands trembled as she reached out, and her knuckles scraped across sharp rock. Was she in a cave?

A shaky laugh escaped her lips as she took another step and kicked something in the dirt with a clang and a clunk. Her sword.

There was *nothing* in the void. Certainly not dirt, caves, and her sword. So where was she?

She took a deeper look into the darkness and realized it wasn't so complete as she'd first thought. There *was* a sliver of light. She slowly walked toward it, her senses picking up on other things as she got closer. Like the musty, damp feel of the air, and the smell of pine and decaying plant matter making her nose itch and her eyes water as she breathed it in.

Allergies. There were no allergies in the void.

There were only allergies in…

At the mouth of the cave, she blinked. The sun was low in the sky, almost below the tree line. One sun. One big *golden* sun. And trees with wide green leaves that created a shaded canopy overhead.

The faeries had promised to send her back to the human world if she helped them. Had they planned to send her back either way?

No. Not just her. Anyone who could stop them. Which meant that maybe she wasn't alone.

Her heart hammered as she peered across the tiny clearing in front of the cave. Isaac leaned a shoulder against a tree a few feet away with his arms crossed, looking as big and infuriating as ever. His hair stuck straight up, and his clothes were torn all to hell. There was a long scratch on his neck.

He looked amazing.

She ran when he straightened and took a step toward her and laughed as she leaped into his open arms and threw her legs around his waist.

His big hands wrapped around her, holding her up, and he ducked his head to kiss her like a shipwrecked man kissing solid ground after washing up on shore. She was just as desperate, needing to know he was real, that this was all real.

"Isaac." Her lips moved against his. She curled her hand around his neck and gazed into his arresting amethyst eyes. It *felt* real. "This isn't a dream, right?"

"Not a dream." He kissed her again but let her legs slide down to the ground until she stood plastered against him from the knees to shoulders. "But we certainly aren't in Mylena anymore," he said with a sharp hint of concern. "Defiant, reckless human. What have you done now?"

That familiar scowl made her want to laugh with joy. She could handle that. She could handle anything but the savage snarl that contained none of the sarcasm and arrogance she'd come to crave so much.

"Me? Why is it always *my* fault when something happens?"

"Because trouble is your middle name." His arms tightened as if he was afraid of letting her go. She felt the same. She didn't dare loosen her grip.

"Actually, it's Matilda, but I've always hated that, so we can go with Trouble if you want."

"Always you make jokes."

She sobered at that. "No, Isaac. The moment you went Lost…there was nothing funny about that. You scared the hell out of me."

He caressed her cheek like she might disappear. "I was Lost in the moons completely. I felt nothing but the thrill of the chase and the taste of blood in my mouth as I brought down prey. I ran and ran, and then the pull of the moons spurred me even faster. I wanted nothing but their sighs rippling through me like the wind, telling me that I belonged with them. I was filled with the power of the earth, even as I crushed it beneath my every step."

His thumb tipped her chin up until she met his gaze through a blurry layer of moisture. "Why are you crying?" He sounded confused.

She bit her lip, angry that she couldn't control her stupid emotions. "You make it sound as if you didn't want to come back, as if you found a freedom in being Lost that was better than anything you had before." She could almost understand it. All the responsibilities of being the goblin king would have meant nothing. "No more weighty responsibilities as the goblin king. No more disappointment. Just freedom."

"In a way, you're right. A part of me didn't want anything but the Great Mother's embrace and the glow of her daughters' regard. I was more at peace than I have ever been…except when I'm with you."

She gasped and blinked up at him. "Really?"

"I didn't feel Lost…until I heard my name. *You* are the only one who says my name. *You* were the tie that couldn't be broken, the one thread binding me to that other life. I felt it holding me back, although it was gentle, like the fragile silk of a Theridian spider." He drew a line down her arm as if tracing that spider's web onto her. "At first it made me angry," he said. "When I tugged against it, I expected it to snap easily enough. But it stretched instead of breaking."

"I felt it, too," she whispered.

He frowned. "But then you were gone again. The moons had their own demands and I couldn't do anything but heed them. I set off once more to run and kill and howl, but after a while I heard your voice calling me again. At first it was only a whisper, and I continued to ignore it, but you wouldn't give up. You kept searching for me, and something in me kept letting you find me."

"You wouldn't have let me go if it was the other way around." She curved her hand around his neck. "I had to try."

"When you touched me, I remembered." He twisted her hair around his fist. "These silly braids, and the way your nose and cheeks get bright red spots of pink in the cold. I remembered how you cock your hip and cross your arms when I'm in for an argument." A fire burned in his eyes as he gazed down into her face, far from crazed or wild, but just as intense.

As his other hand slipped up under the edge of her shirt and opened over her skin like a brand, she gasped. "I remembered the way you look at life as a challenge you must always win, and the way you are both soft and strong in my arms. I remembered the bright blue of your eyes, and how they turn to ice or liquid fire, depending on whether I've just kissed you or made you angry."

"You remembered all that in a touch?" she murmured, breathless.

"I remembered it all. Your touch brings back *everything*."

She bit back a sob of relief as he took her mouth in a kiss so deep she felt it all the way to her toes. When Isaac kissed her it was like tumbling off the edge of a cliff, making her weightless and free, and she kissed him back with everything she had. He wasn't gentle, but she didn't want him to be. She liked her rough, overbearing goblin with a little bit of wildness in him. A *little* wildness, not *all* the wildness.

"Maybe you should let me go. Or I should let you go," she murmured with a chuckle. But neither of them seemed in any hurry to move.

"I'd prefer that you never let me go," he said, suddenly serious. "But if you must, know that because of you I will never truly be Lost. You can always call me back."

She grinned and kissed his chin. "It was just a suggestion, anyway. I'm good right here."

"Would you have come after me if I stayed Lost? Would you have hunted me down and put your blade in my heart?" His voice was low, his lips a mere inch from hers.

She bit her lip. "I don't know." She shook her head, tremors shaking her from the inside out. She didn't want to think about it. The person who'd lashed him with fire and ice didn't feel like her. Now that the magick was gone and she was just Greta... Greta who loved him so much it was hard to breathe...could she make the same choices? "Don't ever make me have to decide something like that again, okay?"

Before she could talk herself out of it, she leaned forward and pressed her lips to his again and opened her mouth, letting his tongue inside to tangle with hers.

In no time at all, the kiss became her whole world. She needed it more than she needed to breathe. They made out like that until she couldn't see straight or stand up without his hands to hold her, until he traced each of the bones marking her rib cage all the way up to the sides of her breasts, and she giggled. Who knew she was ticklish?

He leaned back, and she sighed, trying to slow her racing heart.

"Thank you," he said.

She swallowed. "What for? The Lost thing?"

He kissed her again, lightly this time, but his gaze didn't lighten, and the hot weight of it made her sweat like she'd been running for miles.

"I can't remember the last time anyone saw beyond the magick and curses of the goblin king to me...the man I really am," he said. "They were always so busy either seeking out my gifts for their own benefit or running from them out of fear."

"I won't say I've never been afraid of you." She squeezed his arm. "But I know what it's like to go through life without anyone who can accept you for who you are."

His gaze dropped, following the line of her cheekbone to her jaw and lower until she blushed. "You're so beautiful."

She laughed. "I'm human and covered pretty much from head to toe in scars, Isaac. How could I possibly be anything but horrifying? It's okay, though," she hurried to assure him with a grin. "I don't care. I've gotten used to it."

"I don't see any scars," he said, tracing her cheek and nose and jaw, making her shiver. He dragged his thumb across her lips as if he could smudge the imprint of his kiss like lipstick — even though she'd never worn the stuff in her life, there were some things from that long-lost other existence that were still stuck in her head.

"That's not fair. You can't just pretend they aren't there."

"When I look at you, I don't see anything except the strong female who makes me want to be stronger, too, and matches me in every way."

"Don't ignore reality." She shoved him in the chest, suddenly angry. If he only saw what he wanted to see, how could she ever be sure his feelings were real?

He grinned. "I don't ignore what's truly important. I see your *real* flaws, trust me."

A distinct throat clearing came from behind her. Her hand immediately dropped to her sword belt as she spun around, until she realized she'd left her weapon back in the cave.

She stopped and let out a long sigh of relief when she saw the gangly, scruffy teen standing there with raised eyebrows. Ray.

Behind him stood Sloane. Charlie. Niall. Carter. Leo. And little Jacob. Her heart expanded with relief. They'd all made it.

Jacob ran to her, his little legs pumping. She bent over to catch him before he barreled right into her. When he looked up, his eyes were bright. "We're *home*!" he cried. "Sloane says so." He grinned at her, and she couldn't help grinning back. Thank the Great Mother he was okay.

The rest of the boys approached more slowly. At first she thought they were disappointed in her. They'd have every right to be after the way she'd left them. But then she realized they couldn't take their eyes off Isaac.

"It's okay," she said. "He's with us."

Us.

She looked around. A warm breeze blew all the stray strands of hair escaping her braids across her face. Could it be true?

Isaac squeezed her hand, and she glanced up at him. He nodded over her shoulder and she turned around to see Wyatt with one arm around Siona's waist and his other hand holding her arm across the back of his shoulder as he helped her to her feet. She wobbled, and he gently pulled her closer.

Siona looked up and her gaze met Greta's, then Isaac's. She froze, and the look of pain on her face had nothing to do with physical discomfort.

Wyatt bent his head to hers and murmured something in her ear. Finally, she set her chin and nodded, giving him a shy smile before they made their way over.

"Are you okay?" she asked.

Siona winced, but she nodded. "It's nothing," she said. Her eyes filled with sorrow. "I'm sorry. This is my fault. If I hadn't stopped you from—"

"Despite everything, she was your mother," Greta interrupted, taking her hand. "I totally get it."

Isaac wasn't so quick to let her off the hook. "Because of your constant betrayal, the demon has arisen. Agramon not only has the power of all faeries and commands an army ready to march on all the kingdoms of Mylena, but we are trapped *here*, unable to do anything about it." His voice cut like a knife, causing everyone to wince.

"Hey." Wyatt edged in front of Siona protectively. He glared at Isaac. "Leave her alone."

"It isn't all her fault," Greta interjected. "We all played a part in that fiasco. The demon was in *me*, and I'm responsible for the destruction he will cause now." She swallowed hard. "The lives he will take."

Isaac's expression darkened. "There will be war. Not only in Mylena, but everywhere."

Wyatt frowned. "What do you mean?"

Greta shivered. She knew exactly what Agramon would do.

"Once the demon has conquered my world," Isaac said, "he won't hesitate to come for this one. He'll burn through the human world and move on to the next, and the next. His hunger for blood and pain and power can never be satisfied."

Wyatt's shoulders slumped. "So what do we do now?"

They all looked at each other.

Ray smiled. "I say first we find a burger joint…and then we figure it out."

CHAPTER TWENTY-SIX

They spent three warm, sunny days camped out in the caves where the portal had dumped them—which was really nothing for a group of kids who'd spent *years* fending for themselves in Mylena during the dead of winter. At first they'd just wanted to figure out exactly where they were. But they also searched for a way back. Greta, Isaac, and Siona had all agreed from the start that they *needed* to return as soon as possible, to stop Agramon and prevent as many deaths as possible.

They hadn't found anything, though, and finally, they were forced to make a decision.

Find civilization. Find help.

Isaac didn't object. He didn't say much of anything. Only stood back and let her and Wyatt make plans amid the boys' excited chatter.

When the boys huddled up to sleep that night with Wyatt and Siona standing watch, whispering softly to one another, she took Isaac aside. "Are you sure you're okay with this?" She squeezed his hand. "Just because we're leaving this place doesn't mean we won't be able to get back here when we find out how to open the portal from this side. You know that, right?"

He slipped his hand to the back of her neck and kissed her until she could barely remember what they'd been talking about. When he lifted his head, his smile was soft and guarded. "No matter how much I wanted it to be so, I realize that Mylena may never have accepted you the way you needed to be accepted. Even if we find a way to return, I would understand if you decided to stay here…"

She didn't pretend that the idea hadn't already occurred to her, but she wasn't letting Isaac go anywhere without her. "Wherever we are, if I have you, then I have all the acceptance I need."

She repeated those words to herself on a loop the next afternoon as they walked out of the forest.

Agramon/Queen Minetta's portal had dumped them neither where Greta had originally come through while on vacation in Germany—thank the Great Mother—nor in North Dakota, where Wyatt had come through. In fact, the consensus was that this was nowhere any of them had ever been, although Jacob was too young to be sure.

With the forest behind them, civilization started to creep over the land. Isaac seemed to be taking it all in stride, maybe because he'd already seen some of the differences between her world and his through her dreams.

It didn't take long before they came across a small town called Stroudsburg. Greta realized then that they were only a two-and-a-half-hour drive from…home.

After that, it seemed obvious *where* they would go, but how to get there was a different story. It took a while to find the Greyhound station, and once they did she worried that trying to get the nine of them on a bus without adult guardians would raise some eyebrows. But apparently not enough for anyone to step in and ask difficult questions.

Getting them all on the bus without any *money* was more difficult, and she wasn't proud of what she did to make it happen. There was a guy stranded at the station who wouldn't be very happy when he found his wallet in the restroom and the note she'd tucked inside, thanking him for the use of his credit card.

Once on the bus, Isaac and Siona were captivated. All of the boys delighted in telling them all about the different kinds of motorized vehicles, from buses and cars to trains and planes. It took some quiet explaining about mechanics and gasoline that Greta was sure she'd bungled because she didn't have the knowledge, but Isaac had picked up the theory of it almost immediately, and the sparkle in his eyes made her smile.

A little while later, she gazed out the window as Isaac's warm palm clasped her thigh just above the knee. She welcomed the distraction, because every time the bus stopped to pick up and drop off passengers, she was *this close* to telling everyone to get off.

A ball of dread and uncertainty lodged in her chest. She hadn't seen her family for more than four years. She'd barely been a teenager when she disappeared, only thirteen, but would be returning home a hardened warrior who'd killed with her bare hands and had every intention of leaving them as soon as possible to go back and do it again.

How to explain her disappearance and the things she'd done? Should she even try? How could they not look at her with anything but revulsion and fear? How could they feel anything but horror?

Isaac nudged her with his shoulder. She turned to him and forced a smile. He pointed at the small screens that were mechanically sliding down from the ceiling of the bus every couple rows. She groaned. "Don't even ask me to try explaining television yet. It's just going to freak you out."

Three hours later, Isaac entwined his hand with hers and together they stopped on the sidewalk in front of number thirty-six in a dense residential neighborhood.

The one place she'd given up on ever returning to again.

It was a little row house, tall and narrow. The black-painted front door had thrown her off for a minute. She remembered it as being red. And the tree in the front yard was bigger than she remembered. Its wide branches blocked her view of the upper levels of the house.

Jacob tugged on her hand. "We're going to see your mom and dad, right?"

She looked down at his upturned face and nodded with a solid gulp. "Uh…"

"Do you think they know my mom?" He was so full of anticipation, his little body practically hummed with it. "Maybe she's here, too?"

Wyatt came over and hefted Jacob into his arms. "Hush, magpie," he said in a soothing voice. He'd gotten more like his old self every day they'd been here. He'd been patient with the children, attentive to Siona, and…tolerant of Isaac. There'd been no shadows in his eyes, no vestiges of the violence and anger that had seeped into him in Mylena.

Right now, though, he looked vaguely awkward, the kind of awkwardness that came the first time you went to meet your girlfriend's parents. Ironic, considering he was the type of guy that the parents she remembered would have loved for her to bring home.

Her actual boyfriend—the one any sane parent would freak out to find her daughter dating—didn't look any more comfortable. Despite his interest in everything, he'd been very quiet ever since they left the forest.

Wyatt, Sloane, and the boys crowded up the walk behind her and Isaac. She spared them a quick glance over her shoulder. Jacob waved and grinned from Wyatt's arms. Carter and Niall stood close to one another, holding hands with matching expressions of wariness. They were old enough to realize that coming home might not be as easy as little Jacob thought it would be.

Charlie and Leo lagged behind, staring up and down the street. They were still mesmerized by things like oak trees and squirrels. She'd caught them lying out on the rocks just outside the cave yesterday morning, basking in the sun and chattering about all the things they couldn't wait to do, like go to a playground and play soccer.

Maybe she should have come alone first. A pack of unknown homeless children arriving on the doorstep was a bigger shock than anyone could be expected to handle well. But the boys were nervous—maybe as nervous as she was—and she'd promised that they wouldn't be separated, at least not until all the families had been notified and they felt comfortable leaving.

She paused with a white-knuckled fist outstretched to knock on the door. Her stomach was doing somersaults.

Isaac whispered in her ear, "If Greta the bounty hunter can take on all the races of Mylena and restore a goblin king's soul, she can handle anything this world may throw at us."

Acknowledgments

My street team has been absolutely fantastic. The Goblin Gang is a group of passionate, friendly, amazing people who couldn't be more supportive. Thank you so much for being a part of this crazy, wild journey!

Thank you also to the readers, bloggers, and reviewers who have supported my words. Your dedication and honest enthusiasm for books makes the world a better place filled with possibility and adventure.

Thank you also to my family and my friends, especially my amazing husband and son, who let me live in my fantastic worlds and don't call me crazy to my face.

Finally, thank you to Stephen Morgan, Heather Howland, Liz Pelletier, Melanie Smith, Heather Riccio, Debbie Suzuki, and the entire team at Entangled Publishing. I can't ask for a better home for my books. You all make me a better author, and I'm grateful for the opportunities you give me.

About the Author

Chloe Jacobs is a native of nowhere and everywhere, having jumped around to practically every Province of Canada before finally settling in Ontario where she has now been living for a respectable number of years. Her husband and son are the two best people in the entire world, but they also make her wish she'd at least gotten a female cat. No such luck. And although the day job keeps her busy, she carves out as much time as possible to write. Bringing new characters to life and finding out what makes them tick and how badly she can make them suffer is one of her greatest pleasures, almost better than chocolate and fuzzy pink bunny slippers. You can visit her online at www.chloejacobs.com

Discover more of Entangled Teen's books…

THIEF OF LIES
a *Library Jumpers* novel by Brenda Drake

Gia Kearns would rather fight with boys than kiss them. That is, until Arik, a leather clad hottie in the Boston Athenaeum, suddenly disappears. When Gia unwittingly speaks the key that sucks her and her friends into a photograph and transports them into a Paris library, Gia must choose between her heart and her head, between Arik's world and her own, before both are destroyed.

THROUGH FIRE & SEA
an *Otherselves* novel by Nicole Luiken

There are four mirror worlds: fire, water, air, and stone. And each has a magic of its own. Holly resides in the Water World. When she's called by Holly, her twin "Otherself" from the Fire World, she nearly drowns. Suddenly the world Holly thought she knew is filled with secrets, magic, and deadly peril. For a malevolent force seeks to destroy the mirror worlds. And the only way for Holly and Leah to save them is to shatter every rule they've ever known…